TRENT'S TRUST

LAURA SCOTT

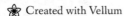

CHAPTER ONE

Trent Atkins put everything he had into his performance yet found it impossible to lose himself in his music. After finishing the song, he sipped his water, glancing surreptitiously at the woman seated near the back of the pub. She was pretty, with straight chin-length blond hair, high cheekbones, and curvy physique, but so far he hadn't seen her smile. The mystery woman had shown up at his last two gigs, but he did not get the groupie vibe from her.

Just the opposite.

She seemed to be sitting there, judging him. Was she someone he'd met when he'd been with the Jimmy Woodrow Band? A one-night stand he'd never contacted again? Or maybe one of Jimmy's one-night stands? He abruptly steered away from thoughts of his buddy's abrupt death or he'd never be able to finish this set.

Trent launched into another song, doing his best to ignore the woman's intense stare. Music had always been his sanctuary. His place of peace. Something he'd lost when he'd joined Jimmy's band. Of course, he hadn't realized it at the time. No, Trent had been drawn toward the lure of raking in big money, being famous, and living large. All of which had come true. At least temporarily. The money had been great, better than anything he'd ever experienced before, but the drinking and drugs soon had the entire band spiraling out of control. He hadn't taken many drugs, but the alcohol? Oh yeah. The booze had been the devil on his shoulder.

But not anymore. At least, not for the past three months. Which he knew wasn't saying much. Trent closed his eyes for a moment and focused on the song. A country rock ballad he'd composed himself after getting and staying sober.

When Trent finished, he tipped his cowboy hat—it was a prop more than anything—to acknowledge the smattering of applause. Then he thanked the crowd for coming and mentioned he'd be playing at the Thirsty Saloon next Friday night too. He stood, looped his guitar crossways over his body, and moved off the small rough plank stage, heading toward the rear door of the bar.

The saloon was a far cry from the high-level clubs the Jimmy Woodrow Band had played in. Jimmy and the band had drawn huge crowds and had more gigs than he'd ever imagined was possible. It had been a roller coaster of a ride.

Until the night Trent woke up, hungover and trying not to puke, only to stumble across Jimmy's dead body on the floor of their hotel suite.

The image haunted him still. Jimmy's wide eyes staring blankly at the ceiling, his body cold to the touch. Since Trent had pretty much passed out, he had no real idea of what had happened.

If he were honest, he didn't want to know. What if he'd somehow played a role in his friend's death? Even after all this time, he was secretly waiting for the police to show up and haul him away in handcuffs.

Especially since Trent had cowardly left the hotel room without waiting around for the authorities to show up. He hadn't even called the police but had huddled in a seedy dive motel room watching TV, waiting for the news to explode.

And it certainly had.

Trent was so preoccupied with his thoughts, ruminating over the past, he didn't notice the figure dressed in a black hoodie coming swiftly toward him until it was almost too late. Trent's street-fighting instincts had him lashing out with his foot in an attempt to kick the guy's groin while throwing a punch with his left hand, his dominant one. He also shouted at the top of his lungs, hoping to draw the attention of people passing by.

Out of nowhere, the blonde from the bar showed up and struck the attacker from behind, bringing two fists down onto the back of his head with surprising force. The hooded man stumbled, dropped a knife, then whirled and ran off, darting between the cars in the small parking lot.

Trent gaped at her, trying to understand what had happened. A mugger tried to steal from him, but his mystery woman had charged to his rescue. Why? He had no idea, but he didn't think it was simply a kind gesture on her part. "W-who are you? What do you want?"

She gripped his arm and steered him toward a dark blue SUV. "We need to talk."

Talk? His paranoid instincts from the time he'd spent living on the streets came rushing back to him. She was even more beautiful up close, but that didn't mean anything. He dug in his heels and roughly shook off her hand. "No way, lady. I'm not going anywhere with you."

"Trent, I have reason to believe the guy who attacked you is no ordinary mugger." She stepped closer, tipping her head back to meet his gaze. For a tiny thing, she'd packed a wallop.

No ordinary mugger? The crime rate in Nashville was such that he found it difficult to believe. Lots of petty crime and worse happened every day. Why would tonight be any different?

"We need to talk," she repeated sternly.

He swallowed hard and eyed her warily. The way she referred to him by name was alarming. As if she knew a lot about him when he didn't know squat about her. "About what?"

There was a long moment of silence before she said, "Jimmy Woodrow's murder."

Murder. The word hit him square in the chest with the impact of a bullet. He staggered back a step, wondering if he'd misheard her. Maybe he was losing his grip on reality. It wouldn't be a surprise to realize the secrets he'd never voiced had instead slowly and surely eaten away at him, causing him to go quietly insane.

Even the role he'd played on the night of the fire when he and his foster siblings had escaped the Preacher's cabin didn't compare to what had transpired with Jimmy. Not for the first time it occurred to Trent he never should have left his foster brother Cooper behind in Gatlinburg.

He never should have come to Nashville at all.

"Please, Trent. I promise I only want to talk."

He shouldn't trust her. He had learned to trust no one, except maybe Cooper, who was still living in Gatlinburg and was of no help to him now. In fact, Trent had ignored his foster brother's phone call a couple of weeks ago, too embarrassed to respond. But that didn't matter right now.

"Who are you?" he demanded.

"My name is Serena Jerash." She paused as if waiting for him to recognize her.

He didn't.

"Why do you care about Jimmy?" he asked harshly.

Her gaze was shadowed in the darkness, impossible to read. "I'm a friend of his. And I just want to talk to you, nothing more."

Yeah, she kept saying that, but he wasn't buying it, not for one hot minute. She must have known he had been there the night Jimmy had died. It was the only explanation.

The steamy September night closed in on him, stealing his breath. He struggled to remain focused, ignoring the keen, desperate desire to go back inside for a shot and a beer, followed by another and another until he could no longer see Jimmy's blank stare in his mind. Yet Trent knew the relief would only be temporary. Staying sober was the only way to survive. He gathered every ounce of willpower he possessed. "Lady, I don't know who you are or what you're up to, but I'm not going anywhere with you." He turned away.

"There's a restaurant that's open all night about a mile up the road." She hurried after him, putting a hand on his arm. She was persistent, he'd give her that much. "We can talk there. It's a public place but won't be too busy at this time of night."

"Why should I?" He stared at her. "Muggings are not unusual in Nashville, and in case you haven't noticed, we happen to be standing in a rough part of town." He was at the point where he couldn't afford to be picky when it came to places willing to hire him to sing and play his guitar. He took any and all gigs he could get. Even then, he was barely making ends meet.

"Because the same person who killed Jimmy Woodrow is likely coming after you."

That blunt statement stopped him cold. "Are you a cop?"

"No. As I said, I just want to talk."

His thoughts whirled. He shouldn't talk to her. To anyone. Trent knew the best thing he could do was get as far away from the blonde as possible. Yet she'd been at his last few gigs. And would likely show up next Friday there at the Thirsty Saloon to see him.

Unless he blew off the gig, which he was in no position to do.

"Please, Trent." Her low, husky voice had him wondering if she was a singer. It would explain her interest in Jimmy's death.

His murder?

His curiosity got the better of him, and he capitulated. "Fine. I'll see you at Connie's Café." Without saying anything more, he twisted out of her grip and walked to his rusty and badly dented Ford truck. After sliding his guitar off his shoulders, he stored it in the back seat, then climbed in behind the wheel. Glancing through the driver's side window, he noticed Serena Jerash hurrying to her much newer and nicer SUV.

Against his better judgment, Trent waited for her to pull out of the parking lot before following behind. The ride to Connie's Café didn't take long, and he seriously considered driving past once they'd reached their destination.

But he pulled in and parked beside her, hoping he wasn't making a giant mistake.

SERENA HALF EXPECTED Trent to make a run for it,
but to her surprise, he parked his battered truck right beside
her. He waited for her to emerge from the vehicle first
before pushing open his door to accompany her inside.

Her hands were sore from where she'd struck the
assailant before he'd dropped the knife and taken off. She'd
been relieved there hadn't been a need to pull her gun.
She'd seriously considered going after the guy in an effort to
understand who had hired him. Yet sticking close to Trent
Atkins had seemed the better choice.

For now.

Because of the late hour, there was no hostess on duty.
Serena led the way to a booth in the back corner of the café.
Trent's expression was grim as he slid in across from her.

The musician was a very good-looking man, or he would
be if he smiled more often. Trent was also very talented,
although her father's best friend's son, Jimmy Woodrow,
had been even more so. The entire family knew Jimmy was
brimming with talent, a shining star, one whose light had
been extinguished far too soon.

As a private investigator, Serena had been hired by
Jimmy's father to uncover the truth about his son's murder.
Granted, the ME's report had deemed Jimmy's death to be
undetermined, mostly because his tox screen had tested
positive for alcohol and cocaine. Not enough to kill him,
however, but still an indicator of his lifestyle. One that may
have contributed to his demise.

Yet the rumor amongst the cops who'd responded to the
scene was that something shady had happened that night.
Without witnesses or much information to go on, the investigation had stalled and become dormant.

There was a fair amount of crime in Nashville, always

another murder to deal with. And the indeterminate conclusion from the ME didn't offer much clarity either.

Trent continued to stare at her, clearly not willing to start the conversation. Once the server had brought waters and had taken their orders, she leaned forward, putting her elbows on the table.

"I know Jimmy Woodrow was no saint. He was an extremely talented musician, but he also partied a little too much."

Trent didn't so much as blink. She took that to mean she hadn't told him anything he didn't already know. Which was true. As Jimmy's lead guitarist, she knew Trent had more knowledge of those parties than she did.

"I don't know if you realize the medical examiner listed the cause of Jimmy's death as indeterminate."

"You said murder." It was the first thing he'd said since leaving the parking lot at the Thirsty Saloon.

"Yes, because I believe he was murdered." She didn't want to tell him too much, but she needed his cooperation, now more than ever. "And I know you were with him that night."

If she hadn't been watching him so closely, she might have missed the nearly imperceptible flinch. "You're wrong."

"No, I'm not." She'd been working on this case for several weeks and had learned from another member of the now broken-up band that Jimmy and Trent had been very tight. It didn't make sense that he wouldn't have been there that night.

Trent sat back in the booth. "You're right about the fact that I was at the hotel for a while after the gig. We typically got together to celebrate finishing up a good run, and that night was the one in which we opened for Luke Bryan, which was huge. We all knew that night was our trip to the big leagues, so of course we were pumped. But I didn't stay overnight. I left at four in the morning."

"Drunk?" she asked pointedly.

He shrugged. "Rideshares are the best invention since sliced bread. No reason to drink and drive."

Interesting that he hadn't denied drinking. Then again, useless to deny something so easily proved as the two former band members she'd spoken to had mentioned how much Trent liked to drink. And how much he and Jimmy had partied the night he'd ended up dead in the hotel room.

Watching Trent for the past few nights, she'd noticed he'd only drank water with fresh slices of lemon. Which didn't mean anything, he could have turned into a closet drinker, hiding his addiction from the prying eyes of the world.

But not from God.

Serena prayed for guidance as she regarded him thoughtfully. "That isn't exactly the story I've heard, but we can set that issue aside for now. The real question here is who killed Jimmy? And why has that same person decided to come after you?"

A flash of impatience crossed his features. "Are you some sort of journalist? Because you're pretty good at making up stories. There's no proof Jimmy was murdered, and there's no reason on earth the killer would come after me. Jimmy died three months ago. I'm pretty sure the Nashville Police Department has already stuck his death deep into their cold case file."

She had to admit he was right about that. With no new leads to go on, the Nashville PD had moved on. The case wasn't necessarily in the cold case file, but it sure wasn't being actively pursued.

But it would be once she found the evidence they needed to keep moving the case forward.

"Why would someone attack you?" She lifted a brow. "Have you made someone mad? Cheated with a married woman? Owe someone money? What?"

He frowned. "None of the above. You're making up stories again. That attack was a random thing." His gaze narrowed. "Unless, of course, you're the one who set it up. I've never been attacked by anyone until tonight. And you've been to my last couple of gigs."

Again, she couldn't help being impressed because she would have thought the exact same thing. And she had no reason to be paranoid, unlike Trent.

Their server brought their breakfast meals, then left them alone. Serena bowed her head and silently thanked God for the food and for guiding her to Trent in time to help him escape the hoodie assailant.

When she lifted her head, Trent was staring at her oddly. "What was that?" he asked.

"A prayer." She didn't understand why he was confused. "Considering the earlier attack, we have a lot to be thankful for."

"Yeah, right." His snide tone surprised her. Trent had been suspicious, blunt, confused, curious, and skeptical, but he hadn't been downright rude.

"I take it you don't believe in God." She picked up her fork and cut into her omelet. Something about eating after midnight always made her want to order breakfast. Apparently, Trent felt the same.

"No, although I lived with the devil for about five years." He turned his attention to his meal, oblivious to her shocked expression.

"I'm sorry to hear that." The words were grossly inadequate. "That must have been terrible."

"Yeah." Trent lapsed back into silence, concentrating on his meal as if his life depended on it. Which made her wonder about what he'd done before joining up with the Jimmy Woodrow Band. Not that Trent's personal life should matter to her one way or the other.

Unless it had some sort of bearing on what had triggered Jimmy's murder. But somehow she didn't think so. No, Trent had been the lead guitarist, but whoever had killed Jimmy must have had a personal reason to do so. On a professional level, Jimmy was worth more alive than dead.

Her father's friend Allan Woodrow had maintained an overly positive view toward his talented son. He'd acted as if the drinking and drugs were smears on Jimmy's good name by those who were jealous of his ability.

But that was not the picture Serena was uncovering through her investigation. Granted, the two band members could have been exaggerating, but she didn't think so. Jimmy had been wild when it came to women and having fun. Finding his tox screen had contained alcohol and cocaine had only confirmed what Jed Matson and Dave Jacoby had told her. Whatever had transpired that fateful night, she was certain Jimmy had been too impaired to fight back or escape.

"Do you remember seeing anything suspicious the night Jimmy died?"

He glanced sharply at her. "No."

She refused to be deterred. "I need you to think back on that night, on what was going on before you left. Any fighting? Arguing? Anything remotely unusual?"

"There was nothing to fight about, we'd just opened for a big-time star, and we were celebrating." He stuck stubbornly to his story. "We drank too much and probably got too loud. I vaguely remember the hotel security coming to ask us to be quiet."

That was something she hadn't heard before. "Do you remember what time that was?"

"No." He dropped his gaze to his empty plate, which he'd devoured in record time, then he dug into his jeans pocket for some cash. "Sorry I can't be of more help, but I need to get home."

Serena didn't want him to leave. "What if I told you that Jed and Dave remembered there was an argument?"

His gaze snapped up to hers. "When did you speak to them?"

"Last week." She eyed him steadily. "Sounds as if you and Jimmy were not in agreement about something, they both mentioned some harsh words between you."

His cheeks flushed, and he tossed a twenty-dollar bill onto the table and stood. "You're mistaken. We were celebrating. Frankly, I don't appreciate you treating me as a suspect. I guess you lied to me about being a cop after all." He stalked away, his long stride taking him quickly across the restaurant.

She winced, realizing she hadn't handled that very well. She pulled out some cash and added it to his before hurrying after him.

But Trent was already in his truck, the engine rumbling to life. She hopped into her SUV and followed. She knew where he lived because she'd tailed him home from his gig last weekend. It was a hole-in-the-wall apartment, a far cry from the plush Grand Ole Opry hotel where they'd stayed the night of Jimmy's murder.

Which was another reason she didn't believe he'd left at

four in the morning. Why would he ditch the swank surroundings for a tiny apartment?

He wouldn't. No one would.

Trent Atkins was hiding something. He wasn't necessarily a suspect, but he was definitely hiding something.

For one thing, he wasn't nearly as forthcoming as Jed and Dave had been. They'd relished talking about the old days and had seemed genuinely upset about Jimmy's death.

They'd also seemed intrigued by the idea of their band leader being murdered, offering up dozens of possibilities.

Including one in which Trent and Jimmy had argued over a woman.

In her humble opinion, both men were handsome enough to hold their own in that regard. Add that to being in a band and she found it hard to imagine either of them resorting to fighting over a woman.

Then again, they'd both likely been drinking and doing drugs, so who knows what had gone through their minds.

Trent slowed near a tavern, but then sped up again. She wondered if he'd given up on the drinking and drugs in the months since Jimmy's death.

She decided to pray that God would guide him on the road to recovery.

When she saw Trent pull into the small parking lot outside his shabby apartment building, she drove past the place, but then pulled over to the side of the road. Getting out of the SUV, she headed back on foot. From her angle, she could see Trent sitting behind the wheel and staring out through the windshield for several long moments.

What was he thinking? She'd have given a hundred bucks for his thoughts. Was he remembering the night Jimmy had died? Jed Matson who was a drummer and Dave

Jacoby who played the keyboard were both members of a new band called Bootleggers. Not exactly an original name for Tennessee and Kentucky, but they seemed to be doing okay. Nowhere near as well as Jimmy Woodrow, but not bad.

So why had Trent struck out on his own?

Serena had more questions than answers after the brief time she'd spent with Trent. And she was keenly aware of the fact that she'd provided far more information than he'd given in return.

Trent pushed open his driver's side door. Something hit the ground, and he bent over to retrieve it at the exact moment a gunshot rang out, shattering the driver's side window of his truck. He hit the ground and shimmied beneath the vehicle.

"Trent! Stay down!" Serena pulled her weapon and crouched down behind a parked car. Using her phone, she called 911 to report the gunfire as her gaze searched for the shooter.

No way was this second attempt on Trent's life a coincidence.

In a few short hours, someone had tried to kill him *twice*.

And with a guilty flush, she couldn't help but wonder if her finding and questioning him had caused this to happen.

CHAPTER TWO

Trent tried to peer out from beneath his truck but couldn't see much of anything except for the shards of glass lying on the ground. He'd managed to scoop up his phone, realizing if he hadn't dropped it, he might be dead.

He tried to listen beyond the pounding of his heart. Serena was talking to someone, maybe the police?

He couldn't believe someone had actually shot at him!

After the attempted mugging at the Thirsty Saloon, he knew this wasn't a random attack. No, as Blondie had theorized, someone was coming after him personally.

Because of Jimmy?

Or maybe because of Blondie. Really, all this started when she'd shown up to watch him perform.

"Trent? Are you okay?" Blondie sounded upset. "Talk to me!"

"Fine," he called back. Why she was worried about him when she was the one who'd brought danger to his doorstep, he had no idea. "I need to get out of here."

"I know, the police will be here shortly."

He inwardly groaned. He didn't trust the police, had

never gone to them for help when he and Cooper had been living on the street. He'd done his best to avoid them over the thirteen years since escaping the Preacher. Of course, picking pockets to eat was a good reason to avoid the law, but even though he'd gone straight, he didn't plan to change now.

No, better to get out of Dodge before they showed up. The wail of sirens could be heard in the distance, an indicator he didn't have much time. Heading inside to his apartment was out of the question, and driving his truck with a shattered window didn't seem like a good idea either. Whoever the shooter was had staked out his apartment and knew what he drove.

Time for plan B. He inched out from beneath the truck and ducked under the vehicle next to his. Lots of people drove trucks or SUVs, so that was helpful. Trent continued that path, moving from vehicle to vehicle, until he found a Honda Civic that was too low to the ground for him to fit under.

Stupid foreign cars, he thought crankily.

He took a risk, belly crawling until he was between the apartment building and the Honda. Once again, he continued his journey away from his truck until he could get around the corner of the apartment building.

For a moment he hesitated, wishing there was a way to head back and grab his guitar from behind the seat. He didn't have the money to replace it and couldn't work without it.

Of course, he couldn't work if he was dead either.

He also wished he could go inside his apartment to grab clothes and extra cash. But he decided the risk was too great.

Blondie had caused this, and she should reimburse him

for his guitar, truck, and expenses, he thought grimly. Not that he planned to stick around to confront her about that.

Running past the apartment building, he headed down an alley, coming out on one of the side streets. He didn't linger, moving in what he hoped was a random pattern. A rideshare would come in handy, but he didn't want to pick it up so close to the scene of the crime.

When he decided he'd gone far enough, he pulled out his phone. The screen was cracked from hitting the pavement, but it still worked. He pulled up the rideshare app and found the closest car, which was thankfully only five blocks away.

He sent the request, then glanced around, looking for a place to wait where he'd be somewhat hidden from view. Out of nowhere, an SUV pulled up next to him. He hadn't seen it because the headlights weren't on. The passenger window opened.

"Get in." Blondie's voice was curt.

"No." He wasn't stupid enough to make that mistake again. He began to walk away, scanning the area for his driver.

The SUV kept pace beside him. "I have your guitar."

He stopped and swung around to face her. "What? Why?"

Her brow puckered. "It's your livelihood, right? I grabbed it when I realized you'd taken off, leaving it behind. Get in, Trent. I'll take you someplace safe."

What was it with this woman? Trent didn't trust easily, and Blondie was no exception. Still, she had his guitar. That she'd even considered getting it for him was amazing. Unless, of course, this was nothing more than a clever trap.

Calling himself all kinds of a fool, he abruptly yanked the passenger door open and climbed in beside her. A quick glance in the back seat confirmed she had indeed brought his guitar from his truck. He'd been forced to leave his first guitar behind when he'd been taken away from his mother and sent to live with the Preacher. He couldn't bear the idea of leaving a guitar behind again.

She hit the gas and sped away. Silence hung between them, solid and impenetrable like the Berlin wall.

"Look, I told you my fears about you being in danger." Serena turned to look at him. "You have to believe me."

"What I believe is *you* brought the danger to *me*. There wasn't a single attack against me until you showed up." He strove to keep his tone even. "Don't bother trying to pretend you care about my well-being."

"I do care," she snapped. "Did you notice the guy dressed in black sitting at the corner table near the front of the stage tonight?"

He frowned, trying to picture the area. "No."

"He was in the crowd when you played at Seekers Thursday, and when you played at Whistlers last Saturday." Serena paused, then added, "I'm pretty sure he's the same man who tried to attack you with the knife."

"And you're just mentioning this now?" Everything Blondie said only made him more suspicious. "Why not tell me that at the café?"

"I should have," she conceded. "But I didn't get a look at the hooded guy's face, so I can't say for sure they're one and the same. After the recent gunfire, though, I'm more convinced than ever that whoever killed Jimmy is now after you."

The whole idea was ridiculous. There was no reason to come after him; he hadn't seen anything. Or heard anything. The memory fragments that floated through his mind weren't enough to paint a picture of what had transpired. He'd been too drunk, and his friend had died because of it.

Trent sat back in his seat and stared out the passenger side window. Thinking back to his earlier performance, he could vaguely remember a man seated alone at a small table. He remembered thinking the guy was waiting for a date but then promptly forgot about him when he'd noticed Blondie in the back. A pretty woman who'd come to see him before had sparked his interest.

He should have known better than to think she'd come because she was interested in him personally.

"Where are we going?" he finally asked.

"My place."

"No way, I don't trust you enough for that." His knee-jerk reaction had him reaching for the door. He could roll out of the SUV, even if that meant leaving his guitar behind, taking his chances on the street rather than ending up at her place. For all he knew, she was working with Jimmy's murderer.

"Okay, then what do you suggest?" Her response surprised him. "A motel?"

"A motel with two rooms," he said firmly. "I'll pick the place."

Serena lifted a brow, then shrugged. "Fine, if that's what it will take for you to trust me, have at it. Tell me where to go."

This could still be a trap, but he decided to go along with her. For now. He thought about the area and gave her directions to a small motel that he knew would accept cash. Not many of them did these days. When Serena pulled up, he watched her closely, but she didn't wrinkle her nose in distaste or say anything derogatory.

Not that he could blame her if she had. The place barely ranked two stars, if he was feeling generous.

"Park in the back of the building," he instructed. "I don't want your vehicle visible from the road."

"Okay."

After parking the SUV, Trent slid out of the passenger seat, then took a moment to grab his guitar. It felt like an old friend in his hand, and he gratefully slipped the strap over his shoulder. Those years of living with the Preacher had been extremely difficult to suffer through without his music to keep him grounded.

Together, they walked into the small lobby. The clerk was behind a shield of plexiglass, not unusual in high crime areas.

"Do you have connecting rooms?" Serena asked.

The guy smirked. "Really? You're joking, right?"

She narrowed her gaze. "Not joking. Do you have connecting rooms or not?"

The guy lifted a shoulder. "Yeah, I've got a pair that aren't in use. You want them?"

"We do. I'll pay in cash." Serena removed several bills from her front pocket.

The clerk didn't argue, and within moments, they each had a room key.

"Why connecting rooms?" Trent asked as they walked down the sidewalk in front of the motel doors. Their connecting rooms were the last ones from the end of the row.

She used her key to open the door, then turned toward him. "Please open your side of the connecting door. We need to continue our conversation and then figure out our next steps."

Our next steps? "Sure, Blondie, whatever you say."

"Serena," she corrected curtly before disappearing inside.

For some odd reason, her flash of anger made him want to smile. An inexplicable response since he appeared to be walking around with a target on his back. Which was nothing to smile about.

He unlocked his door and went inside. After placing his guitar on the bed, he went over to open his connecting door.

If this was all related to Jimmy Woodrow's death—his murder—then they did need to talk.

But he wanted Serena to answer his questions rather than the other way around.

SERENA LET out a small sigh of relief when Trent opened the connecting door. She hadn't been sure he'd do as she'd asked. She waved him in. "Let's sit down."

He took a seat on the edge of the bed across from the only chair in the room. Swallowing the flash of nervousness, she lifted her chin and met his gaze directly. "I'm afraid I may have inadvertently caused the guy in the bar to come after you."

His eyebrows rose. "Inadvertently? Or on purpose?"

"Why would I do that on purpose?" She was shocked by his accusation. "Trent, I'm trying to understand what happened to Jimmy Woodrow. I never wanted you to be in danger because of it. Please, I need you to tell me what you know."

"Yeah, so you said." He crossed his arms over his chest. "And I already told you, I wasn't there all night."

She sighed. "Why do you keep lying to me? Don't you

understand that your safety depends on us figuring out who killed Jimmy?"

"Jimmy?" His tone was suspicious. "Sounds like you were on a first-name basis."

Having a conversation with Trent was like pulling her hair out one fistful at a time. "I told you he's the son of my father's friend. So yes, I knew him. We were closer as kids, before we went our separate ways."

"You were in a relationship with him." The statement hinted at jealousy, which was ridiculous. From what she could tell, Trent didn't like her. And he certainly didn't trust her.

"Never." She rolled her eyes. "Why would Jimmy be interested in someone like me?"

He stared at her for so long she felt her cheeks flush with embarrassment. She knew she wasn't beautiful, at least not the way Jimmy's girlfriends had always been. Yet for some reason, the way Trent stared at her made her feel pretty.

Or maybe she only wanted to believe that he thought her pretty.

Whatever. She'd been burned by a guy who had claimed to love her in the past, and she had no interest in trying again. Especially not with a musician. That lifestyle didn't interest her in the least. She gave herself a mental shake.

"What's in it for you?"

His question surprised her. "What do you mean?"

He uncrossed his arms and spread his hands wide. "What are you getting out of this? Money? Fame? A story? What?"

Twice now, he'd assumed she was a journalist. His being a member of the Jimmy Woodrow Band meant being exposed to reporters and photographers, vying for the big scoop. Music artists, sports players, and the Hollywood crowd were always hounded by the gossip rags.

The idea she was doing this for money rankled, yet she couldn't deny it was true. She had been hired by Allan, Jimmy's father, to uncover the real circumstances surrounding his son's death. Her motivation was a bit more complicated than earning a paycheck.

Her dad was a former detective and had been horrified when Serena had become a private investigator. Then again, her father hadn't spoken to her much over the past three years as he blamed her for her mother's death. Yet as crazy as it sounded, she longed to prove herself worthy.

Finding Jimmy's killer would go a long way in earning her father's respect. Maybe not his forgiveness, but his respect.

"I'm not a journalist. And let's just say that as a friend of the family, I'm interested in seeing justice served."

"Let's not just say that." Trent leaned forward. "There's something you're not telling me. And I have no intention of talking about this until you come clean."

His perception was right on target. Frankly, she wasn't used to having anyone read her so easily. Then again, Trent had picked up on her being at his last few gigs. She needed to give him credit for that, even if he'd missed the guy dressed in black.

She stared at him, knowing that if she didn't tell him everything, he would likely take off. After all, he had his guitar and hadn't paid for the room.

"Okay, I guess you deserve the truth."

"You think?" His sarcastic tone cut deep.

Keeping her expression impassive, she pulled her

license out of her pocket, along with a business card from her jeans pocket, and handed them to him.

He scowled when he read the information printed there. "You're a private investigator?" The incredulous tone was the same as if she'd admitted to being a lion tamer for the circus.

"Yes." She took the papers back. "Although I don't know why that surprises you."

"Maybe because I've never met a PI before."

His testy attitude was getting old. "Well, there's a first for everything, right?"

"Are you armed?"

"I am, yes. And I have the appropriate concealed carry permit." She lifted her sweatshirt to show him the gun holster she wore over the T-shirt beneath. "I've been hired by Jimmy's father to find his son's murderer."

"So money, then." The sneer was unmistakable and made her bristle.

"You don't play at the Thirsty Saloon for free, do you? Same difference."

He grimaced and looked away. "I guess."

"We all need to make a living," she said quietly. "And some of us don't have your voice and talent with a guitar. Regardless, this is more than a job to me. I knew Jimmy, but even more than that, our fathers were very close. They went to college together and stood up in each other's weddings. Even all these years later, they've stayed friends. This is personal, and I really need you to tell me what you know about that night."

Trent didn't say anything for a long second. "I told you I don't remember anything. I'm not lying about that. We drank a lot, more than usual. Everything was great, we knew we were on our way to being a success."

"Until Jimmy died."

His expression was pained. "Yeah. I have to tell you, that was a complete shock. Guys our age don't just drop over dead."

"They do if they abuse alcohol and drugs," she calmly pointed out. "As a matter of fact, a lot of musicians have died at a tragically young age."

"I know. It's one of the reasons I gave up drinking." His voice was subdued now rather than confrontational. "But I don't think Jimmy drank that much or overdosed on drugs. If he did, you wouldn't be here." He looked at her. "I'm sure the autopsy results show what was in his bloodstream."

"They do. His alcohol level was 0.20, and he had cocaine in his system, but not at levels high enough to make the ME believe it was an overdose."

"What about the two levels combined?"

"I asked that too. According to the ME, there was evidence of long-term drug use, such that he did not believe the levels of cocaine combined with the alcohol caused Jimmy's death. They were, however, contributing factors."

Trent nodded slowly. "Jimmy used drugs more than he should. We all drank, but I stayed clear of the drugs. We warned Jimmy, but he claimed the drugs helped him shine on stage."

"He was a functional drug addict," she said softly. "Nothing shiny or glamorous about that."

"I know, as I was the same way." He blew out a breath. "What did he die of, then?"

She watched his face closely. "I was hoping you could tell me."

His jaw clenched, and his gaze narrowed, but there was no flash of guilt. "I don't know. I don't remember."

At least he didn't try to say he wasn't there. Not remembering is different than not being in the hotel at all. "He died of a head injury."

Trent looked surprised. "A head injury?"

"Yes." She waited a moment, then added, "He was found face upward with the back of his head a bloody mess."

"Well, if he fell and hit the back of his head on the tile floor, it would be a bloody mess. If someone hit him on the back of his head, he'd fall face first, wouldn't he?"

"Yes, logically he would. Only his head was on an area rug, not the tile. And while he wasn't far from the edge of a table, the amount of blood on the corner didn't seem to be enough to have caused the injury. Head wounds bleed like crazy. Most of the bleeding was internal."

He nodded slowly. "Hence the indeterminate conclusion by the ME."

"Yes." She waited, hoping he'd say more. After a full five minutes, she said, "Tell me about the argument."

"You're making a big deal out of nothing." Trent sighed and scrubbed his hands over his face. "Jimmy was sleeping with a woman who was married. He didn't know that at the time, but after the truth came out, Jimmy said he didn't care and continued the relationship."

Finally, they were getting somewhere. "What was her name?"

"Heidi Stout. Although I don't think that was her married name. In fact, it may not be her real name at all."

She frowned. "Then how did you find out she was married?"

He looked sheepish. "I overheard Heidi talking on the phone. She said something like, 'go ahead and file for divorce, you won't get a dime.'"

"Wow." She couldn't help being impressed. "Heidi wasn't just married, she was also rich?"

"That's what it sounded like to me." He shrugged. "I told Jimmy she wasn't being honest with him, but he only laughed. Said he couldn't care less if she was married or not as long as he was having fun." Trent used air quotes around the word *fun*.

Serena couldn't deny that description fit Jimmy Woodrow to a T. "If that's all the argument entailed, why did Jed and Dave make it sound like something more?"

"Beats me. You'll have to ask them." Trent hesitated, then said, "You should know they were both a little jealous of me and Jimmy. We tended to get more of the attention. Especially Jimmy."

"I would think that everyone would have their share of the ladies," she said dryly. "It's not as if you aren't all very good-looking and talented guys."

"Maybe, but Jed in particular had a chip on his shoulder. As the drummer, he felt as if he wasn't getting the attention and accolades he deserved. Dave often sided with Jed, the two of them against me and Jimmy over one issue or another."

Discord amongst the band members was an angle she hadn't seriously considered, mostly because they stood to make more money by sticking together. "Killing Jimmy only put Jed and Dave on the street, looking for work. Doesn't make sense they'd have motive to kill him."

"You're thinking about this from a logical perspective," Trent pointed out. "When emotions run high, arguments break out and things can quickly spiral out of control."

She stared at him. "Are you insinuating that Jed or Dave killed Jimmy?"

"No, I'm just saying the argument about Heidi wasn't

the only thing going on. There was always an undercurrent of, I don't know, dissatisfaction between the band members."

"Even though you'd just opened for Luke Bryan?" she asked.

"Yeah, even then." He slowly shook his head. "We were on our way to the big time, but Jimmy made it clear it was all about him. That caused some resentment, even though he was right. People paid to see and hear him, more so than the rest of us. We were part of the package, but not the main draw."

She could see what he was getting at. "Okay, so tell me this, Trent. Why on earth would someone want to kill Jimmy and then come back to kill you?"

"I don't know." The words were flat, but a shadow flickered over his eyes.

"You were there all night, weren't you?"

He nodded. "Yeah. But I'm telling you, I drank a lot and don't remember anything. Except waking up to find Jimmy's dead body."

She believed he was finally telling her the truth. She thought about that for a moment, then sat up straighter. "Trent, if you were there that night, whoever killed Jimmy would have seen you, right?"

"Yeah." He paled. "I hadn't considered that possibility."

She felt a surge of compassion for him. "Think about it, Trent. If the killer saw you, he or she must think you saw something you shouldn't have."

Now it made sense. No wonder there had been two attempts to kill him. And she very much feared the killer wouldn't stop until Trent had been silenced, forever.

CHAPTER THREE

Trent stared at Serena, his thoughts whirling. "If that's true, why wait three months to come after me? Why not take me out of the picture right away?"

She flushed, her dark eyes shadowed with guilt. "Because of me."

He tamped down a flash of anger as the realization struck home. "When the cops stopped investigating, the killer thought he was in the clear. Only you've taken up the cause, and now the killer is afraid you'll find something. The way you tracked me down to talk must be making him or her nervous."

She tipped her chin to her chest and closed her eyes. "Yes. I'm so sorry. I can't believe I did this to you."

It wasn't that long ago that he'd accused her of bringing danger to his doorstep. Which turned out to be true. But the sheer angst on her face made him want to reassure her. "Not your fault, Serena. It's possible the killer would have come after me eventually, without you investigating the case. Jimmy's father could have hired anyone, right? The end result would be the same."

"I feel terrible." She put a hand on her stomach as if she might throw up. "The killer must have followed me."

"The man in black, right?"

She lifted her grim gaze. "It's hard to say for sure. He may not be the same man who killed Jimmy. I think it's possible the real killer has hired someone else to the job."

Great, Trent thought with a sigh. The only good thing in this entire scenario is that he must not have contributed to Jimmy's death. If he'd done something, he wouldn't be walking around with a target on his back.

Small consolation, but one he was glad to have. Still, so much had happened in the past few hours that he felt as if he'd been smacked by a semitruck. A wave of exhaustion hit hard. He rose. "We need to get some sleep."

"Trent?"

He paused at the threshold of the connecting door and glanced over his shoulder. "Yeah?"

"I'm going to do whatever I can to make sure you're safe." She stood and moved toward him. "Until we can figure this out, we need to stick together."

Up close he could see her eyes weren't dark brown or black as he'd originally thought, they were a light desert brown. It irked him to realize he was attracted to this woman, especially since he still didn't really trust her.

"We'll talk about that later." He wasn't going to blithely agree to anything at this point.

"Please, Trent." She rested her hand on his arm, and he shouldn't have noticed the strange tingle of awareness at her touch. "I don't want anything to happen to you."

It was a little late, considering his truck window was shattered and he couldn't go back to his apartment. But she looked so miserable he didn't voice his thought. "We're safe here for now, right?" Against his will, he reached up to brush a strand of hair off her cheek. "Best thing we can do is get some rest. Good night, Serena."

A slight smile creased her features. "Good night."

He quickly ducked into his room in an effort to resist the temptation to kiss her. Ridiculous reaction, he didn't want or need that sort of complication in his life.

After taking a quick shower, he stretched out on the bed and stared down at his phone. It had been a couple of weeks since Cooper had left him a message asking for help. Trent had been playing back-to-back gigs at the time, but even when he'd gotten a day off, he couldn't bring himself to return Coop's call.

Trent set the phone aside knowing the battery would likely be dead by the morning and stretched out on the bed to stare up at the ceiling. He clearly remembered the night over three years ago when he'd left Cooper to head out with the Jimmy Woodrow Band. There had been a flash of hurt in Cooper's eyes upon hearing the news, but his foster brother had encouraged him to go. To follow his dream of hitting it big as a musician. To be honest, Trent would have gone with Jimmy even if Cooper had put up an argument. Deep down, Trent had wanted nothing more than to start over with a new life. To leave everything related to those five years of living with the Preacher behind.

Even Cooper.

The Preacher and his wife, Ruth, had taken in seven foster kids. Jayme was the oldest, then Sawyer, Hailey, Cooper, Trent, Darby, and Caitlyn. Caitlyn had been the youngest and the most vulnerable to the Preacher's rage. Their lives had gone from bad to worse under the Preacher's tutelage. The man was a lunatic, making them kneel for hours as he ranted and raved about how they were sinners and God would send them all to rot in hell while he beat them with a switch. Ruth homeschooled them and made them do chores, which were the highlight of their days because they'd been away from the Preacher. Sometimes they'd argued over who got to do which chores outside, as being outdoors was the biggest treat of all.

Then came the night of the fire. Trent didn't know who'd started it, but he'd played a role in the outbreak as he'd brought in wet logs for the fire. On purpose, even though he knew he'd get a beating. He clearly remembered thinking he hoped the Preacher's cabin would fill with smoke so that they might be able to escape.

Trent hadn't caused the fire, but the cabin had filled with smoke. And even now he wasn't sorry it happened. All seven foster kids had managed to escape, despite being forced to sleep in the cellar. He recalled being woken by Hailey who whispered urgently about the smoke and needing to get out as soon as possible. Sawyer helped them up the rickety stairs, then Jayme was there, helping them up and through the smoke-filled and fiery cabin until they'd all gotten safely outside.

The Preacher and his wife hadn't made it. When they heard the wail of fire engines coming to the rescue, the seven foster kids had looked at each other. In a heartbeat, they'd all agreed they weren't going back into the system. Instead, they'd melted into the Smoky Mountains, keeping out of sight.

Trent had gone with Sawyer and Cooper. Jayme had taken little Caitlyn, while Hailey and Darby had left together. Trent had often thought they'd all meet up at some point, but that hadn't happened.

In fact, they'd never seen each other again. He and Cooper had ditched Sawyer after about a year, annoyed with his bossing them around, as if being two years older mattered one way or the other. He and Cooper had stuck together, and Cooper had helped him buy his used guitar. They'd lived together, hung out together for many years, until slowly, gradually, they'd drifted apart.

Just over three years ago, he'd left Cooper to come to Nashville. The break had seemed inevitable. At least, that's how it had felt at the time. Yet looking back, Trent realized how much he missed his foster brother.

What would Cooper think of him now, sitting in a dive motel room after performing in a dive bar hiding from someone who'd tried to kill him not just once but twice?

Coop certainly wouldn't be impressed, that's for sure.

He closed his eyes. How had his life gone so wrong?

His drinking.

Deep down, Trent knew that his excessive drinking had been the beginning of the downward spiral. Prior to joining Jimmy's band, he hadn't had money to spare for booze. He and Cooper had barely managed to work enough and steal enough to eat and pay for a tiny apartment. Cooper had started drawing for tourists, which had brought in some extra cash, while Trent had done some restaurant work between music gigs. Which was how he'd met up with Jimmy Woodrow. Jimmy had heard him practicing and brought him into their group. Trent had instantly realized that together they were way better than anything he'd done alone.

With Jimmy, Jed, and Dave, there was suddenly more than enough money to go around. And while he'd still kept a secret stash of cash hidden away, the guys were always bringing in alcohol and drugs. He clearly remembered drinking the booze while being secretly glad he hadn't paid for it.

Except he had paid for it, with the damage that had been done to his mind.

To his soul.

The fleeting success was over, never to be recaptured again. And most of the time, he preferred being sober. He knew that if he'd stayed with Jimmy's band, he'd have never been able to stay straight.

Somehow, Trent must have fallen asleep because he was in the cabin again, clawing at the top of the cellar door, shouting for someone to let him out. The fosters had left him alone down there, and he didn't know why.

HELP ME!

He woke up, drenched in sweat. Serena burst through their connecting doors holding a gun, her eyes wide with concern as she raked them over the room. "What happened?" she demanded.

"I—had a dream." He couldn't seem to tear his gaze from her weapon. "You don't need the gun."

"I thought Jimmy's killer found you," she said curtly. But she lowered the weapon so it was pointing at the floor. "You scared me."

"I pretty much scared myself." He rolled up so he was sitting on the edge of the bed and scrubbed his hands over his face. His throat felt raw, and he realized he must have screamed out loud. Talk about embarrassing. "Sorry about that."

She set the gun aside and sat down next to him. "Dreaming of the night Jimmy was murdered?"

He laughed harshly. "No. I told you, I don't remember much about that night."

"Then what?"

He shook his head. "Never mind."

"Oh," she said softly. "Must be when you lived with the devil."

He sighed, knowing he shouldn't have mentioned that. At the time, her praying over their meal had caught him off guard. He didn't know anyone who did that. For some reason, he found it strange that a woman who carried a gun and worked as a private investigator believed in God. Then again, he hadn't been around anyone who believed in God. He turned a bit so he could see her better. "Yeah, although I haven't had a nightmare like that in a long time. Sorry I woke you."

Serena regarded him steadily. He was all too aware of her sitting so close, her sleep-tousled hair framing her face. He had to drag his gaze away lest she see how much he wanted to kiss her.

"You sounded so scared," she finally admitted. "I've never heard that much agony in a person's voice."

"It's nothing." He really didn't want to have this conversation. His remembering the fire and Cooper must have brought the memories cascading back. "I'm fine. Again, sorry I woke you." He glanced at a spot over her shoulder, unable to come up with a polite way to kick her out of his room.

"Trent." She put her hand on his arm, his skin tingling from her touch. "I'm here if you want to talk."

"I don't." He winced at his blunt tone and added, "Thanks, Serena. But living with the Preacher is part of my past and has nothing to do with Jimmy's murder."

"The Preacher?" Her voice rose in shocked surprise. "You mean a real preacher?"

"Oh, he liked to preach all right," Trent drawled. "About how we were all horrible sinners and God was sending us straight to hell as he hit us with a switch."

"Oh, Trent. God is not like that."

He wasn't convinced. "It's not important. What happened back then has nothing to do with Jimmy's murder."

"But it has to do with you as a person." She squeezed his arm, then stood. "I know you don't believe in God, but I do, and I know He is watching over you, Trent. He is watching over both of us."

He shook his head, not sure why she'd think such a thing. "You, maybe. Not me." He'd done so many things wrong since escaping the Preacher that he felt certain there was no hope for him.

"Yes, you, Trent. We're all sinners, but God is good and gentle and kind. God loves us no matter what we've done."

Uncanny the way she'd read his mind. He watched her pick up her gun and cross over the threshold into her own room. Then he let out a pent-up sigh and hung his head for a moment. That was a close call. He couldn't afford to get emotionally tied up with Serena.

One minute he was singing to a crowd of roughnecks in a tavern, the next he was hiding from a killer, accompanied a beautiful woman. If there really was a God, He must have some sort of warped sense of humor.

One that deliberately put Trent in the position of wanting someone he couldn't have.

SERENA COULDN'T GET the heartrending sound of Trent's scream out of her mind, the image of him being tortured by a man who was supposed to be preaching the word of God. Not just for a short while, but for five long years.

No wonder he didn't believe.

And had started to drink.

She climbed back into bed, but sleep didn't come easily. She prayed that God would help Trent find his way home and that he'd continue on his path to stay sober. Her prayers brought a measure of peace.

The following morning, she awoke to the tantalizing scent of coffee. After washing up in the bathroom, she made her way through the open connecting door to find Trent sitting and sipping from a cup of coffee he'd made with the small pot in the room.

"Help yourself." He lifted the cup and gestured to the pot. "Makes two cups."

"You're up early," she said with a yawn as she did as he'd suggested. "I thought all musicians were night owls."

"Not me." Trent shrugged. "At least, not anymore. Being sober changes things."

She inwardly winced. Back when Trent was partying with Jimmy, she imagined he had been a night owl. It made her glad that he'd given up alcohol.

"Are you hungry?" She eyed him over the rim of her coffee cup. "I know we ate last night, but we'll need to check out of here soon."

A wry smile tugged at his mouth. "I can always eat."

"Okay, but first we need to come up with a game plan."

All hint of humor faded from his face. "What kind of plan?"

She sank down onto the edge of the bed. "If my poking around in Jimmy's case has brought the killer here, then it must be because someone told him about it." Her gaze turned serious. "I have to think Jed or Dave said something about my theory to someone who doesn't want the truth to come to light."

His scowl deepened. "Who did Jed or Dave talk to?"

She needed to tread lightly here. "I need you to think back to that night. You argued over Jimmy's affair with Heidi, but was there anyone else at the celebration that night? Anyone who seemed out of place?"

To his credit, Trent pursed his lips and considered this. "Our band manager was there, Brett Caine, but he wouldn't have a reason to kill Jimmy. Brett made money when the band made money; he took a percentage of the profits. There were a lot of groupies there, but that wasn't unusual."

Serena could only imagine the girls who'd come to party with the band. Not her scene at all, but plenty of others would have jumped at the chance. "Was Heidi there?"

Trent frowned. "I don't think so, at least not right away."

"Wasn't that unusual?"

"She wasn't always around. Heidi and Jimmy hardly kept to any sort of schedule. They were both more likely to hook up when the opportunity presented itself."

"How can we find Heidi Stout?"

Trent sighed. "I told you, I'm not even sure she gave us her real name. She was very secretive about stuff, which we all thought was odd until I overheard her conversation with her husband. Then it made sense."

"She never mentioned her husband's name?" Serena pressed. She knew Trent had been drinking back then, but she couldn't help but think there were suppressed memories that he didn't even realize he had.

"No." He hesitated, then said, "Rob."

Her pulse spiked. "Rob? As in Robert?"

Trent stared into his coffee as if the dark brew held all the secrets of the world. "All I heard was Rob. She said it almost in a derogatory tone, as if wondering why he was bothering her."

"Tell me again about the conversation you overheard between Heidi and her husband."

She half expected him to balk, but he straightened and met her gaze. "She was in the bathroom, her voice echoed off the walls. She answered the phone with his name, Rob. Then there was a brief silence as she listened, before she let out a harsh laugh and said, 'I don't care what you do. Go ahead and file for divorce, you're the one who'll be sorry. I'll make sure you don't get a dime.'"

It was more than he'd mentioned before, which only made her think that he knew more about that night than maybe he realized himself. "That's good, Trent. Rob could be Robin, I suppose, but I think it's more commonly a short-ened form of Robert."

"She wasn't a nice woman," Trent said.

"How so?"

He drained his cup and set it aside. "Heidi liked to have fun and could party most everyone under the table, except maybe Jimmy. But she would treat the rest of us like we were dirt under her feet. She'd order us around, tell us to get her food, or booze, or whatever. As if she was the queen of the castle and we were there to serve her needs. Jed lost it one day and snapped at her." A faint smile tugged at his mouth. "Dave and I were secretly glad to hear it, but Jimmy was mad. Told us to do what Heidi wanted or else."

"Or else what?"

He shrugged. "Get kicked out of the band. It wasn't as if there weren't other drummers, keyboard players, or guitar players out there who couldn't have replaced us in a heart-beat. And Jimmy made sure we knew it too."

She was horrified to hear her former childhood friend

described in this way. Her opinion of the type of man Jimmy had turned into changed for the worse. From what Trent described, Jimmy had started to believe in his own omnipotence. And that was never good.

Not that his being a jerk meant Jimmy deserved to be murdered. Still, it opened up a wide range of additional possibilities.

With that attitude, Jimmy could have ticked off any number of people.

But she was still thinking of Heidi's husband, Rob. What if Rob found out about Jimmy Woodrow being the guy his wife was cheating with? Sounds as if divorce would cost him money, maybe good old Rob thought it would be better to simply eliminate the competition.

It wasn't necessarily a great motive because Rob had to know that if his wife cheated once, she'd do it again. Killing all the men she'd chosen to have affairs with wasn't exactly a viable long-term plan.

Unless Rob had targeted Jimmy because he felt threatened by the musician. Maybe Rob was seeking revenge against Jimmy for busting up the marriage.

A theory, but impossible to look into without knowing who Heidi and Rob really were. Was Trent right about the last name of Stout being an alias? It seemed a stretch that the woman would make up a different last name, yet anything was possible. Much of her clientele involved spouses who wanted proof of suspected infidelity. Serena needed to do some digging with her computer.

"You said something about breakfast," Trent reminded her.

"Yeah." She finished her coffee. "We should go, but we're going to need a place to stay. I know you didn't like the idea of going to my place, but it's probably better than hotel hopping."

Trent didn't say anything for a long moment. "Fine. We can go to your place, but I'd like to stop by my apartment to pick up a few things."

"That's not a good idea," she protested. "Remember the gunfire? There could still be someone watching the place."

"I'll find a way in through the back and be in and out before anyone is the wiser." Trent stood. "I need a change of clothes and more cash. Oh, and I have a gig later tonight."

Was he kidding? "No, Trent. You can't go on as if your life hasn't changed. You'll need to cancel."

"Not going to cancel." Sheer stubbornness darkened his green eyes. "This is my life, my career, Serena. And I highly doubt someone will shoot me off the stage at Whistlers."

Whistlers was a step up from the Thirsty Saloon, so she could understand his desire to keep the performance. She'd been there last Saturday when he'd played. "Trent, you have to think this through. If they found you at your other gigs, they'll find you tonight too." A horrible thought occurred to her. "You have a website, don't you? A site that lists all the places you're performing."

"Yeah, that's how I let my numerous adoring fans know where I'll be." There was a hint of sarcasm in his tone.

"That's exactly my point." She narrowed her gaze. "Jimmy's killer will know he can find you at Whistlers tonight."

"That gives us a chance to figure out who he's working for, right?" Trent led the way out of the motel room.

She ducked into her room to grab her keys before heading out to the SUV. "They only do that kind of stuff on TV," she complained as she backed out of the parking spot. "And I'm not a cop, remember? I can't call the SWAT team in for backup."

"It's still better than sitting around, doing nothing."

His stubbornness made her want to scream. She drew in a deep breath and looked at him. "Breakfast first? Or your apartment?"

"My apartment."

Yeah, she figured that would be his choice. She headed to Trent's apartment building.

"Remember, we're going in from the back," he said. "Don't take the main street."

She headed down the side streets Trent had taken on foot in order to escape the gunman. She hoped the police weren't still hanging around, but as she pulled up in the alley, there was no sign of law enforcement.

A gunshot and shattered truck window apparently didn't warrant much of a response in this area of the city.

"Stay here, I'll be back shortly." Trent pushed open his door.

"Wait." She grabbed his arm. "You are going to come back, right? You're not going to ditch me again?"

"I don't have wheels, so ditching you wouldn't be easy. My phone is dead; I need my power cord. And I don't have anywhere else to go." The simple statement caused a pang in the region of her heart. "I'll be back."

"Okay." She released him and tried to smile. "Thank you."

He shook his head wryly and closed the door behind him. She gripped the steering wheel tightly, trying not to imagine all the ways this could go wrong.

The gunman could actually be in his apartment waiting for him.

Serena pushed out of her SUV and hurried after Trent. But he was already gone from view. Biting her lip, she spied the rear door. Was it locked? Only one way to find out.

Hurrying over, she grabbed the door handle, surprised when it opened easily. There was a lock, but apparently, no one bothered to use it.

She didn't know which apartment was Trent's, so she made her way through the building to the lobby. Names were printed above the mailboxes there, and she found Atkins listed above apartment number 2 1 4.

The stairs creaked ominously, although she hoped the twang of country music blaring from one of the apartments masked the sound. Then she heard a loud thudding noise.

Trent!

She sprinted the rest of the way. The door to Trent's apartment hung open, but she couldn't see all the way inside. She pulled her weapon and stealthily approached. She saw a shadow and shouted, "Stop!"

There was another crash, then a man bolted from the apartment, hitting her hard enough to send her flying backward against the wall before he disappeared.

CHAPTER FOUR

"Trent! Are you okay?" Serena's panicked tone had him struggling to sit upright. He groaned, his head pounding much like it used to when he'd overindulged.

"Yeah." He forced himself to look up at her. For a moment there were two faces, but then they thankfully merged into one. "Did you get a good look at him?"

"Unfortunately, I didn't." She dropped to her knees beside him. "We need to get you to the hospital."

"I'm fine." His head hurt like the dickens, but he wasn't about to go to the hospital. He looked around his apartment. "At least he didn't wreck the place."

"Huh?" Serena frowned. "Your head injury is bad, Trent. The place is a disaster. It looks like the assailant was searching for something."

"No, I, uh, tend to be a slob." He grimaced at her shocked expression.

"You . . . live like this?" She was truly horrified.

He decided this line of conversation wasn't going anywhere. He pushed himself up to his feet, staggering a bit. "That guy was hiding in here, waiting for me."

"But he didn't use a knife or a gun," Serena observed. "Which doesn't make any sense, considering the previous attempts were much more significant."

"I know." Everything had happened very fast, but he knew he only had himself to blame. He should have anticipated someone might be inside his apartment. The door had been locked. Still, he knew the locks were flimsy and could easily be bypassed.

"What happened?" Serena took his arm and led him over to the sofa. She had to move a pile of clothes so they could sit down.

"I came inside and headed toward my bedroom. I sensed movement behind me. I ducked and turned so that the blow glanced off the side of my head rather than hitting me dead-on." Grimly, he realized the attempted attack mirrored what had likely happened to Jimmy. Only the star singer had been too impaired to realize what was about to happen.

"What did he hit you with?" Serena reached up to gently palpate his temple.

"Not sure, but possibly a gun. Maybe he thought the gunfire would bring too many people out from the other apartments."

"Very likely," she agreed. "You need some ice for this bump."

"You can check the freezer." He had several full ice cube trays as he liked his water icy cold. Maybe a remnant of his drinking days.

Serena jumped up and rummaged in his minuscule kitchen. He could hear her muttering about the stack of dirty dishes in the sink and couldn't help but smile. Cooper had been a neat freak, too, and had always made comments about Trent's mess in their apartment.

His smile faded as he thought again about Cooper. He should have called him back. Should have gone rushing down to Gatlinburg to help him out.

He was a sorry excuse for a man, thinking only about himself. Granted, he'd been fighting to stay sober, to keep on the straight and narrow, but that wasn't a good reason to let Cooper down.

Now, so much time had passed that he couldn't bring himself to return his foster brother's call. Deep down, Trent feared his call would go unanswered because Cooper was dead.

That maybe all the fosters had died. And that his turn was coming soon.

"Hold this against your temple." Serena pressed a dish towel full of ice cubes into his hand.

He did as she asked, the cold temperature helping to ease the ache. "I guess you were right. Coming back to get my things wasn't a good idea."

"I never should have let you come up here alone." Her desert brown eyes were full of self-recrimination. "If I hadn't followed when I did, so that I was here in the hall-way . . ." She didn't have to finish the thought, it echoed through his mind.

He'd be dead. Just like Jimmy.

He shook off the depressing thought. Three strikes and you're out, right? This was the third attempt against him, and he couldn't ignore the threat any longer.

However, it had happened, someone decided he knew something about Jimmy's death and wanted to silence him, forever.

Too bad he didn't know who had killed Jimmy. It would be easier for both him and Serena if he did.

"Yeah, well, obviously we can't stay." He handed the

makeshift ice pack back to her and stood. "I'll get my stuff."

It didn't take him long to grab some clothes and toiletries and his phone charger, stuffing them into a small rolling duffel bag. It was the bag he'd used when traveling to various gigs with the band. He quickly returned to the main living area.

Serena handed him the ice pack and tried to take the bag. He tightened his grip on it. "I've got it."

She sighed, mumbled, "Men," then led the way back out through the rear door of the apartment building. Her SUV was still blocking the alley, but thankfully there was no sign of a ticket.

He stored his bag in the back next to his guitar, then slid into the passenger seat. He leaned his elbow on the door and pressed the ice pack to his head. The cold helped deaden the pain.

"I'm thinking we shouldn't go to my place either." Serena drove through the neighborhood, glancing frequently at the rearview mirror. "The killer must know I'm involved in this by now. Better we stay off grid."

He straightened and turned to glance back through the window. "You think someone might be following us?"

"I don't know, but I'm still going to do my best to shake off anyone who might be back there." True to her word, Serena made an abrupt right-hand turn, then a quick left, barely skating through a yellow light.

He had to give her credit, she was taking the most recent attack on him to heart. Probably because she still felt guilty for whatever role she may have played. Odd, but he didn't blame her. Not any longer.

Finding the person who'd killed Jimmy was the right thing to do. He should have called the police back then rather than hiding out like a coward. Unfortunately, going back to fix the mistakes he'd made wasn't an option. But now he could help Serena find the killer.

And she was right in that they needed to track down Heidi Stout and her husband, Rob.

"I know plenty of low-level motels," he offered wryly. "They're all in high crime areas, though."

"I'm surprised." She shot him a quick glance. "Jimmy preferred nice, expensive hotels, didn't he?"

"Yeah, but in our earlier days, we couldn't afford that." He thought back to those first few gigs that hadn't paid well, especially after cutting the money four ways, with Jimmy getting a higher percentage than the rest of them. "Take another left up ahead."

Serena followed his directions to another motel that was similar to the place they'd stayed in the night before. She drove by it, then went around the block and pulled over to the side of the road. "It's too early to get a room, so we need to find a place to hang out for a while. Something that offers free Wi-Fi so I can use my laptop."

"There aren't many nice coffee shops around here," he pointed out. "You're better off heading into the city."

She nodded and pulled back into traffic. The ice began to seriously melt, so he opened his window and shook out the bits of ice that remained before dropping the wet towel between his feet.

"We'll get more ice at the coffee shop."

"Don't bother. I'm fine." The initial stabbing pain had subsided to a dull throb. "At some point, we should go to the police."

Her glance was sharp. "I thought you didn't want that?"

"I didn't." Trusting anyone was difficult, but this guy seemed bound and determined to do him harm. "But shouldn't we get these attacks on record?"

"We should, yes." She sighed. "But we'll need to head back to the police station closest to your place to file a report."

"Maybe later." He shouldn't have brought it up. "You really think you can find Heidi or Rob by searching online? There have to be millions of people with similar first names out there."

"Yes, but they may not be linked together, as a couple. I figure it's worth a shot. You thought there was a significant amount of money involved, that may help us narrow them down too."

"Okay." He figured she must know what she's doing. "If you find a picture of Heidi, I should be able to recognize her."

Serena flashed a smile. "I'm counting on it."

For the first time since the knife attack outside the Thirsty Saloon, Trent felt as if they might actually learn the truth about what had happened to Jimmy. Even though he was often lonely, he didn't want to go back to those days of being in the band. Certainly, he didn't trust himself to stay straight in that environment.

His failures were his problem. Maybe Jimmy partied more than he should have, but that didn't mean he deserved to be murdered.

For a moment, he thought back to Jed and Dave. He'd often wondered why they hadn't stayed longer at the post-gig celebration, but they'd left just after midnight. He'd been too buzzed to care, but the more he thought about it, their early departure had been odd.

He frowned, trying to remember if they'd left with a couple of groupies. It was a rational explanation, but he didn't remember women hanging on the two men.

Or maybe he just had been too drunk to notice.

There was no reason for either Jed or Dave to kill Jimmy. And since they'd left the suite, the fight angle didn't make sense either.

If only he could remember what had happened.

As Serena navigated traffic he thought back to that night. Three months was a long time, worse when your memory was tainted by alcohol. He did his best to remember the moment when Jed and Dave had left. Was it his imagination or had they looked upset? Had Jimmy said something stupid, the way he sometimes had? Jimmy liked to brag that he was taking them along for the ride, as if they wouldn't be anything without him.

Which was true, not that they'd appreciated hearing it all the time.

He remembered there were two beautiful girls fawning over Jimmy. Their faces were a blur. Had one been Heidi? Or had she shown up to find two women and Jimmy enjoying themselves?

It didn't take much imagination to imagine Heidi clubbing Jimmy in the back of the head. He'd always thought her to be mentally unstable. Maybe it was the drugs, but he'd seen her go from laughing one minute to ranting and raving the next.

Kinda like the Preacher, except the Preacher had never smiled, much less laughed. No, the Preacher had various stages of rage, which had gotten worse when he drank. A fact that should have deterred Trent from succumbing to alcohol.

Except it hadn't.

"This will work." Serena's voice cut into his thoughts. "They offer food and free Wi-Fi."

"Okay." He knew the food and coffee would cost twice

as much because of the free internet, but getting a line on Heidi and Rob was important.

The place was crowded. They stood in line, but when a table opened up, Serena nudged him. "Grab it, quick."

He did as she asked. She returned with two coffees and two egg sandwiches a good fifteen minutes later.

"Hope this is okay." She sat with a sigh, setting her laptop on the table between them.

"I'm not picky." Once, Trent had picked through garbage for a meal; he and Cooper had been that desperate. It was about the time they'd resorted to stealing, something that had bothered Cooper more than him.

Trent's father had given him a guitar before he'd died. Trent had taught himself to play, escaping the apartment as often as he could, especially once his mother's new boyfriend had come into the picture. The guy had physically abused Trent, which is how he'd ended up in foster care. To be honest, he still carried a lot of anger about that.

The Preacher's hitting them with a switch hadn't been as bad as being struck with a heavy belt buckle, but it had brought back memories he'd rather have forgotten.

Serena bowed her head again, silently praying over their food. He didn't quite understand her. She was different from anyone he'd met.

Then again, considering the trajectory of his life, that wasn't saying much. He didn't hang around with "good" girls like Serena.

Which only made him circle back to his foster sisters. Jayme, Hailey, Darby, and Caitlyn. If he believed in God, he'd ask Him to watch over the women.

Over all the fosters. If it wasn't already too late.

SERENA SENSED Trent was uncomfortable with her praying, but that only made her more determined to show him there was another way to get through the difficulties in life.

By leaning on God's strength, His guidance.

His love.

"Again, we have a lot to be thankful for." She eyed Trent as she unwrapped her breakfast sandwich.

He didn't agree or disagree. He just took a long sip of his coffee, then took a bite of his sandwich. "Where do you usually start when searching for someone?"

"Social media." She set her food aside and powered up the computer. "I'm hoping that by using both names, Heidi and Rob, we'll find something relatively quickly."

"If they're on social media," he pointed out. "I'm not."

"But Jimmy was," she said. "I know because I checked his page right after his death. Thousands of people posted condolences before someone took the page off-line."

"Who did that?"

She shrugged. "I figured his manager, Brett. Or maybe Jimmy's father asked someone to take it down. I wouldn't blame him."

"I guess that must have been hard to see," Trent agreed somberly. "And now that you mention Jimmy's social media, my picture must have been plastered all over, along with the rest of the band." He looked a bit stunned by that revelation.

"You were, yes." She wanted to mention how much better Trent looked now, compared to those pictures. He looked healthy and fit sitting across from her.

Although far too handsome for her peace of mind.

After taking another bite of her meal, she went to work. She looked at multiple responses for Heidi and Rob, rejecting those who weren't in the state of Tennessee. Kentucky was a possibility, but she figured the pair had to be living in either Nashville or Memphis.

That's where most of the money was anyway.

"What can I do to help?" Trent asked after he finished his meal.

She glanced at him. "Hopefully, I can find someone for you to identify soon."

"There has to be something more I can do." He looked frustrated. "Sitting here doing nothing is making me antsy."

"What would you normally be doing?" Certainly not cleaning, that was for sure.

"Practicing, composing." He drummed his fingers on the table. "Don't forget, I have to perform at Whistlers tonight."

She swallowed a sigh and rubbed her temple. Why Trent was being so stubborn about keeping that gig was beyond comprehension. "I thought you'd call that off after the assault at your apartment."

"No, I'm going." The stubborn glint was back in his green eyes. "And for your information, I don't have a website. That was a joke. Nobody cares when and where I'm playing, which is why I'm not turning this opportunity down."

She decided to let it go for now. Turning her attention back to the screen, she continued her search. It wasn't easy to ignore Trent's impatience radiating toward her, but she did her best. This kind of thing was tedious and time-consuming. The life of a private investigator wasn't nearly as exciting as TV portrayed it.

At least, not usually. The past twelve hours with Trent was exactly like something out of a movie.

"I'll get us more coffee." Trent cleared the garbage from

their table, then stood in line.

Serena continued going through pictures, one after the other without success. Was it possible Trent was right about Heidi using an alias name? Maybe her real name was Penelope or Trudy.

She smiled to herself as she searched. There weren't many Rob and Heidi's mentioned together, so she was left with just Heidi as the first name, of which there were many. None, of course, with the last name of Stout.

This could take all day.

Trent returned with two coffees. He watched over her shoulder for a few minutes before taking the seat across from her.

"Nothing yet?"

She started to shake her head when a striking redhead caught her eye. Clicking on the image, she was shocked to see a beautiful woman dressed in a scanty bright blue bikini. There was no mention of Rob, but something about the way the woman laughed into the camera made her turn the computer toward Trent, watching his expression closely.

His eyes widened, and he choked on his coffee. "That's her," he sputtered. "That's Heidi. Only when I saw her, she was a brunette, not a redhead."

"Easy enough to change hair color." With a surge of satisfaction, she turned the screen back for a deeper dive. "This site lists her as Heidi Law, every single photo that I'm able to see is a bit risqué."

"Not surprised," Trent said. "That fits Heidi's description perfectly."

"No mention of a husband either. In fact, her status is single." She frowned at Trent. "Wouldn't Rob be upset to find her social media lists her as single?"

"I would assume so," he agreed. "Unless she didn't

change her status until after Jimmy's murder. And if her last name is really Law. Honestly, it sounds fake to me, just like Stout. No reason for Rob to look up a woman named Heidi Law, right?"

"You make a good point." She couldn't see all the posts, but most were of Heidi alone, no husband or boyfriend in sight. Not even a picture of her and Jimmy together. But the location on the main page did list her as living in Brentwood, which was one of the wealthiest suburbs of Nashville.

If Heidi was rich, it made sense she lived in Brentwood. Yet the discovery wasn't nearly as helpful as she'd hoped. She could try looking into property records to see if she could find anyone with the last name of Stout or Law, but that would take even more time. She closed the computer and sat back in her seat.

"We know Heidi lives in Brentwood and has a social media site that lists her as single. I tried looking up a Rob Stout, but nothing came up." She abruptly opened the computer again. "Give me a minute to try Rob Law."

"Or maybe the famous Rob Lowe?" Trent joked.

"Why not?" Unfortunately, neither name brought up anyone living in Brentwood, although there was a Robert Lawson in Nashville. She stared at the image of the good-looking guy for a long moment, before showing the picture to Trent. "What do you think? Is Law short for Lawson?"

He stared at the photograph, then shook his head. "Maybe. You could try looking for a Rob or Robert Stout, see if that brings up something."

She pulled up a property search she paid for on a monthly basis, but the name Robert Lawson didn't come up as owning property in Nashville or Brentwood.

Another strikeout.

"The staff are sending us dirty looks," Trent said in a low voice. "We've been hogging their table for two hours now."

"Okay, let's go." She closed the computer again. "I have more areas to search, but we can wait until we're settled in a motel room."

"I was thinking we should pick a place closer to Whistlers." Trent held the door open for her as they returned to the SUV.

She tried not to grimace. Whistlers was nicer than the Thirsty Saloon, but it wasn't downtown Nashville either. Any motel nearby wouldn't be very appealing. "Okay, but it's still too early to check in."

"How about we sit at the park?" He gestured toward it. "I'd really like to practice a bit. Especially my new songs."

"Sure." She couldn't bring herself to refuse such a simple request. Listening to Trent play and sing wasn't a hardship. "I'm not familiar enough with your work to know which songs are your newest ones."

"I'm not as good at composing music as Jimmy, but he used some of my stuff when we hit the clubs."

"Really?" She turned to look at him in surprise. "I didn't know that."

"Well, it's not as if Jimmy gave me much credit," he said wryly. "In fact, he always called them our songs, as if he'd contributed half the vocals and music."

She was beginning to understand the real dynamics of the Jimmy Woodrow Band. "And what about Jed and Dave? Did they contribute too?"

"Sometimes. Mostly Jed. He insisted we have at least one drum solo in every performance." Trent shook his head. "Jimmy argued about that, but Jed insisted that was something that people had come to expect."

The more she heard about the music business, the less she liked it. "I think I'd rather read a book."

Trent looked startled, then grinned wryly and nodded. "I see what you mean, too much drama. I don't miss that part at all."

She found a place to park, and they headed across the lawn to an isolated spot near a large oak tree. Trent sat with his back against the trunk, his guitar across his lap. He drank from a water bottle, then began to strum. She sat close beside him, listening intently as he played.

Despite her earlier annoyance, the music called to her. And when Trent began to sing, a chill rippled down her spine.

He was good, no doubt about that. She was actually surprised he hadn't been scooped up by another band after Jimmy's death. Especially if he could write songs like this one, songs that reached deep into a person's soul.

The lyrics were haunting, lost love and desperation. It made her wonder if that's how Trent felt after everything that had transpired in his life.

When he finished, she instinctively clapped. So did several other parkgoers nearby.

"That was incredible," she said softly. "Really amazing, Trent."

"Thanks." She was surprised at the way his cheeks went pink. "I, uh, didn't realize it would be more difficult to sing to one person rather than to a crowd."

Their gazes locked, and she felt as if she couldn't breathe. For a long moment, tension shimmered between them until Trent surprised her for the second time by bending close, lowering his head, and capturing her mouth in a warm kiss.

CHAPTER FIVE

Trent couldn't explain why he'd kissed Serena, but the moment his lips had touched hers, flames sparked and heat rose in a wave that was impossible to ignore. In the back of his mind, alarm bells rang, but he shut them out. Instead, he drew Serena into his arms and deepened the kiss.

She kissed him back until she abruptly broke off from their embrace and scrambled to her feet, glancing around as if to make sure no one had seen them. "I, uh, don't do this kind of thing."

Maybe it was the impact of her kiss, but he didn't understand. He slowly rose and faced her. "What kind of thing? Kiss a guy?"

"This." She waved a hand and took several steps back. "I'm not one of those women who trails after musicians."

Call him slow, but he still didn't get what she was talking about. "I never thought you were. I don't do the groupie thing anymore either. I'm hardly famous, just trying to earn a living." He hesitated, then added, "It was a simple kiss, Serena." Okay, so that was a lie because there had been nothing simple about it.

No, this woman who looked like a pixie and packed a gun had complication written all over her.

A dichotomy that he ironically wanted to unravel. Why had she become a private investigator anyway? It wasn't a likely career path for a young woman. He estimated Serena was roughly his age, twenty-five or twenty-six. She was clearly smart, so why choose PI work? There must be a story there.

"Look, we can't afford to become distracted." She blew out a breath. "We need to find Jimmy's killer, remember? That's our focus."

"Okay." He could tell she was embarrassed by their brief embrace, and it made him sad. Not that he was looking for a relationship any more than she was. Suddenly, it hit him. "You have a boyfriend."

"What? No!" Her eyes widened with horror. "I'd never kiss you if I was involved with someone. That's not it. It's just—you're not my type."

"Because I play the guitar and sing for my supper?" For some reason, her comment stung. "It's an honest way to make a living."

"No—yes, it is, but . . ." She shrugged helplessly. "Let's just pretend it never happened."

Yet another blow to his ego, but he nodded. Maybe she was worried about a relapse in his drinking. Whatever. He wasn't one to push where he wasn't welcome. Although her response to his kiss made it clear she'd felt something other than revulsion. "Okay, if that's what you want."

"Thank you." She eyed her watch. "How much longer would you like to practice?"

"Does it matter? It's still too early to check into a motel," he pointed out.

"Maybe not, depends on how busy the place is." Serena

looked everywhere but at him. "I think we should give it a try."

"Fine with me." He did his best to sound nonchalant. He adjusted the guitar strap so the instrument was over his back. "Let's go."

She took a few steps forward, then stopped and turned to face him. "Have you ever considered hypnosis?"

He felt as if she'd tossed a brick at his face. "What? Why would I?"

She licked her dry lips. "I believe you might have repressed some memories from the night Jimmy died. Being hypnotized would be a way to get those memories to resurface."

"No." He was fundamentally repelled by the idea. "Forget it. Not happening."

She stared at him for a long moment, then turned and continued walking toward the area where they'd left the SUV.

Hypnosis? Over his dead body. For a moment, a memory fragment flashed in his mind. Loud voices. His? Jimmy's? Or the killer's?

Did it matter? He wasn't going to be able to ID a killer from a fuzzy memory of a voice.

For all he knew, he'd imagined the whole thing. Hallucinations weren't uncommon while drinking. Especially the amount he'd consumed.

They rode in silence as Serena made her way back to the area where Whistlers was located. In the bright light of daytime, the place looked worse than he remembered. The paint on the outside was peeling and the open sign hung crookedly in the window. Yet he knew that by later that evening, the place would be packed with people determined to have a good time. Whistlers did a brisk business on Saturday nights.

"There's a motel to the east about five blocks from here," he said, breaking the prolonged silence.

She nodded but didn't comment. It didn't take long for them to arrive at the run-down motel that looked even worse than Whistlers. When he pushed open his door, she lifted a hand.

"Wait."

He looked at her over his shoulder. "For what?"

"I'd like to go in alone." Her expression was serious.

"Why?"

"You're in danger. Better to keep you hidden, don't you think?"

"I'm not going to be hidden tonight at Whistlers," he felt compelled to point out.

"Yeah, don't remind me. I still haven't figured out how to handle that." She pushed open her door and jumped down. He watched as she disappeared inside the lobby.

He couldn't seem to pry her request to be hypnotized from his mind. He didn't want anyone poking through his memories. Not just the night Jimmy died, but those years he'd lived with the Preacher. And the years before that when his mother's boyfriend whipped him with a belt buckle. Bad enough to send him to the hospital. Then into foster care.

Too many bad things were hiding in the recesses of his mind. Trent worried that if one memory was brought to the surface, the others would soon follow, cascading over him until he crumpled beneath the weight.

Something like that could send him back to seeking solace in the bottom of a bottle.

No, the risk was too great. He was doing okay now and

planned to keep on the straight and narrow. They'd have to find Jimmy's killer some other way.

Frankly, it was a job for the police. Not a PI like Serena. Certainly not for a musician.

Serena returned to the SUV holding two motel room keys. "We're all set."

"Connecting rooms again?" He hoped she hadn't asked for two rooms just because of their brief but intense kiss.

"Yes." She glanced at him. "It's not that I don't trust you, Trent. I just think it's better for us to have some privacy."

"Sounds good." He wasn't sure why the arrangement bothered him, he preferred having privacy. Besides, he was oddly reassured that she actually trusted him not to pounce on her like a starving man at a buffet. "Did you have to pay extra?"

"You mean for an early check-in?" She shook her head. "Nope. The guy was happy enough to have two customers. Sounds like the place is pretty much empty, which seems strange for a Saturday night."

"September means kids are headed back to school." He shrugged. "Tourist season starts winding down by now. Things will stay low-key until closer to the holidays, when tourism tends to spike again."

"True." She parked off to the side of their rooms, there wasn't a back parking lot available here, and slid out from behind the wheel. Trent paused to grab his guitar and his duffel, feeling a little bad that she didn't have a change of clothes too.

"We should have stopped at a shopping mall so you could pick up a few things." He took the key she offered. "I have a bag, you don't."

"I'll think about it." Serena disappeared into her motel room, closing the door behind her.

He went inside and unlocked the connecting door between their rooms. He should practice some more, but the musty smell inside the room made him long to return to the park.

"I've decided to make a quick stop at the store we passed along the way," Serena said, coming into his room through the open doorway. "But I'd like you to stay here while I'm gone."

"I'm not a prisoner." His tone was sharp, so he tried to soften it, adding, "Why don't I ride along with you? Two of us watching out for possible danger is better than one."

"Okay." She glanced around his room. "I can see why you wouldn't want to hang out here. This place is worse than the last one, and I didn't think that was even possible."

"Exactly." He opened the windows to help air the place out, then picked up his guitar. "Let's get out of here."

The trip to the store took less than ten minutes. "Do you mind waiting out here?" Serena asked.

He could imagine she didn't want him seeing the personal items she'd need to buy, so he nodded. "Sure."

"Thanks." She left and headed inside.

He opened the door, then took his guitar and once again strummed a few notes. He normally didn't have to deal with threats against him before a performance, and he was disconcerted at how difficult it was to concentrate. With an effort, he pushed the recent incidents aside to focus on the music.

As the lyrics echoed in his mind, he found himself thinking about Serena. About how she'd looked so beautiful and engrossed by his song. About how she'd tasted so sweet when he'd kissed her.

Twang. His fingers slipped off the strings, making a jarring sound. He inwardly sighed and turned to store the guitar in the back seat.

Somehow, he'd need to get his mind off Serena and centered on his music. Or tonight's gig might be his last.

SERENA FLEW THROUGH THE STORE, picking out a new set of clothes, underwear, toiletries, and a power cord in record time. Partially because she didn't like leaving Trent outside and vulnerable, but also because she didn't want him wandering in to find her.

There was no doubt in her mind Trent had seen his share of women's underwear. But not hers. And not after that devastating kiss.

She'd been seriously knocked off balance by his embrace, to the point she was tempted to call Jimmy's father and tell him this case was a dead end and that he should go back to bothering the police.

Only the recent attempts against Trent made it clear the case wasn't a dead end. There wasn't a doubt in her mind that Jimmy had been murdered and that the killer was now focused on Trent.

But who? And why? Understanding the motive would help find the killer.

Jealousy? That would put Jed, Dave, and Rob at the top of the suspect list. All three of them had a reason to be jealous of Jimmy.

Yet there was also the possibility of Heidi herself losing control and killing him. Maybe they'd argued about her being married. Or maybe Jimmy had wanted to break things off and that sent Heidi into a rage.

Or maybe it was just an overzealous fan who'd gotten upset over something trivial. With a guy like Jimmy, the possibilities were endless.

She paid for her purchases and headed back outside. Trent was sitting with the door open, staring moodily at nothing in particular. "Are you okay?"

He glanced at her and nodded. "Get what you need?"

"Yes, thanks." She tossed the bag into the back seat. "You want me to take you back to the park?"

"No, I'll practice in the motel room." He forced a resigned smile. "Should be aired out by now."

Serena wanted to broach the subject of hypnosis again but couldn't think of a way to make him change his mind. After hearing only the barest of information about his time with the Preacher, she could understand why he didn't want anything to do with it.

But if the attempts to kill him continued, she'd have to find a way to get him to cooperate. Reliving bad memories might be bad, yet how did that compare to being injured or dead? The goal had to be to find the killer, before he or she succeeded in silencing Trent forever.

"Are you worried I'll go back to drinking?"

His question caught her off guard. "Should I be?"

"It's a reasonable assumption, but no. You shouldn't. I didn't drink until I hooked up with Jimmy." A shadow crossed his green eyes. "I don't plan to go back to that lifestyle ever again."

"I believe you." She smiled. "And I'll pray for you too."

He didn't say anything more. Upon returning to the motel, they each stayed in their own rooms. She could hear Trent playing as she worked on her computer, trying to find property owned by Heidi Law, Lawson, or Stout.

But she came up empty.

She also verified that Trent didn't have a website. Since she hadn't seen a computer in his apartment, it wasn't a surprise. Yet Whistlers did have a website and listed Trent Atkins as the performer playing there that evening.

Anyone following Trent would know to search in places offering live music. Granted, live music was everywhere in Nashville, yet these places wanted to advertise who would be there. It was likely that's how he'd been found at the Thirsty Saloon last night.

And it made her worry about another attack happening again. Maybe Trent was right in that it was time to call the police.

Only she didn't honestly think the cops would be much help. Especially when the attacks had been so varied, with too many suspects and absolutely no proof that any of this was related to Jimmy's death.

The music stopped, and she imagined Trent was trying to get some rest. Neither of them had slept much the night before. At six o'clock, Trent poked his head through the doorway. "I'm hungry."

"Me too." She hadn't wanted to interrupt but gladly shut down the computer. "You want to eat at Whistlers? Or somewhere else?"

"Somewhere else," he said without hesitation.

"Okay." Trent stored his guitar in the back of her SUV. She was getting the impression he never went anywhere without it. "What about that family restaurant near the store?"

"Works for me," he agreed. He glanced at her. "Find anything useful?"

"No." She frowned and pulled out of the small parking lot. "Nothing on Heidi Law, Heidi Lawson, or Heidi Stout."

"Lawrence?" he asked. "Or maybe a hyphenated name?"

She frowned. "Those are good ideas, but I searched on every single Heidi in the entire Nashville area. Either her last name Stout or any form of Lawson, or her first name isn't Heidi at all."

He grimaced. "Wouldn't surprise me if she lied about that."

Serena tried not to feel disheartened by the setback. She kept a wary eye on her rearview mirror as she drove, yet her thoughts spun around in her mind. Would the police have a better way of tracking Heidi Law down? Maybe. If they believed her to be a viable suspect.

Based on the word of Trent who'd been intoxicated at the time of Jimmy's murder. And who'd left the scene of the crime.

She inwardly winced. Yeah, maybe it was better to hold off on that. At least for a while. She pulled into a parking space, then shut down the engine. "I noticed on the Whistlers website you play at eight o'clock."

"Till midnight," he confirmed. "As usual."

Yeah, the same timeframe he'd performed at the Thirsty Saloon. Predictable enough for the killer to know too.

"Do they have a bouncer?" she asked as they walked toward the restaurant.

"Yeah, why?" Trent held the door open for her.

"Just trying to think of who we might have as backup." The hostess quickly crossed over to greet them. "Table for two, please."

"This way." She led them to a table in the corner. Serena wondered if they looked like a couple who wanted privacy.

Don't go there, she warned. Repeating their earlier kiss wasn't an option.

Trent waited until their server came by to take their order before leaning over the table. "The assailant isn't going to try something while I'm on stage performing," he said in a low voice. "All we need is an escort to the car afterward, and we should be fine."

"Should be, but no guarantee." She noticed he was rubbing his injured temple. "Does your head still hurt?"

"I'm fine. The nap helped." He seemed uncomfortable with her concern. "Trust me, I've endured far worse."

"I hate knowing you've suffered at the hands of a man who should have been following God's word," she said in a low voice.

"The Preacher hit us with a switch, but that wasn't as bad as the belt buckle Rogan used," he said with a shrug. "Besides, that's all in the past."

"Rogan?"

"My mother's boyfriend."

She stared in horror. "That's awful. You could still press charges against them."

Trent let out a harsh laugh. "No use. It's been too long, I don't even know Rogan's last name. They took me away from her after I landed in the hospital. I never saw him or my mother again, although I missed having my guitar. Oh, and the Preacher is dead."

She choked on her water. "You killed him?"

A flash of hurt darkened his eyes. "I've never killed anyone."

"I'm sorry." She reached across the table to touch his hand. "To be honest, I could understand if you had. In self-defense," she added.

"The Preacher and his wife, Ruth, didn't survive the

fire." He took a long sip of his water. "And it's partially my fault they didn't get out in time."

"What happened?"

"I don't know exactly." He toyed with his paper straw. "We were forced to sleep on pallets in the cellar. Hailey woke us up, and we could smell the smoke and hear the crackle from the fire. Sawyer was at the top of the stairs, and somehow Jayme was there, too, helping us up and out of the cabin. The smoke was so thick I couldn't see anything. We held hands as we stumbled out of the cabin. Then we hid in the woods, watching as the flames engulfed the place."

"Doesn't sound like you did anything, Trent."

"I brought in wet wood for the fire." He met her gaze straight on. "In fact, I specifically searched for wood that had been soaked in the nearby river."

"Why would you do that?"

He lifted a shoulder, then glanced away. "We all rebelled in our little ways. Bringing in the wood was my job, so I thought why not bring in wet wood? I figured the Preacher wouldn't notice until the interior of the cabin filled with smoke."

"Because you wanted to escape," she said, reading the expression on his face.

"We did. We talked about it late at night sometimes, but it seemed impossible. Especially since he locked us in the cellar."

She couldn't imagine living like that for a week, much less five long years. A spurt of anger hit hard. "He deserved to die that night."

"I thought so," he agreed. "Although that wasn't my intent. I had some half-brained idea that the Preacher would come down to yell at me. We talked about ganging up on him, that all seven of us working together could probably take him. But Caitlyn . . ." His voice drifted off.

"What about Caitlyn?"

"She was the youngest and scared to death. We tried to shelter her as much as possible, but the Preacher made sure to threaten her enough that the rest of us fell in line."

Her stomach rolled at the image he'd painted. "I'm so sorry."

"Well, it was shortly after that discussion that the fire broke out, so it worked out in the end."

"Worked out?" It sounded like something straight out of a horror flick. "Seven kids running off in the middle of the woods isn't exactly a happy ending."

"It was to us. We made a pact not to go back into the foster system and disappeared into the woods." He offered a lopsided smile. "And while we made a lot of mistakes along the way, especially since living on the streets wasn't easy, we managed to survive. I even managed to get another guitar, which helped more than anything else."

That Trent was sitting across from her right now was nothing short of a miracle. "You're an amazing man, Trent Atkins."

He flushed and looked away. "Hardly. But I'm trying to turn my life around, so that has to count for something, right?"

"Very much so." Their server returned with their food. Serena bowed her head and silently thanked God for protecting Trent over the past twenty-four hours and back when he and the other foster kids escaped the Preacher. When she finished, she looked over at Trent who was staring down at his clasped hands.

"Did you ever think that maybe God had a hand in the fire that enabled you and your siblings to escape?" She reached for her chicken sandwich. "I think it's incredible that the fire broke out on the same night that you brought in wet wood."

"No, I can't say the possibility ever occurred to me." He picked up his burger. "But I can see you truly believe in God. I'm happy for you. It must be nice."

"It's wonderful, especially because I often need His guidance and support."

He didn't say anything more yet seemed curious about the possibility. Which was all she could ask for, considering what he'd been through.

She was glad Trent had escaped. And had rediscovered his music.

They finished eating and then headed to Whistlers. There was less than an hour before he was scheduled to play, but she wanted to be sure to have a table nearby. No more sitting in the back row.

As they sat and sipped water, Serena kept an eye out for the guy dressed in black who'd shown up at Trent's previous gigs. If the guy continued his pattern, he'd show up there.

But there was no sign of him.

At a quarter to eight, Trent left the table and took his guitar up to the stage. He spent some time tuning the instrument, then prepared to play.

The crowd tonight was rowdier, so he opened with a popular country rock song that had everyone clapping along. A couple of people jumped up to dance in the aisle, bumping into Serena as they tried to do a two-step.

She moved out of the way but couldn't help but smile at the crowd's reaction to Trent's music. He was smiling and singing as if he were having the greatest time of his life, but she knew most of it was an act.

A really good act, judging by the way he easily transitioned into the next song, another one with an upbeat tempo that kept the crowd engaged.

Serena couldn't help but wonder why Trent hadn't been the lead singer of the band rather than Jimmy. He certainly seemed to have captured the attention of every woman in Whistlers.

All the more reason to keep her distance from him. How many musicians were faithful to their partner? Not very many.

A man pulled a woman up out of her seat and twirled her around. Serena only caught a glimpse of his face, but the flash of recognition was unmistakable. He kept his back toward her as he swayed with the girl, but she felt certain he was the same guy who'd sat near the front of the Thirsty Saloon all alone.

The same one who'd attacked Trent with a knife?

She wished she knew for sure. Pulling out her phone, she took a picture of Trent, then moved so that she could get the man and his girlfriend in another photo. The man was wearing a loose-fitting shirt buttoned only halfway, a different look than last night. She stood and made her way around so that she was able to get a better look at the guy who was now glancing at Trent.

It was the same man. It had to be. Only this time, he'd brought a woman along. As a prop for some sort of cover? Or was she armed the way Serena was?

Her weapon was in a holster beneath her denim jacket, but she couldn't pull it unless she or Trent were threatened. Whistlers did have a bouncer at the front door. Jerry was a big man who carried more fat than muscle on his large frame. But he'd agreed to keep an eye out for trouble and to call the police if anything happened.

She prayed that wouldn't be necessary. It could be she was overreacting and the guy was doing nothing more than having fun with his date.

Yet her instincts told her otherwise. And watching the pair, she had the distinct impression they were trying too hard to look as if they were having fun.

The dancing couple sat back down and sipped their drinks.

Serena kept her position to Trent's right, near the stage, her gaze locked on her suspect. If she hadn't been watching so closely, she might have missed the subtle way the man reached beneath his partially buttoned shirt. Her heartbeat spiked, and she jumped toward Trent the moment she saw him pull his weapon.

"Gun!" She threw herself at Trent just as the gunshot reverberated through the room, sending the crowd into wild chaos.

CHAPTER SIX

Trent wasn't expecting Serena to plow into him, and the two tumbled off the stool and crashed to the floor. It took a moment for the gunfire to register, then people started screaming and making a mad dash for the door.

"Are you okay?" Serena accidentally elbowed him in the gut as she struggled to her feet. "I have to go after him."

He reached up to grab her arm. "You're not going anywhere."

"He's getting away!" She tugged herself free, looking around wildly for the shooter.

"I'm sure he's long gone." Trent pushed himself upright, looking down at his guitar he'd managed to tuck behind his back. Thankfully, the instrument hadn't been damaged in the collision. How, he wasn't sure.

"Stay here." Serena's tone was curt. She whirled and waded into the mass of people clamoring for the exit. He set his guitar aside and followed, unwilling to let her out of his sight.

He'd caught a glimpse of the gun a nanosecond before Serena had screamed and launched herself at him. He was furious at how she'd put herself directly in the line of fire and could hardly believe she hadn't been hit.

Neither had he, thanks to her quick reaction.

The crowd of people pushed and shoved as if doing so would have them getting out of the tavern quicker. In reality, it slowed them all down.

When they finally made it outside, Serena stopped on the sidewalk and slowly made a circle, looking in all directions.

He joined her. "See them?"

"No." She blew out a frustrated breath. "I don't understand. They were in the front row watching you, how did they manage to cut through the crowd to escape so quickly?"

He shook his head. "Maybe there's another way out we don't know about."

She snapped her fingers and once again pushed through the crowd to head back inside. She stopped near the bouncer. "Jerry, where's the other exit? In the kitchen?"

"Yeah, but there's also a side exit this way." Jerry's expression was grim as he showed them the side exit located near the restrooms.

"That's it," Serena said on a sigh. "That's how they got away so quickly."

"I know you told me to be alert for signs of trouble, but gunfire?" Jerry shook his head. "Wasn't expecting that."

Trent eyed Serena who looked dejected. "The couple dancing and laughing, right?"

"Yes." She lifted a brow. "You noticed them too?"

"Yeah. Something seemed off." He wished he'd taken Serena's advice about canceling the gig. "They weren't drinking that much but acted as if they were drunk."

"My fault." Serena raked her fingers through her short

straight hair. "I should have anticipated they'd know the place well enough to have an escape route planned."

He hated seeing the self-recrimination in her eyes. "You saved my life, again."

"Again?" Jerry scowled. "If you suspected this might happen, you shouldn't have come tonight putting everyone else in danger."

"I didn't expect it," he said tersely. Jerry didn't look convinced. Trent knew that he wouldn't get another gig at Whistlers anytime soon.

Maybe not anywhere at all, once this incident hit the news. He could hear the wail of sirens getting louder, and he knew there was no getting out of reporting this one. They'd have to hang around to talk to the cops.

If he tried to leave, Jerry would likely sit on him.

Trent quelled a hint of panic. He wasn't the scared kid stealing from tourists while living on the street. He wasn't going to be arrested for Jimmy's murder either. If he'd killed Jimmy, why would someone be trying to kill him? Revenge? No, the timing was such that he knew the person who'd killed Jimmy believed he knew what happened that night.

"Did you get a good look at the shooter?" Jerry asked.

Trent shook his head and glanced at Serena. "You?"

"I took a picture on my phone," she admitted. "Although it wasn't easy to get a clear view of his features the way he kept dancing and making out with his co-conspirator."

"Co-conspirator?" Trent stared at her. "You think the woman was in on it?"

"Yeah, I do," Serena admitted. "And I hate to admit I wasn't expecting that."

Through the window, Trent could see several police

cars pulling up outside Whistlers. Jerry went over to greet them, but he and Serena didn't move.

"It's my fault; I didn't listen to you." He put his arm around her shoulders. "I couldn't believe it when you threw yourself in front of me. You're a private investigator, Serena, not a bodyguard."

"I thought he was going to kill you." She turned to look up at him. "I was closer to you than to the shooter, or I would have tackled him."

The thought made him shiver. He carefully drew her into his arms and hugged her. He lowered his face to her hair, trying to wrestle his emotions under control. "If anything had happened to you . . ."

"I feel the same way," she whispered. They clung to each other for a long moment before breaking apart. "Time to talk to the police."

"Yeah." He wasn't looking forward to it but forced himself to buck up. A crime had taken place, and innocent lives had been put in harm's way.

It was his duty to let the police know everything that had happened in the past twenty-four hours.

Hard to believe how much his life had changed in one day. Not just the previous twenty-four hours, but three months ago, the night of Jimmy's murder too.

And also the night of the fire.

God's hand? He didn't believe that. Did he?

"Mr. Atkins?" Trent looked over to where Jerry was escorting two uniformed police officers to where he and Serena stood. They closed the gap, meeting them halfway. "This is Officer Newman and Officer Jonas. They'd like to hear what happened," Jerry said.

"Of course." Trent tried to relax. Serena put her hand

on his arm, which helped keep him steady. "Maybe we should sit down. It's a long story."

"Not at that table, though," Serena hastily interjected. She pointed to the table the shooter and his girlfriend had used. "The table and chairs all need to be dusted for prints."

The two officers exchanged a look. "Are you a police officer, ma'am?" Newman asked.

"No, but I have a degree in criminal justice," Serena said. "And it's common sense since lifting prints is your best chance to find out who did this."

Trent glanced at her, surprised to hear she had a degree in criminal justice. Again, he wondered why she hadn't gone the route of being a cop. Not that her decisions were any of his business.

They sat at the table Serena had used. For a long moment no one spoke. Trent cleared his throat. "The attempt to shoot me wasn't the first attack against me. Last night, after I finished playing at the Thirsty Saloon, a man attacked me with a knife. Ms. Jerash came up behind him and struck him in the back of the head to stop him. He dropped the knife and took off."

Jonas narrowed his gaze. "Did you report that to the police?"

"No." Trent shrugged. "I honestly didn't think much of it. But then later that same night, after Ms. Jerash and I had a late dinner, gunfire shattered the driver's side window of my pickup truck."

"Why on earth didn't you report that?" Newman demanded harshly.

He didn't have a good answer, so he dodged the question. "Ms. Jerash and I escaped and stayed in a motel. When I returned to my apartment to pick up a few things, someone hit me on the side of the head."

Both officers looked grim. "You are definitely being targeted," Jonas said.

"Yes." He glanced at Serena. "I should have canceled tonight, but I thought we'd be safe enough in a crowded tavern. But I was wrong."

"Go on," Newman urged. "Explain what happened."

"It might be better if I tell you what I saw," Serena interjected. "I noticed the couple at the table there." She gestured toward it. "To me, their laughing and partying seemed like an act. Their drinks were barely touched, yet they were acting drunk. If I hadn't been watching them so closely, I wouldn't have noticed the guy pull a gun from beneath his loose and only partially buttoned shirt."

"You saw the gun?" Jonas demanded.

"Yes." Serena met his gaze straight on. "I was closer to Trent and knew he was the target, so I yelled gun and threw myself onto the stage to protect Trent."

"She barreled right into me, and we both hit the floor," Trent said, picking up the thread of the story. "I noticed the couple, too, but didn't really think much about it. Other than they seemed overly into the music."

"I have a picture of them." Serena showed them her phone. "I'll text you copies."

"Why is this guy trying to kill you?" Jonas demanded. He seemed to be the officer in charge.

This is where things got tricky. A bead of sweat rolled down his face. "I used to play guitar in the Jimmy Woodrow Band."

Jonas frowned. "Who's he?"

Trent was shocked these guys didn't recognize Jimmy's name. Then again, just because they'd opened for a famous country singer didn't mean the band was that well known.

"Jimmy is dead," Serena said bluntly. "And I believe he was murdered."

"So how does that connect to this guy?" Newman jerked his thumb toward Trent. "He a witness?"

"I was drunk and passed out the night Jimmy was murdered." Trent decided there was no point in beating around the bush. "I don't remember much, but it seems that the killer believes I can identify him."

"Hence four attempts on Trent's life in the past twenty-four hours," Serena said. "We need those fingerprints run through AFIS to see if we can ID the shooter."

"*We* aren't doing anything," Jonas said. "The crime scene isn't your concern."

"Yes, it is," Serena argued. "You must realize by now that Trent is still a target in this."

"Yes, which is why you and Atkins are going to come down to the station to talk to a detective," Jonas said firmly. "And if this is related to an active ongoing murder investigation, the detective will work with those involved."

Another bead of sweat rolled down the back of his neck. Trent didn't like the thought of going to the police station, but it was clear they weren't going to be given a choice.

"That's just it," Serena said with a weary sigh. "The ME deemed Jimmy Woodrow's death to be undetermined. He didn't straight up call it a homicide, so I don't think anyone is working the case."

Jonas narrowed his gaze. "You seem to know an awful lot about this."

Serena flushed. "I'm a private investigator, hired by Jimmy's father to look into his death."

"Great, just what we need," Newman muttered. "A cop wannabe."

Serena bristled, but Trent put a warning hand on her

arm. "Ms. Jerash has uncovered more information than anyone else related to Jimmy's death. If you were smart, you wouldn't dismiss her skills so quickly."

Jonas continued to look intently at Serena in spite of Newman's skepticism. "I'll escort the two of you to the station. We'll sort everything out there."

Trent rubbed his damp palms on his jeans. There was no reason to be nervous. They hadn't done anything wrong and weren't in custody or under arrest.

But as Jonas rose and ushered them outside to his squad, Trent couldn't help but think that he'd somehow end up behind bars regardless.

He and Serena were put in the back of the squad. He reached out to take her hand. To reassure her and maybe to reassure himself.

Trent hadn't killed Jimmy, at least he didn't think so. He'd been too drunk to do anything, right? His biggest transgression was leaving the scene of the crime. Followed by not reporting Jimmy's death, even though he'd seen the lead singer's body and his open dead eyes.

And as he clutched Serena's hand, he couldn't help but wonder if this was the beginning of the end. For years he'd worried about being tossed behind bars.

He hoped it wouldn't happen today.

SERENA NOTICED Trent's pale skin, the tension in his muscles, and the sweat rolling off him as they were driven to the police station.

She understood he might be nervous, but the panicked expression in his eyes made her wonder if there was something more going on.

Was it possible Trent knew Jimmy's killer? That he'd kept her in the dark on purpose?

She didn't want to believe it. Yet something was definitely off about his reaction.

When Jonas parked the car and slid out of the driver's seat, she leaned forward. "We're going to be okay," she whispered.

Trent gave a jerky nod but didn't say anything. Jonas opened the rear door so they could slide out.

The police station looked similar to the one where her father still worked. He was a captain now, leaving his role as a detective to climb the leadership ladder. He wasn't out on the streets as much as he used to be. But when she was young, her dad would bring her into the station to show her off to his cop buddies.

That was before her mother had died, leaving a wide gulf of grief between them. Her father had changed into someone she didn't recognize. A man who hadn't cared about what she did. At least, not until she'd been forced to drop out of the police academy. Then he'd lost his temper, saying all kinds of terrible things.

Blaming her for her mother's death.

Knowing it was only his grief talking didn't take the sting from his words. And he'd dismissed her career as a PI much the way Newman had.

The way most cops did.

Jonas opened a door and gestured for them to go inside. The interview room was dreary and had no window. She sat, but Trent stood in the corner as if looking for a chance to escape.

"What's wrong?" she asked.

"Nothing." He looked at the four walls, then at the

camera mounted in the corner. "I tend to get claustrophobic at times."

Remembering how he'd been forced to sleep in a cellar, she now understood why he'd seemed so nervous. "Hopefully, this won't take long."

"Yeah." He continued staring at the camera as if he could see the person watching on the other end.

They waited almost twenty minutes for a detective to show up. Detective Grayson looked as if he'd just rolled out of bed, but Serena knew there were detectives working on every shift.

Trent pushed away from the wall to sit across from Grayson. He repeated the story he'd told the officers, and to Grayson's credit, he listened without interrupting.

Serena added what she knew of Jimmy's death, and by the time they'd finished, an hour had gone by.

"Who is the detective who worked on Woodrow's death?" Grayson asked.

"Coakley, out of the fifth district." Serena paused, then added, "He refused to tell me anything about the case. Everything I've learned is through my own investigation."

"Including the autopsy report?"

"Yes. Jimmy's father received a copy and gave it to me. I spoke personally to the ME." She eyed Grayson. "You must admit these attacks on Trent indicate Jimmy's death is murder."

"One that isn't yours to solve," Grayson shot back. "It's a police matter, not something a PI should be looking into."

"Someone had to," she snapped back. "The case had gone ice cold."

"You don't know that for sure," Grayson pointed out. "Coakley could very well be working the case as we speak."

"He's not." She stood. "Although he probably will open that dusty file now that someone has been trying to kill Trent." She edged toward the door. "Better late than never, right?"

"Hold on, you can't leave," Grayson protested. "I need contact information for the both of you."

"Here." Serena gave him her business card.

Trent leaned forward, took the pencil, and wrote down his phone number on the back of it. "You can reach me at this number."

Grayson eyed them warily. "Where are you staying?"

"Someplace safe," Serena said, turning and opening the door. "Oh, and we'll need a ride back to my car."

"I'll have someone drive you back." Grayson tucked the card into his breast pocket. "You'll be hearing from Coakley soon."

"I hope so." Serena couldn't seem to rein in her annoyance. Reporting these incidents to the police was the right thing to do. Especially after the guy had been so bold as to shoot at Trent in a crowded tavern. Yet she knew this meant the investigation would soon be out of her hands.

So much for proving herself worthy. Not that her father much cared what she did these days anyway. He'd made it clear he despised her career choice.

Trent didn't say anything until they'd been dropped off outside Whistlers. There was yellow police tape strung over the door, and several officers were still standing outside the establishment.

"I need my guitar," Trent said. He'd relaxed the moment they'd left the police station.

"They're not going to let us back inside," she warned.

"I'm not leaving without it." Trent's jaw flexed, and he approached the officer standing in front of the door. She hurried to catch up, fearing an argument, but to her surprise, the cop let him inside.

"Really enjoy your music," the cop said with a shy grin. "I heard you play last weekend."

"Thanks." Trent's smile was strained.

She trailed after Trent, pausing at the shooter's table. Despite the time that had passed, there was no sign of the crime scene techs who should be testing it for fingerprints. She frowned, then waved a cop over. "I told Jonas and Newman that this table was used by the shooter. It needs to be dusted for fingerprints."

The cop shrugged. "Lots of crime in the area. They'll get here eventually."

Serena couldn't believe that a gunshot occurring within a restaurant and bar didn't merit a quicker response. She stared at the two glasses sitting on the table for a long moment without touching them.

Even if she wanted to, she didn't have the proper equipment to test for fingerprints. It was frustrating, but she had to trust that the cops would do their job.

Trent came over to join her, his guitar looped over his back. "Ready?"

"Yes. But let's go out the side door." She steered him toward the area where the restrooms were located. "I want to check it out."

She used her elbow to open the side exit, which led to a narrow alley. There was another building adjacent to Whistlers, but the windows were dark. It was some sort of secondhand store.

"I can't believe they got away," she muttered as they took the alley to the rear of the building. The parking lot was directly behind the two structures, and she knew the shooter and his gal pal had likely hopped into their car and driven away.

"I don't see any cameras," Trent said as they walked toward her SUV. "You'd think in an area like this they'd have them."

"Maybe that's the reason the shooter and his girlfriend took the risk." She glanced at Trent. "You didn't recognize him or the woman, did you?"

"No." He looked as frustrated as she felt. "I wish I did. I'm sure I won't get paid for tonight, and I am not likely to get any other paying gigs in the near future."

She winced, suspecting he was right. She took a circuitous route back to their dive motel, although she suspected the shooter and his girlfriend were long gone. The motel was close enough to Whistlers that she felt certain they wouldn't want to risk running into one of the many cops who were still on scene.

"I'm sorry," Trent said as she parked as far away from the lobby as possible. "I should have listened to you."

She reached over to squeeze his arm. "I feel bad that your career is being impacted by this. When are you supposed to perform again?"

"Not until Thursday." He glanced at her. "I doubt the cops will have that guy behind bars by then."

"Probably not. And even if they do track him through fingerprints, I don't think he's the same person who killed Jimmy."

She pushed open her door and slid out of the SUV. Trent joined her, and they went into her motel room as the connecting door between their rooms was still open.

"You really think Jimmy's killer hired that guy to kill me?" Trent asked. "He's not even close to being a professional hit man."

She chuckled. "No, he's not. But yeah, I think he's a hired gun. I also believe that somewhere in the dark recesses of your brain, you know who killed Jimmy."

"I'm telling you, I don't." He turned and carefully placed his guitar on the bed, before raking a hand through his dark hair. "I swear to you if I did, I'd tell you, the police, the entire world. I want this nightmare over as much as you do."

"I said in the deep recesses of your brain, Trent," she reminded gently. "I know you were drinking and were pretty much passed out at the time, but I still think you saw something. If you were truly out cold, there would be no reason for anyone to come after you." In her mind's eye, she could almost imagine how it may have happened. The killer struck Jimmy, then turned him over and realized he was dead. Then the killer must have looked over toward Trent where he was stretched out on the floor, maybe watching through an alcohol-induced haze. The killer left and then waited to hear what would happen.

Only Trent had left, too, without saying a word to anyone.

Until she'd stirred the pot, bringing the past boiling over into the here and now.

He sighed and dropped into the closest chair. He stared down at his clasped hands before meeting her gaze. "You just won't give up this hypnosis idea. Which won't work."

"You don't know that it won't work." She knew he hated everything about the idea. "I think you're afraid it will."

"What I'm afraid of is looking like a fool." Trent stared at her. "You don't have any idea how many horrible memories are buried in my subconscious. Call me crazy, but I don't want to relive any of them."

Her heart broke for what he'd suffered. Who was she to

ask him to do such a thing? Watching him in the throes of a nightmare was bad enough. She really didn't have a right to ask him to do that again and again through who knew how many hypnosis therapy sessions.

"You're right. I'm sorry." Time to let that idea go. She stood and paced. "We'll have to go back to researching Heidi and Rob. One of them likely knows something that will help us get to the bottom of this."

"Social media didn't work, so I'm not sure what else we can do."

"Social media did work to a certain extent," she protested. "We found Heidi, didn't we?"

"With a fake last name," he countered. "And no sign of Rob."

"We'll just have to dig deeper." She tried to smile. "Come on, Trent. Let's put our faith in God's hands."

She expected him to scoff at her comment, but he looked at her with a hint of uncertainty shadowing his gaze. "I have to admit, the fact that we're both here, unharmed, makes me wonder if there is someone watching over us."

Tears pricked her eyes, and she went over to kneel beside him. "He is, Trent. Believe me, God cares about us. About *you*."

"When you came flying toward me, I worried you'd be killed." His words were so low she could barely hear him. "I wanted to scream at you, but then we were hitting the floor. I thought for sure my guitar would be broken in half, but it was barely scratched." He shook his head, looking dazed. "It doesn't make sense that God would care about me, but I don't have another explanation for what happened tonight."

"Oh, Trent." She wrapped her arms around his neck and hugged him. "I'm so happy to hear you say that because

I know it's true. We'll figure out who is behind these attacks."

He pulled her close and buried his face in her hair. For long moments they simply clung to each other, reveling in the miracle of being alive.

When her phone rang, she was forced to let him go in order to reach for it. When she realized the caller was her father, she hesitated, his calling was unusual. Must be an emergency? She quickly answered. "Hello? Dad? Are you okay?"

"No, I'm not okay!" he roared. "What's this I hear about you interfering in an active police investigation?"

She sighed. Bad news sure traveled fast. "I didn't—" she began, but he cut her off.

"You're going to drop this thing right now, understand?" he thundered. "No child of mine is going to get in the way of a cop doing his job! You should be ashamed of yourself!"

Before she could say anything more, he disconnected from the line.

She slowly replaced the phone in her pocket. Apparently, her attempt to solve Jimmy's murder had caused the strained relationship she had with her father to deteriorate even further.

Something she hadn't thought possible.

CHAPTER SEVEN

"Problems?" Trent watched as Serena's expression morphed from frank concern to resignation. He hadn't realized she had a dad. Stupid, really, as most people had parents.

Most kids didn't grow up the way he and the other fosters had.

"Not really." She grimaced. "My dad has been disappointed in me for a few years now, so this isn't anything new."

"Why would he care if you investigate this case?" Trent didn't understand that part, which had been easy to hear despite the call not being on speaker. "I thought Jimmy's dad was his best friend?"

"They are friends. But my dad is also a cop, he carries the rank of captain. And I didn't exactly tell him that Allan Woodrow came to me about his son's death."

"I see. I'm sorry to hear that." He could tell the relationship between father and daughter was complicated. Which was too bad because having a parent who cared for you was a gift.

One he hadn't been blessed with. Well, he'd had his

father, but the guy hadn't given him much of anything other than the guitar. Even now, Trent couldn't really picture his dad. Or his mother.

More repressed memories he had no intention of reviving.

"My father blames me for my mother's death." The words shocked him. "I was driving the car when we were T-boned by a guy who blew through a red light. My mom took the brunt of the crash and didn't survive."

He reached out and drew her close, wrapping his arm around her shoulders. "Her death wasn't your fault, Serena."

She shrugged. "If I'd have seen the other car earlier . . ."

"No one expects a car to blow through a red light," he said firmly. "Even if you'd have seen him, would you have been able to get away? Or would he have just hit someone else?"

"Maybe." She continued staring at the ugly stained carpet of their dive motel room. Then she raised her gaze to his. "Truth is, we'll never know. I didn't see him until it was too late."

"How badly were you injured?" He sensed there was more to the story.

"My injuries were minor in the big scheme of things. My right ankle still hurts sometimes." She offered a wan smile. "I couldn't pass the fitness portion of the police academy because running made the pain worse."

Ah, now he understood. Being her father's daughter, she'd wanted to follow in his footsteps. Only she couldn't. And their grief over losing her mother only widened the gap between them.

"I'm sorry," he murmured, wishing he could come up with something better. "I'm sure it's difficult for you."

Serena surprised him by leaning against him. "Well, you've suffered much worse, Trent. And honestly, hearing your story has helped me put my own issues into perspective."

"But we all have a story," he argued softly. "What you suffered is horrible, and just because my experience was different doesn't lessen the importance of yours."

"You're a wise man." She slipped her arm around his waist. "I'm sure you don't want to hear this, but leaning on God has helped me tremendously over the past four years."

"You're wrong, Serena. I'm very glad you've gotten the support you need." Talking about God wasn't easy, especially since he hadn't believed in His existence, yet he also knew that some people did.

And hearing her talk about God, he'd found himself wondering if he'd missed something. Logically, the Preacher was wrong to physically and psychologically abuse him and his foster siblings, so why not accept that the Preacher may have also been wrong about God?

"I really wish you would have that same support." Her words were muffled against his western-style shirt. "I believe God brought us together for a reason."

"To find Jimmy's killer?" He wasn't sure God would care about a sinner like Jimmy. Trent knew he'd sinned a lot too, but Jimmy had been worse. Although maybe when it came to sinning, there wasn't a better or worse. Maybe all sins were created equal.

"No, although I think we need to do that in order to keep you safe." She lifted her head. "I think He brought us together because we needed something from each other."

He wasn't entirely sure what she meant, but looking into her tawny eyes made it difficult to think clearly. He wanted very badly to kiss her again, yet he managed to hold himself in check. She'd pulled away from him before, and he wasn't the kind of guy who pushed himself on women. To be honest, he'd never needed to.

Serena wasn't anything like the women he'd been with. If he'd had a real family, she'd be the type of girl he'd bring home to meet his parents, if he had them.

To meet his siblings.

He thought about Cooper and how he'd ignored his brother's call. Trent wanted to talk to Cooper, but being in the bull's-eye of danger probably wasn't the time to reach out. Maybe when the guy who'd tried to shoot him had been arrested, he could reunite with his foster brother.

The idea gave him hope. Something he hadn't experienced in a long time.

"Trent?" Serena reached up to cup his cheek. "You looked really happy there for a moment."

"I was thinking about my foster brother Cooper. I haven't seen him in three years."

"I'm sure Cooper would love to see you again." She stared deep into his eyes in a way that made him uncomfortable.

"I'm not so sure about that. We spoke a year ago, but I was pretty drunk and don't remember much of the conversation. Then, out of the blue, he called me a few weeks ago, but I was too busy and too embarrassed to respond."

"Family is important. I know my relationship with my dad is rocky, but I still care about him. And if he calls me, I'll always answer, even if it means getting yelled at."

"I should have answered Cooper's call," he admitted. "But now isn't the right time. I can't do anything that will bring danger to his doorstep."

"That's true," she admitted. "You're a good man, Trent."

"Not nearly good enough." In his mind, he added, *for you.*

She leaned forward and kissed him. The shock of her lips touching his held him still for a moment, wondering if he was imagining it. Then he instinctively pulled her closer, molding his mouth to hers, deepening the kiss.

A simple kiss had never before made him feel like this. Like he was holding something priceless in his arms. Then he remembered how he'd just acknowledged he wasn't good enough for her, so he forced himself to ease back.

"I, uh, don't know what got into me." Serena's tone held a note of apology.

"Please don't think I'm upset. I enjoy kissing you, more than I should." He cleared his throat and forced himself to stand, putting distance between them. "I think we're better off as friends, though."

Was it his imagination or did she look dejected by his comment? Must have been because she quickly smiled and nodded. "You're absolutely right. We need to stay focused on finding Jimmy's killer. I'll do more research in the morning, see if we can find a lead to follow up on."

He frowned. "Are you sure? Doing that only puts you in danger. And your father said to stay out of it."

"My father doesn't get to tell me how to run my business." Her tone held an edge. "I'm being paid to find Jimmy's killer, and that's what I intend to do."

"Just—be safe, Serena."

"Me? You're the one who's been in the crosshairs more times than I can count."

"And you're the one who threw yourself in front of a bullet. Which, by the way, I'm still not happy about. You'd better not do something so irresponsible and reckless like that again."

"I'm fine," she protested.

"Yeah, but next time you might not be." He glared down at her. "This idiot wants me dead, not you. Stay out of it, Serena. Work the case, but no acting like some sort of bodyguard."

"I'm not going to stand by and watch while someone tries to kill you," she said wearily.

"You're not a cop," he shot back.

She stared at him, looking wounded. He felt bad for hitting a nerve, but it was true. She wasn't a cop.

Maybe she was licensed to carry a gun. Yet if she shot at someone, injuring or worse, killing them, she'd be held to the full extent of the law.

He couldn't bear the thought she'd take that level of risk because of him.

"No, I'm not." She stood. "Good night, Trent."

For a long moment they stared at each other. Finally, he grabbed his guitar and turned away, raking a hand through his hair in frustration. "Good night, Serena."

He crossed the threshold into his motel room and sank onto the edge of the bed. First a kiss, then an argument.

Oh yeah, he sure had a way with women.

Not.

Proof he wasn't cut out for a relationship. Wouldn't know how to have one, even if he was looking for something long term. Which he wasn't.

He propped his guitar in the corner, washed up in the bathroom, then crawled into bed. He was mentally and physically exhausted, but memories of Serena's sweet kiss made it impossible to fall asleep.

THE FOLLOWING MORNING, Serena showered and changed before getting back to work. The argument with her father lingered in the back of her mind, but she pushed it aside. Nothing she did now would change her father's opinion, of that she was certain.

She had a job to do, and failure was not an option. She hit the computer again, searching for information on Heidi Law, Lawyer, Lawson, Lawrence, and every other variation she could come up with. Somehow, she stumbled across a Lynn H. Lawrence. She pulled up the picture and audibly gasped when she recognized the woman as the same one wearing the barely there bikini on the Heidi Law Facebook page. Only this picture showed her as a brunette.

Lynn Heidi Lawrence, aka Heidi Law. She sat back in her seat, stunned that she'd finally found the mystery woman. Serena reached for her coffee cup, forgetting it was empty. She'd already depleted the small amount of coffee that came with the room, so she rubbed her eyes and went back to the property searches.

This time, she found what she was looking for. Lynn H. Lawrence owned a 3.6 million dollar mansion in Brentwood, Tennessee. When she pulled up a three-dimensional map on the screen, her eyes widened at the lavish dwelling.

And she knew there were probably even bigger houses in the area owned by a variety of stars.

Interesting that Lynn, aka Heidi, who lived in a fancy-schmancy place like this would spend time with Jimmy Woodrow. Partying with him and sleeping with him. Jimmy was good-looking and talented, but he wasn't in the same league as the other country stars. Judging by the house on the screen, Serena guessed that many of those big stars were likely her neighbors. Being the opening band for a famous singer wasn't the same as being equally famous. Sure, some did go on to hit it big, but others were nothing more than a brief flash of light, a comet streaking across the sky.

Gone in the blink of an eye.

Was that what would have happened to Jimmy Woodrow's band? If Jimmy hadn't died, would they have made it big?

She wasn't convinced.

Trent poked his head through the connecting door. "Hey, are you hungry?"

"Come look at what I found." She waved him over. "Heidi's real name is Lynn Heidi Lawrence, and this is her house."

Trent whistled. "Wow, that's some place."

"Isn't it though? And while it's expensive, I'm sure there are plenty of others in the area that are even bigger and better." She tapped the screen. "So now we know who she is. I'm wondering if we should show up on her doorstep and ask a few questions."

His eyebrows hiked up. "She's likely to kick us to the curb. If we can even get close. I'm thinking she lives in some sort of gated community."

"Doesn't mean we can't try." Then an idea came to her. "What if Heidi used her wealth as a way to convince Luke Bryan to allow Jimmy's band to open for them?"

Trent looked surprised, then slowly nodded. "That actually makes sense. I mean, Jimmy was good, and we played a lot of gigs, but Luke Bryan was a whole different level."

"What did your manager say about the Luke Bryan thing?"

He shrugged. "I don't remember what Brett Caine said. He made the announcement, and everyone went into major celebration mode."

"I can imagine," she said dryly.

He grimaced. "Yeah, everything was nuts for a while. But it honestly never occurred to me that Jimmy may have gotten help obtaining that gig from someone other than our manager."

"What I'm not sure I understand, though, is why she'd do it? I mean, it's a nice thing to give a recommendation to a friend, yet her social media posts portray her as fairly self-absorbed." She shook her head. "Getting Jimmy's band help seems out of character. Unless she paints this picture of herself on social media on purpose."

"No, self-absorbed is a good description of her. At least from what I saw." He straightened and rubbed a hand over his jaw. "My view could be jaded, though. But if she's married, why would she risk bringing Jimmy to a friend's attention? Wouldn't anyone famous know she had a husband named Rob? They'd have to know Jimmy and Heidi were involved, if only by watching the way they acted together."

"I don't have any answers. At this point, all we can do is see if we can convince Heidi to talk to us." She minimized the screen and stood. "Are you ready to go?"

"Yeah, let me get my stuff."

While Trent got his things together, she did the same, using the store bag in lieu of a suitcase. Allan Woodrow was paying her a small fee for daily expenses, but she was blowing through that extra money faster than she'd antici-pated. Then again, she hadn't considered the possibility that the same person who'd killed Jimmy would come after Trent.

Trent stored his guitar and his duffel in the back, then took her bag too. It wasn't until they were on the road that she asked, "Did the Nashville PD talk to you about Jimmy's death?"

"Yes. I told them I was too drunk and passed out to know anything." He glanced at her.

"The cops knew you spent the night there?"

"No." He shifted in his seat. "I told them I left at four in the morning and took a rideshare home without seeing or talking to Jimmy."

"That's what you told me too," she said slowly. "But it doesn't make any sense that the police wouldn't have checked your phone to verify if you did in fact take a rideshare."

"I told them I was about to use my app when I saw one drive by and flagged it down. Offered the guy cash and he took it."

"They're not supposed to do that." She frowned. "The driver could have gotten in trouble."

"Yeah, well, since I wasn't being truthful about it, no one got in trouble," he pointed out dryly. "Why are you asking about this now? I told you I lied back then."

"You did, yes." She hoped he wasn't lying to her now. "I guess that explains why the police dropped it. And why the killer didn't come after you until now."

Trent glanced at her. "Who did you talk to?"

"Jed Matson, Dave Jacoby, and some of the hotel staff." She swallowed hard. "I keep coming back to whether or not Jed or Dave killed Jimmy."

"They don't really have a motive," Trent said. "I mean, yeah, there was discord, but killing Jimmy doesn't help them out. However, I do think they talked to others about Jimmy's death. I can just imagine how the story may have changed by now."

"Changed how?" She saw a family restaurant and made

the turn. She could hear Trent's stomach growling, and she was hungry herself. Besides, it was too early to knock on Lynn's aka Heidi's, door, especially if the woman still did a lot of partying. Who did she hang out with these days, now that Jimmy was gone?

"By now they're claiming my argument with Jimmy blew up and I killed him in the heat of the moment."

It was similar to what the two musicians had told her. She pulled into a parking space and twisted in her seat to face him. "Doesn't that concern you? What if the police believe that too?"

"There's no proof. Besides, while we did argue about Heidi being married, that happened earlier in the evening. Jimmy was still alive and well, and there were plenty of witnesses."

"But someone might think that same argument resurfaced later," she said, a feeling of dread uncurling in her gut. "I don't like it, Trent."

"I brought up Heidi because I was worried about Jimmy," he said stubbornly. "When he told me he didn't care, there was nothing more to say. If he didn't care, there was nothing I could do to sway him. Besides, why would I do something as drastic as killing a man over a woman who isn't remotely faithful to her wedding vows? My opinion at that point was that they pretty much deserved each other."

"I guess." She couldn't necessarily disagree. Still, she couldn't help but wonder if they were operating under a flawed theory. The motive for the various attacks could be related to the fact that someone out there thought Trent had killed Jimmy when he really hadn't.

Making the motive revenge rather than eliminating a potential witness.

"Serena? Are you okay?"

She flushed, realizing she'd been staring blankly out the window. "Yes, sorry. I need more coffee."

"You and me both."

They entered the restaurant and were seated without delay. Their server brought coffee and water. "Thanks, you read my mind," Serena joked.

"Here's our breakfast menu." The woman set two laminated cards on the table. "Enjoy your coffee and I'll be back soon."

Serena sipped her coffee with gratitude. Trent's intense green gaze made her flush. "What? Do I have something on my face?"

"No, you look great." His green gaze was serious. "I'm just trying to figure out if you really believe I had something to do with Jimmy's death."

"No, I don't think that at all." She carefully set her cup down. "But I would be pretty upset if someone else thought I'd killed someone."

"Ah, so my reaction bothered you." He wrapped his hands around his mug. "Jed and Dave are all talk, Serena. And they weren't happy when I declined joining the new band."

"You were included in that offer?" She leaned forward. "Bootleggers wanted all three of you?"

"Yeah. Maybe they thought the three of us would bring some of the Jimmy Woodrow magic along."

She tipped her head to the side. "Why didn't you go with them?"

He took a moment to drink his coffee. "It wasn't my scene anymore. I had quit drinking. Getting back with the group would make it impossible for me to stay sober."

She reached out to take his hand. "I'm happy you made

that choice, Trent. You're looking out for yourself and still entertaining others."

His smile was lopsided. "Well, I may not be doing much entertaining in the near future. No one will want me to come and perform on the chance of attracting a crazy dude with a gun."

She winced. "We'll get to the bottom of this."

Their server returned and took their orders. For long moments neither of them spoke, each lost in their thoughts. Finally, Trent said, "There's only one way we might be able to convince Heidi to talk to us."

"How?"

"You tell her that Jimmy's dad hired you because he's agonizing over his son's death."

She considered that. "You think if she cares about Jimmy at all, she'll want to help his father find some peace?"

"Maybe. If she cares about him at all." Trent shrugged and took another sip of coffee. "Not saying it will work, but I can't think of another scenario in which she'll agree to answer any of your questions."

"It's worth a shot." The idea of approaching such a beautiful and wealthy woman was intimidating, but she was determined to see this through. Then she snapped her fingers and rose. "I need to get the computer."

"Why?" Trent asked.

She hurried back outside to the SUV. She took the computer inside and powered it up. "I forgot about Rob," she said, tapping the keys.

"Forgot what?"

"To see if they're divorced." She found the site she needed and typed in Lynn H. Lawrence as one of the legal parties. The information she was looking for popped up on the screen. "There he is, Robert Furrier."

"How did you find him?"

"A divorce will be listed as a civil suit in the circuit court system." She turned the page to show him. "Lynn H. Lawrence, aka Heidi, filed for divorce from Robert Furrier."

"I had no idea that type of site existed." Trent looked a bit shell-shocked.

"Don't worry, I won't look you up," she teased.

"You can, I won't be in there." He pushed the computer back toward her as their meals arrived. "I was never caught."

She wasn't sure what to say to that. On one hand, she didn't approve of anyone breaking the law, but considering how Trent had lived on the street at such a young age, she knew he must have broken dozens of them.

And ironically, that didn't bother her. What if her parents had both died and she'd ended up in a horrible foster home? If she'd run away, she likely would have done whatever was necessary to survive.

Exactly as Trent and his foster siblings had done.

Acting on impulse, she reached over and took his hand. Then bowed her head and whispered, "Dear Lord, we ask You to continue watching over us, keeping us safe in Your care. And bless this food we are about to eat. Amen."

Trent didn't say anything verbally in response, but he squeezed her fingers and smiled. "Guess it can't hurt to ask for protection, huh?"

"We need it," she agreed. "And I know God will provide for us. Although we need to do our part too. Which reminds me, are you going to call off your next gig?"

"It's not until Thursday, we still have a couple of days yet." He dug in to his eggs with relish.

She didn't point out that if Heidi didn't talk to them, they were fresh out of new leads. Unless they went back to

Jed and Dave, questioning the two band members together. Would either of them say anything different if Trent was with her?

Doubtful, but again, there was only one way to know. And they didn't have anything to lose.

And if none of these ideas worked? Serena tried not to be a negative Nellie. Trent agreeing to hypnosis was a nonstarter. She'd brought it up twice and had been shot down both times.

He knew the importance of getting to the truth, but she couldn't force him into being hypnotized either.

"Wait a minute." Trent reached over and grabbed the computer. He used the touch pad to bring the screen to life, then looked over at her. "Did you notice the date?"

"The date?" She turned the computer so she could see what he was talking about. A chill snaked down her spine. "The divorce filing was the day before Jimmy's death." She couldn't believe she hadn't noticed that right away.

The filing of the divorce could have been the motive for Rob to kill Jimmy. Maybe the soon-to-be ex-husband had gone over to confront Jimmy and lost his temper, lashing out and ultimately killing him.

And if Rob thought Trent saw him, he could have hired someone to kill Trent too.

CHAPTER EIGHT

Trent watched Serena's expressive features. It was easy to see what she was thinking. He ate some of his eggs but noticed she hadn't done the same. "Rather than questioning Heidi, we should track down Rob. If he was upset about the divorce and found out about Jimmy, he might be our guy."

"I know. We'll need to find him and talk to Heidi." She picked up her fork and toyed with her food. "We should talk to Jed and Dave again. See what they remember about Heidi and/or if they noticed Rob hanging around."

"Not sure those guys will be much help." He wasn't opposed to talking to his former bandmates, but he didn't trust them. Both Jed and Dave would lie to save themselves. They'd also throw anyone else under the bus to save themselves, including him.

They already had, since they'd mentioned his argument with Jimmy to Serena, which had sent her coming to see him. He could imagine how that conversation went down, with both of them giving each other sly looks as if they were hesitant to pinpoint him as the possible killer while they did just that.

Yeah, the guys weren't going to help them. Not even a little bit.

Serena finally began to eat. She seemed preoccupied with her thoughts, and he wondered if she planned to bring the police in on their latest theory. He still felt bad about the argument she'd had with her father. After he and Cooper had spent years running from the cops, it was rather ironic he was sitting across from a cop's daughter.

A woman who would have been a cop if not for her inability to pass the physical required by the police academy.

"You could try again." He finished his eggs and reached for his coffee.

"I know, that's why I'm planning to talk to Jed and Dave for a second time."

"Not that, I meant the police academy." He met her gaze. "It's been a few years, right? Your ankle may be better healed by now."

She frowned. "I'm doing okay as a private investigator."

"You're a great PI," he agreed. "But your skills are going to waste, Serena. You would be an amazing cop. And I'm just saying it's worth a try."

She seemed to consider his words, then shrugged. "I'll think about it. For now, let's stay focused on the case at hand."

A case the police should be investigating, he thought. And they were, at least as it related to the gunfire at Whistlers. Trent thought of the gig he had on Thursday, playing at one of the large hotels. Not the Grand Ole Opry but a nice place just the same.

He really didn't want to cancel. It was a biweekly gig, one that he was fortunate to have. The pay was good, and he was concerned that if he canceled this week's event, he'd never get back on the schedule.

As it was, he didn't think Whistlers would invite him back. The Thirsty Saloon probably would, but they paid rather poorly. Not that he was in a position to be picky.

Serena finished her meal and pulled the computer over. "I'm impressed they have internet access here."

Since he didn't have a computer, Wi-Fi wasn't something he'd paid much attention to. He used his phone for basic stuff, like finding the locations of his various jobs.

He didn't even have a television back at his apartment. Paying for cable wasn't high on his list of priorities, not like food, water, and electricity.

Even when he'd been playing with Jimmy, Trent had kept his low-rent apartment. Partially because he'd wanted to have a place to be alone if needed, but more so, he realized now, because he'd secretly feared the band would fall apart. Even if Jimmy hadn't died, he didn't think they'd have stayed together much longer than another year or two at the most.

Too bad he hadn't socked more money away. Oh, he'd put some away, but he had been forced to live off his savings while he got his solo career up and running.

"I have a location for Rob Furrier." Serena's voice broke into his thoughts. She met his gaze over the top of the computer. "It's about as opposite of Heidi's home as you can get."

"Not surprising since it sounded like the money was hers, not his." He frowned. "I wonder why they bothered to get married in the first place? Especially since Heidi didn't appreciate being tied down."

"That's something we'll need to ask her and Rob." She closed the computer and glanced around for their server.

"We should hit the road, see if we can catch Rob at his apartment."

"Okay." He flagged their server over.

The woman smiled and set down their tab. "Thanks for coming today."

"Thank you," Serena said, picking up the bill.

"I've got it," he said gruffly. He didn't like the idea of Serena paying for their meal. For his meal. He quickly pulled cash from his wallet and set it on the table.

"No, really, my treat." She thrust the cash back toward him. "I have a daily expense allowance, and you're helping me solve this thing. Buying breakfast is the least I can do."

He frowned. "You've been paying all along, it's my turn."

"Maybe later, but let me do this, Trent. Please?"

He wasn't destitute, and knowing Jimmy's dad was actually paying for the meal only made him feel slightly better. "You saved my life several times, Serena. You can expense this one, but I'll buy our next meal."

"I'm glad I could be there for you." Sincerity shone brightly from her eyes. "I told you God brought us together for a reason."

They left the restaurant and climbed back into her SUV. "Where are we headed?" he asked, glancing at her. "You didn't mention Rob's address."

"His apartment isn't far from yours." She pulled out of the parking lot and headed east.

"That is as far from Brentwood as you can get." He wondered again about how Heidi and Rob had ended up together in the first place. Realizing the guy was living at about his own income level only added to his motivation to kill Jimmy. At least in his mind. Although the reality of the situation was that Heidi would have continued to cheat with or without Jimmy, making their divorce a foregone conclusion.

Why would Rob risk his freedom for a woman like that?

"What if Rob isn't home?" he asked, peering at the apartment building in the distance. "The guy must have a job, especially if Heidi kept her word about not giving him a dime."

"We'll talk to the neighbors, see if anyone knows when he'll be back." She didn't look perturbed by the possibility. He'd noticed before how much she seemed to enjoy investigating the events around Jimmy's death.

Maybe as much as he enjoyed playing guitar and singing.

Ten minutes later, Serena pulled into an empty parking space near the apartment building. It looked similar to where he lived, maybe a slight step up. He glanced around curiously as Serena led the way inside.

The lock on the outer door was intact, verifying his opinion that this place was better than his. A woman holding a baby girl in her arm while lugging a stroller came through the door. He held the door for her as Serena offered her a hand with the stroller.

"Let me help you with that." Serena unfolded the stroller.

"Thanks," the woman said breathlessly. "Some days two hands aren't enough."

"I can only imagine." Serena beamed. "Your daughter is adorable. What's her name?"

"Abigail." The woman smiled as she placed the baby in the stroller seat.

"Such a cutie." Serena paused, then said, "We're here to see Rob Furrier. Do you know him?"

"Rob?" The woman frowned. "Is he the new guy?"

"Relatively new, he may have moved in about three or four months ago. He's tall with longish dark hair, broad shoulders, looks like he works out."

"Oh yes, Rob." The woman shrugged. "He's cute but clearly not interested in kids. I think he complained about Abby's crying to the manager." She looked annoyed. "As if he could keep a baby quiet."

"I'm sorry to hear that," Serena said. "Especially since Abby is such a pretty baby."

"Yeah, it takes all kinds. He lives on the second floor, right above me in 210." She clipped the safety strap around the baby. "I haven't seen him in the past few days, which has been a blessing."

"Okay, thanks." Serena joined Trent at the door, watching as the woman pushed her daughter's stroller down the sidewalk.

"I'm amazed at how much she talked to you," Trent said as they went inside. "If she had known Rob better, I'm sure she would have told you everything you needed to know."

"It's just a matter of chatting with people." She eyed him as they headed for the stairs. "Although somehow I don't think chitchat is something you indulge in very often."

"Rarely," he agreed. You didn't invite chitchat while living on the streets. That was the kind of thing that could get you noticed by the wrong people, in a very bad way.

They hiked to the second floor and made their way down to apartment 210. Serena knocked on the door, and they both waited expectantly. Pressing his ear to the door, he listened intently but didn't hear any signs of movement coming from inside.

Trent doubted the guy was home. There were a lot of musicians in Nashville, but other people normally worked during the day. Whatever Rob did for a living, he was likely off earning a paycheck.

"He's not here. We'll have to come back later," he said with a sigh.

"Give me a minute." She took something from the purse she wore crossways over her chest. It took a moment for him to realize she was picking the lock. "What are you doing?" He glanced around nervously. "That's illegal."

"But I'm not a cop, and I only want to check the place out. Make sure he's okay." She jiggled the silver tools, and the lock sprung open.

"You've done this before?" Trent had broken his share of laws in his life, but this seemed different. However, he followed her inside and quickly closed the door behind them.

The place was a pigsty, much like his, he silently acknowledged. But as he followed Serena through the living room, he noticed a wedding photo sitting on an end table.

"Guess he really loved her," he said, peering at their smiling faces. Maybe it was his imagination, but he sensed that Heidi's smile wasn't sincere, the way Rob's was.

For some people, love was a one-way street.

He glanced at Serena. Like maybe for him.

"Don't touch anything," she warned as she moved through the apartment. "But keep your eyes open for any indication of where he might work."

He spied a pair of work gloves on the counter. "Construction is a strong possibility. May even explain where he and Heidi met."

"Hmm." Serena moved into the bedroom. Oddly, he felt uncomfortable being in the guy's house. He hadn't liked it when he'd found someone lurking in his apartment. Messy or not, it was still his personal space.

Apparently, Serena didn't have that problem. She emerged a few minutes later. "He definitely works construction. I found a T-shirt with a logo over the front pocket. OC, which stands for Overman Construction."

In a way it was crazy to think Heidi would have married a mere construction worker. Then again, she hadn't hesitated to divorce Rob either. Had she married him in a moment of weakness? The whole thing didn't make a lot of sense.

"We'll have to return later," he said. "I'm sure he'll be back sometime this evening."

"Yeah." She stood in the middle of the room for a moment, then walked to the door. She opened it, peeked out, and then gestured for him to follow.

Soon they were back in the SUV. "Time to visit Heidi." Serena put the car in gear.

"I guess." He didn't look forward to that conversation. Heidi wasn't a nice person. As much as the poor guy may have loved Heidi, in Trent's humble opinion, Rob was better off without her.

And he found himself hoping the guy hadn't killed Jimmy. From the looks of the apartment, he didn't think Rob had the cash to hire someone to shoot at him.

No, if anyone had ice for blood, it was Heidi. He wasn't a cop, but he still felt the woman was involved, one way or another. He only hoped that poking that sleeping tiger wouldn't get them killed.

SERENA TOLD herself there was no reason to worry about talking to Heidi. Trent was right, the woman wouldn't likely give them much time. Unless she truly cared about helping them find Jimmy's murderer.

"Hey, there's a sign for Overman's," Trent said as she drove past a small construction project. "Looks like they build homes."

"Wonder if they built Heidi's house?" She turned at the next intersection so they could head back to the site. "No way to know if Rob is working here."

"True. But we can ask, right?"

She pulled into the gravel driveway behind the large white Overman Construction van. "Maybe you should let me go up alone."

"No way. We're working as a team." Trent's expression settled into the all too familiar stubborn lines. "Besides, it might be better if I pretend to know him."

As much as she wanted to argue, Trent had a point. As chauvinistic as it was, construction workers were mostly men, and they would probably respond better to him asking casual questions about Rob than to her.

She trailed behind Trent as they approached the house. There was no front door yet, and she could see the interior was rough. A country song blared from a radio, and she figured none of the guys inside had heard them approach.

"Yo, Rob around?" Trent projected his voice to carry above the music.

There was a loud clatter as someone dropped something. The decibel of the music lowered as someone exclaimed, "Man, don't creep up on me like that! I nearly had a heart attack."

"Hey, Rob, long time no see." Trent stepped forward and offered his hand.

Serena could hardly believe that they'd stumbled right

into Rob Furrier. The guy eyed Trent with confusion. "I'm sorry, have we met?"

"Trent Atkins, you quoted me on a job a while back," Trent said, clearly ad-libbing. "A house remodel."

"Sorry, I do a lot of quotes, don't remember your project in particular." Rob glanced over at her. "You must be Ms. Atkins."

The title nearly made her choke on her own spit. "Serena," she said, stepping forward to shake his hand. "We had a delay in financing but are interested in moving forward with the project now."

"Well, I'm tied up for the next few months." Rob gestured to the house he was building. "I'm running on a skeleton crew these days. My helper didn't show up for work today."

"This looks nice." Serena couldn't really tell what the house would look like when it was finished, but the floor plan was bigger than the others nearby. "I'm surprised you don't have a larger crew."

"Yeah, well, things change." Rob shifted his gaze to Trent. "If you can wait a few months, I'd be happy to provide a new quote for your project."

"That would be great." Trent pulled out his phone. "What's your number again?"

Once Rob gave his contact information, she stepped closer. "You did Heidi Lawrence's house, didn't you?"

Instantly his expression closed. "Yeah. Sorry, but I need to get back to work. Give me a call in a few months, okay?" Rob turned away, cranked up the music on the radio, and went back to hammering two-by-fours.

She and Trent turned and headed back outside. "He's running his own business as a one-man show," Trent murmured.

"I see that." She glanced back over her shoulder, but Rob wasn't paying them any attention. "Isn't it dangerous to work a site by himself?"

"Yeah, but as he said, he normally has someone helping him." Trent paused outside the SUV. "Possibly the same guy who shot at me last night."

"Wouldn't your name have tipped him off?" Serena had watched Rob's face when Trent had introduced himself. "He'd have to be a pretty good actor to hide his reaction."

"True." Trent grimaced as he opened his door. "Honestly, I don't think he's our guy."

She nodded. "Well, maybe Heidi can shed some light on the situation."

Trent's expression was skeptical, but he didn't say anything more.

They drove for nearly an hour without reaching their destination. Traffic was crazy busy, and she belatedly realized there was a Tennessee Titan professional football game going on.

Football was huge in the south, and Nashville citizens were proud of their team. Thinking about the stadium made Serena wonder if her dad had gone to the game today. He had season tickets, so if he didn't go himself, he'd have sold them to someone else.

Once they'd attended games together, but not since her mother died.

She pulled her thoughts away from her personal problems. At some point she'd have to contact the detective looking into Trent's case. Her dad's rebuke rankled. It wasn't that she was trying to interfere with the cops doing their job, but if they weren't working Jimmy's murder, then why shouldn't she look into it?

If she made headway where they'd failed, that was their problem. Not hers.

Yet she also knew that the detective assigned to Jimmy's case should be updated with her findings. Coakley hadn't called her, so she'd have to find him. Trent had mentioned the argument over Heidi to her, but law enforcement assigned to the case didn't know anything about it. Or about the divorce being filed the day before his murder. Which may mean nothing as she tended to agree with Trent that Rob wasn't involved in either the murder or the attempts against Trent.

Detective Grayson hadn't called either. He hadn't seemed interested in her theory of the cases being related. Still, a good cop would cover all his bases.

At least, that's what her dad always said.

She sighed. Times like this, she didn't enjoy her role as a PI. Female cops rarely experienced the respect they deserved. Female PIs received even less.

Normally, her cases revolved around cheating spouses or finding people who'd skipped out on paying their bills. There were also insurance jobs where she tracked down people who claimed to be disabled but weren't. Mundane stuff most of the time.

Solving a murder would get her more recognition. Which should lead to better paying clients.

"I think that's Brentwood up ahead," Trent said, breaking the silence.

"Finally." She lightly pressed the accelerator as the cars around her picked up speed. "That football traffic was a nightmare."

"It was." Trent turned in his seat. "Listen, we need to discuss our strategy with Heidi."

"I thought we agreed I'd play to her emotions by emphasizing how much Jimmy's father needs answers." She hesitated, then added, "While you stay behind."

"Yeah, that's the part I don't like." Trent put a hand on her knee. "She's dangerous, Serena. I don't trust her. She doesn't show a lot of emotion."

"Everyone has emotions." Her protest was weak because narcissists didn't have them. All they cared about was themselves. "But she's less likely to be threatened by me than if you were there."

"She doesn't like me, that's for sure." Trent rubbed his jaw. "Maybe we should call the cops, let them question her."

"I plan to update Detective Coakley soon. But I want to approach Heidi before they do. If she has information, I'd like to hear it. And you know as well as I do the cops won't share anything they uncover about the case with me."

He sighed. "True. Just—be careful."

"I will." His concern for her welfare was sweet, if misplaced. He was the one in danger. And it irked her that he hadn't canceled his Thursday gig. In fact, he hadn't even told her where he was scheduled to play.

After she was finished interviewing Heidi, she'd have to do a search on Trent's name. Those who were featuring him likely had that advertised on their respective websites. Shouldn't be too difficult to find out where he was planning to perform.

A familiar song on the radio caught her attention, and she turned the volume up as she crossed into Brentwood. "This is one of my favorites," she admitted.

Trent listened for a moment, his fingers tapping to the beat. "I haven't heard this artist . . . oh, it's a Christian song?"

"Yes." She glanced over in time to catch his grimace. "What's wrong with that?"

"Nothing, other than I've never listened to Christian music."

"Well, then you shouldn't be wrinkling your nose in disgust. In fact, Christian music has a fairly big market here in Nashville. Maybe not as big as country rock," she added when he scoffed, "but it's solid."

"If you say so."

"I do. And you can't argue since you've admitted to knowing nothing about it." She wasn't sure why she was so annoyed. "I guess you haven't attended church services to be exposed to this type of music."

"Never." His tone was clipped. "And I don't plan to change that anytime soon."

"Too bad because your voice would be a perfect fit." She could easily hear Trent's baritone belting out some of her favorite songs.

"We're looking for Lily Road," he said, changing the subject. "All the streets in this particular section of the subdivision are named after flowers or trees."

"Okay, I think we're close." Well, close was relative. Some of these homes were perched on three-acre lots. As far from the kind of home Rob was currently building as you could get.

Their romance puzzled her. Even if Rob had been part of a larger construction company, one assigned to do work for Heidi, why on earth would the rich woman have married him? Especially since the relationship was clearly doomed from the start.

When she found Lily Road, Heidi's house immediately came into view. The imposing structure sat on a hill, looking regal like a queen overlooking her court. To her surprise, there was no gate preventing her from pulling into the driveway, although she suspected there were plenty of cameras on the property.

She drove past Heidi's driveway and found a spot between houses to pull over. She shut down the car and turned toward Trent. "Stay here. I won't be long."

"I want you to call me if anything looks hinky." His gaze was troubled. "In fact, you may want to record the entire conversation with your phone."

"Good idea. And I'll be fine." She smiled, then slipped out from behind the wheel.

She quickly covered the distance back to the long driveway. As she approached the house, she kept a pleasant expression on her face, hoping that whoever was watching through the cameras wouldn't send a pack of rabid dogs after her.

The idea of Heidi having any animals seemed ridiculous. The worst that could happen was that Heidi's staff, assuming she had one, would call the police to haul her away.

To her surprise, she made it all the way to the front door. She used the brass knocker, then pressed the doorbell. The house was so airtight she couldn't hear the responding chime.

Or maybe the doorbell was just for show.

After waiting a full minute, she tried again, leaning harder on the doorbell. Then she reached out to try the door handle.

The door wasn't locked.

The tiny hairs lifted on the back of her neck as she pushed the door open. The foyer was huge, a high cathedral ceiling with a sweeping staircase off to the side. But there was no sign of anyone. This was wrong. Very wrong. People who lived in million-dollar mansions didn't leave their front door unlocked.

"Hello? My name is Serena, is anyone home?" Her voice bounced off the walls, echoing loudly. Not her kind of place, that's for sure. She stepped up and into the house, taking several steps toward the showcase-ready living room before she saw the spilled red wine seeping into an otherwise pristine white carpet, a scattering of pills, and the supine figure of Heidi Lawrence lying on the sofa.

She rushed over and felt for a pulse.

It was there, but barely. Frantic, she pulled out her phone to dial 911. Hoping and praying the ambulance would get there before it was too late.

CHAPTER NINE

Trent waited for all of two minutes before he got out of the car. He didn't like it that Serena was going to talk to Heidi alone. He didn't trust Jimmy's former lover. The woman didn't care about anyone but herself, and if something bad happened to Serena, he'd never forgive himself.

If he'd have been honest with the police from the beginning, none of this would be happening. Or maybe the real killer would have come after him sooner. Which would have been better for Serena who was involved in this mess up to her pretty neck.

He strode quickly down the street toward the mansion. As he headed up the long driveway, Serena came running out of the house. When she saw him, she frantically waved him forward. "Hurry!"

"What's wrong?" He raced toward her, surprised to see the open front door behind her. "Did Heidi say something nasty to you?"

"No, she's not saying anything at all." Serena turned and led the way back inside. The lavish interior wasn't a surprise, and he felt a surprising sense of dread. Following

Serena into the living room, he took note of the alcohol and the pills. Why was it that people who had the most couldn't seem to find happiness?

He crossed over and checked Heidi's pulse. It was there, but weak. He watched her chest rise and fall with shallow breaths and wondered how long she'd been lying there. It was early in the day. Was it possible she'd partied this hard last night?

"I called 911, the ambulance should be here soon." Serena held on to his arm for a moment. "Two wine glasses, Trent. She had company at some point."

"Yeah." He stared at Heidi, hoping she didn't stop breathing. What if she didn't wake up? They'd never find out the truth about what happened with the divorce. And whether or not she was at all involved in Jimmy's death.

"Heidi! Wake up!" Serena crossed over and shook the woman. "Come on, wake up."

Heidi moved but didn't respond.

"Rob is worried about you." Serena continued shaking the woman. "Remember Rob?"

Heidi moved her head from side to side as if she didn't like what she was hearing. Trent wanted nothing more than to get out of the house, away from the pills and the booze. It was a little like watching someone waking him up from an all-nighter, and the memory made him feel sick to his stomach.

"Heidi! Wake up!" Serena lightly slapped Heidi's face. "Stay with us, okay?"

He had to admit, Serena's attempts to wake her up seemed to be working. Her breathing appeared stronger now, and she was moving restlessly on the sofa. "Robbie?"

Serena glanced at him, then leaned closer to Heidi. "Yes, Robbie is worried about you. You need to wake up."

Heidi tried to open her eyes but then turned away without saying anything. As he watched, her breathing slowed again.

He swallowed hard, wondering if they'd be forced to perform CPR. Not that he'd been trained in rescue, but he felt certain Serena was.

Outside, the wail of sirens indicated the ambulance was on the way. Trent watched out the large living room window. Less than a minute later, two police cars and an ambulance came barreling through the quiet neighborhood.

"Pretty good response time," he murmured. Unlike the delayed response to the shooting at Whistlers.

"Anything for the rich and famous." Serena glanced up at him. "Will you go out and show them the way in?"

"Yeah." He moved through the ridiculously large mansion, secretly glad to get out of there. The place reminded him of his life before he'd stopped drinking, and frankly, he wanted nothing more than to head back to his low-rent apartment.

"Where's Serena Jerash?" the officer demanded.

"This way, please. We found the owner of the house passed out on the sofa. We haven't been able to rouse her." He led the way inside.

Four cops and two EMTs entered the house. Again, he was reminded of the delay they'd experienced at Whistlers as the cops surveyed the scene.

"Who are you?" one of the officers asked, eyeing him suspiciously. Trent knew that he and Serena didn't fit in these luxurious surroundings.

Trent made sure to keep his hands where they could see them. "Trent Atkins. Ms. Lawrence used to come and see us play when I was with the Jimmy Woodrow Band."

The cop's expression didn't change, clearly he didn't recognize Jimmy's name.

The two EMTs began providing care to Heidi. Serena backed off, crossing over to stand beside Trent.

"Okay, we need to take your statements," one of the officers said. The expression in his gaze indicated he didn't believe they were innocent bystanders in all this. "Let's go outside."

"Of course, but you should know that I'm armed," Serena said calmly. "Thirty-eight is in my shoulder holster beneath my shirt."

"I'm not armed," Trent added dryly.

The cop removed Serena's gun, then patted them both down. After reviewing her gun permit and her PI license, the cop handed everything back to her. "Private investigator, huh?"

"Yes, that's correct." Serena tipped her chin as if daring him to make a snide comment.

"I'm Officer Ryan Green. I'd like the both of you to start at the beginning."

"There isn't much to tell," Serena said. "I came here to talk to Ms. Lawrence about a case I'm working on. When I arrived, the front door wasn't locked."

"And you went inside?" Green asked with a frown.

"Yes, because I sensed something was wrong." Trent gave Serena credit for keeping her cool. "People around here wouldn't leave their door unlocked. And as it turned out, I was right. If I hadn't gone inside, Ms. Lawrence might be dead."

That fact had Officer Green scrambling to back off. "Yes, of course, it's good you found Ms. Lawrence when you did. Clearly the outcome could have been much different if you hadn't gone inside." Green eyed Trent. "What is your role in all this? You mentioned a band?"

"Yeah. I knew Ms. Lawrence from when she used to come watch our band perform." Trent was conditioned to tell the least bit of information as possible when it came to talking to the cops. He and Cooper had been stopped on occasion, but they had never been arrested.

Green stared at him for a long moment as if sensing there was more to the story, but then he shifted his gaze back to Serena. "What is this case you're working on?"

"I'm sorry, but I'm not at liberty to say anything about the case or my client, it's confidential." Serena's secretive response surprised him. "However, be assured I only wanted to ask Ms. Lawrence a few questions, that's all."

A commotion from behind them had him glancing over his shoulder. The EMTs had Heidi strapped to a gurney. There was an IV in her arm, and a monitor beeped in time with her pulse, which he felt certain was much faster than normal.

"Robbie? I'm sorry . . ." Heidi's eyes were open, her expression confused. Trent assumed the EMTs had given NARCAN to counteract whatever medication she'd taken on top of the wine. His gaze locked on hers, and he thought a flicker of recognition flashed in her eyes.

But then she was gone, the EMTs hustling Heidi away toward the waiting ambulance. He stared after her, wondering if she knew what had happened to Jimmy. And if she was the one behind the attacks on him too.

The cops made them repeat their story before letting them go. Green insisted on taking one of Serena's cards so he could get in touch with her again if needed. He fell into step beside Serena as they walked to where they'd left the

SUV. If the cops thought the location of their vehicle odd, they hadn't mentioned it.

"What do you think?" he asked in a low voice. "Who was Heidi with last night?"

Serena blew out a sigh. "I don't think it was Rob, he was up early and working on the house this morning. From what I could tell, he didn't look the least bit hungover."

"I agree." He turned to glance back at the imposing mansion. "I still think it's odd she didn't have live-in help, someone who would have found her before we did. What if we'd have waited another hour to show up?"

She nodded. "It would have been too late. God was guiding us here. Thankfully, we arrived in time to save her." Serena opened the driver's side door and looked at him. "Interesting how she responded to Rob's name. Her apology sounded as if she still truly cares about him."

"Maybe. Or maybe the drugs in her system made her see someone who wasn't there." Trent wasn't about to give Heidi credit for having feelings for anyone but herself. In some ways, the woman reminded him of his own mother, who only cared about herself. "We should swing by the hospital later. We still need to talk to her."

"We can try, but I'm not sure how long it will take for her to recover from her overdose." Serena slid behind the wheel. He quickly climbed in beside her. "And honestly, I'm more interested in who might have been there with her. Maybe that person is involved in this somehow. Maybe that person was even the one who had been hired to attack you."

"You think so?"

"Yes. Which means we need to go back and search her social media posts again. See if we can find someone who fits the bill."

Serena's plan made sense, but he couldn't help feeling

frustrated. As she drove away from the mansion, the tension that had curled through him eased. In that moment, Trent knew he never wanted to go back to that lifestyle.

It could have easily been him lying on the sofa. He probably should have died from the amount of alcohol he used to drink.

But he hadn't. Why? He wasn't sure. To be honest, his life was rather pathetic. His music entertained, but was that enough? It wasn't as if people came in droves to hear him play.

He reminded himself that he was doing better now than he had been. And he had no intention of going back to his old ways. Just being in Heidi's house had made him feel uncomfortable, to the point he couldn't wait to leave.

But was this all he had? His apartment and his music?

Glancing at Serena, his heart squeezed in his chest. Once they uncovered the truth about Jimmy's murder, he wouldn't see her anymore.

And that was for the best. She deserved someone far better. Someone with a brighter future.

Yet he'd miss her, more than he would have thought possible.

SERENA GLANCED AT TRENT. He'd been unusually quiet since leaving Heidi's home. He seemed lost in his thoughts, and she couldn't help but wonder if he was thinking about the night of Jimmy's murder.

The night he'd been passed out, much like Heidi had been.

"I'm proud of you, Trent."

He lifted a brow. "I didn't do anything."

"You're here, aren't you? Staying sober while helping me find Jimmy's killer. That's a lot to be proud of." She risked a quick glance at his somber expression. "Most guys would have told me to take a hike."

"I tried that, but you ended up saving my life."

She let out a weak laugh. "True, but I think you'd have handled that guy outside the Thirsty Saloon all by yourself."

"Maybe." His tone was noncommittal. "But the attack at Whistlers was all you. I owe you more than I'll ever be able to repay."

"There isn't a scoreboard," she chided softly. "I'm glad to have been there when you needed me. We're in this together."

"So where are we going?" Trent clearly wanted to change the subject. "Another motel?"

"Yes. I have a question, though. When's the last time you saw Brett Caine?"

His brow furrowed. "The band manager? Probably at Jimmy's funeral. Why?"

"I was thinking we should talk to him too." She headed out of Brentwood, leaving the million-dollar mansions behind. "Is he still representing Jed and Dave?"

"Yes, he's managing the Bootleggers." He shrugged. "That's how Jed and Dave got their positions."

"But their lead singer isn't as good as Jimmy was, right?"

"Not from the handful of songs I heard." He turned in his seat. "Why all the questions about Brett? He lost a big meal ticket when Jimmy died."

"As you pointed out, Brett could have lost his temper with Jimmy. Maybe he saw how the drugs and alcohol might bring him down." She hesitated, then said, "I'm thinking Jimmy's death wasn't preplanned. I mean, I doubt someone came to the celebration that night to kill him."

"Probably not." He was silent for a long moment. "I still have Brett's number."

"You do?" She was surprised. "Are you willing to reach out to him? Set up a meeting?"

He nodded and fished his phone from his pocket. Without hesitation, he made the call. "Brett? Trent Atkins, here. Was wondering if you have time to chat?"

She couldn't hear Brett's side of the conversation, but it didn't take long to figure out the meeting was a go. "Great, we can meet at Hathaways for lunch, no problem. Oh, I'm bringing a girlfriend along too."

Girlfriend? Her chest tightened as she realized she liked the sound of that, even though she knew Trent wasn't serious. No doubt, he didn't want to warn Brett about the true nature of their meeting.

"Okay, see you then." Trent disconnected from the call. "Hathaways is a fancy restaurant in downtown Nashville. I have plenty of money, no need to worry about your expense account."

This wasn't the time to argue about who was going to pay for the meal. "Is Brett thinking you've changed your mind about joining Bootleggers?"

"I hinted at that, yes," Trent admitted. "Either joining the guys or getting representation from him on my own."

"But he'd get a cut of your income if you let him rep you, right?"

"Yeah, which is why I have no intention of going that route." Trent shrugged. "But he doesn't know that."

She nodded and turned to head toward downtown Nashville. Serena hoped this meeting would turn out better than the last one. Finding Heidi barely breathing had been a shock.

So far, they weren't making much headway on the case.

And she needed to update Jimmy's dad too. Not that she had any good news for him.

If anything, the suspect pool had only gotten deeper compared to when she'd started her investigation. Heidi, her mystery friend, Jed, Dave, even Brett could be involved.

Or someone else entirely, she thought with a grimace. The only good news was that there hadn't been another attack on Trent.

At least, not so far.

"We're early, so let's find a place to wait." Trent gestured to the coffee shop. "They have Wi-Fi. You mentioned searching through Heidi's social media again."

"Okay, we'll stop there." Thankfully, parking wasn't too much of a problem since it was Sunday.

Fifteen minutes later, they settled at a small table to work.

Serena was hyperaware of Trent sitting beside her, watching as she poked through Heidi Law's social media.

"What about this woman?" She scrolled through various pictures of Heidi alone, posing like the cover model of *Sports Illustrated*, until she found a few candid shots. She turned the screen so Trent could see the image more clearly. "Does she look familiar?"

He nodded slowly. "Anna Weiss. She's the daughter of Wayne Weiss, the owner of Country Blues Records."

It was the first she'd heard of Country Blues Records. "How do you know them?"

"Brett was trying to convince Wayne to give us a record deal." He shrugged. "Anna used to come to some of our parties."

Yet another name to add to the list of potential suspects. Although she didn't see why Wayne Weiss or his daughter would want to kill Jimmy. "Did you know her well?"

"No, she was a nice kid, younger than most of the groupies but old enough to get into the bars. And she liked Jimmy." Trent met her gaze. "Most of the women who attended our gatherings sought out Jimmy's attention."

"Their mistake," she said lightly. She tapped the computer screen. "Did the record deal ever come through? Or get close enough to sign off on a contract?"

"Not that I'm aware of. Although we can ask Brett, he might know more." Trent's casual attitude about the whole thing surprised her. Any musician would love to land a record deal.

Wouldn't they?

"I'm surprised you weren't more excited about the possibility of recording music for a label like Country Blues," she said as she turned the computer back to continue her search. "That seems like a really big deal."

Trent was silent for a long minute. "Back then, yeah, we were all into it. Jimmy especially was pushing Brett hard to make it happen. But now? I can't help but feel that things turned out this way for a reason. When I saw Heidi unconscious on the sofa . . ." His voice trailed off.

"I know, it must have brought back some terrible memories." She wrapped her arm around his shoulders. "You're in a better place now, Trent. This is God's plan for you."

"What, playing low-level gigs barely making enough to get by?" Sarcasm laced his tone. "I think it's more likely this is my punishment rather than a plan for the future."

"God isn't punishing you, Trent." She eyed him thoughtfully. "But I think you're trying to punish yourself."

He frowned but didn't say anything to refute her claim.

For the first time, she understood that Trent didn't trust himself. He'd been sober for three months, but that wasn't long in the big scheme of things. It seemed as if he avoided doing anything that would draw more attention to his talent, as if he didn't trust himself to have a bigger and better career.

She could understand to a certain point. Being semi-famous as a part of the Jimmy Woodrow Band had nearly ruined his life.

But God had given Trent musical ability for a reason. Each time she heard him play, she grew even more impressed. And his original songs made her heart weep. Maybe she could find a way to help him put his skills to good use.

After they figured out who was trying to kill him.

Turning her attention back to Heidi's social media, she found one additional photo. But the guy was clearly Rob Furrier. She showed the image to Trent. "They look happy here. I wonder what happened?"

"Heidi is happy because Rob adores her," Trent said curtly. "I'm telling you, the woman I overheard talking on the phone couldn't have cared less about him."

She looked at the photo again, then closed the computer. "We should head over to Hathaways."

"Yeah." Trent looked as if they were heading to the dentist for a root canal rather than lunch with his former band manager.

The walk didn't take long. Even in September, the sun beat mercilessly down on them. When they entered the restaurant, the air conditioning felt amazing against her skin.

"Nice place," she said in a low tone.

Trent nodded but didn't look impressed. She wondered

how often he and Jimmy had met Brett here as they attempted to scale the music business.

Brett Caine made them wait a full five minutes before joining them. He immediately shook Trent's hand. "Trent, it's good to see you."

"Brett. This is Serena Jerash. Serena, this is Brett Caine, my former manager."

"Hopefully soon-to-be current manager, right, Trent?" The man beamed. "Nice to meet you, Serena." Brett had the personality of a used car salesman. "Are you a singer too?"

"Oh, no. Sorry." Truth was, she didn't have any musical talent whatsoever.

"Well, that's too bad, you'd look great on stage."

Serena was sure he'd meant it as a compliment, but it was difficult to ignore the leer in his gaze.

There was an awkward silence, until Brett said, "Well, let's sit down, shall we? This way." He walked through the tables as if he owned the place. Which, for all she knew, he did. There was a table for four overlooking the Grand Ole Opry hotel, and he waved at it. "Sit, sit. Would you like something to drink?"

"Water," she and Trent said at the exact same time. For a moment, the corner of Trent's mouth curved up in a smile.

"Oh yeah, I heard you gave up alcohol," Brett said, his gaze zeroing in on Trent. "Good for you."

"Heard how?" Trent asked.

"Oh, you know." Brett waved an impatient hand. "The guys said something."

They'd only just met, and Serena already didn't like the band manager. Easy to understand why Trent had no intention of using Brett in the future.

"Better to stay sober than to end up like Jimmy." Trent never took his gaze from Brett. "Don't you agree?"

The manager looked taken aback by the comment. "Yes, of course." Brett glanced around and waved someone over. "Water all around, and we'll start with the escargot."

"Of course, Mr. Caine." The young woman quickly filled their water glasses, then hurried off to bring the appetizer.

"Jimmy's father has been devastated by what happened." She did her best to smile at the man she was beginning to think of as a snake in the grass. A poisonous one.

"Well, any father would be." Brett tried to sound sincere, but his sharp gaze belied any true concern. "Unfortunately, Jimmy isn't the first man to succumb to the lure of drugs and alcohol." He shifted to look at Trent. "Right?"

Trent lifted his water and took a sip. "You were there that night. Maybe you should have shared your concerns with him."

Brett scowled. "I wasn't there for long, and Jimmy wouldn't have listened to me anyway." His gaze narrowed. "And if I remember correctly, you didn't listen to that sort of advice either."

"That's funny. I remember you filling up my glass, not telling me to slow down." This time, there was no mistaking the animosity in his tone.

"Your memory is clouded by alcohol," Brett said.

"In fact," Trent went on as if he hadn't spoken, "I also remember Jimmy called you when he needed something more, and you were only too happy to oblige."

Brett's face flushed with rage, but somehow he managed to wrestle it under control. "You're wrong, Trent. And I thought you wanted to talk about joining the group, not blame me for Jimmy's death."

"Yet you are at least partially responsible for the way Jimmy spiraled out of control," Trent shot back.

"I'm not." Brett turned to look at her as if wondering why she was just sitting there saying nothing. "I'm sorry, Ms. Jerash, but it appears Trent is still harboring ill feelings toward me. It's probably best if we skip lunch."

"What time did you leave the party that night?" If Brett was going to call an end to the meeting, she wanted to get a couple of questions asked.

"Why do you care?" Brett asked, his gaze turning suspicious. He glanced between the two of them. "Is this some sort of setup? Are you a cop?"

"No, I'm not a cop," Serena said honestly. "But you should know that Jimmy's father is determined to get to the bottom of what happened that night." She smiled without any hint of humor. "So be prepared for the Nashville PD to question you again, Mr. Caine. Especially since Jimmy's death could still be ruled a homicide."

The man's jaw dropped in shock. "Homicide? That's ridiculous. Jimmy abused drugs and alcohol, that's what caused his death."

"Not according to the medical examiner," she gently corrected. "He did have drugs and alcohol in his system, but the levels weren't enough to call his death an accidental overdose."

Now Brett looked a little like a mouse caught in a trap. "What are you insinuating? That I'm responsible for Jimmy's death? That's slander!" Brett jumped to his feet so fast he knocked his chair over. "If I read about this in the newspapers, I'll have my lawyer file a lawsuit against the both of you. Understand? Everything you own will be mine!"

Before she or Trent could say anything more, he stalked off, practically running from the restaurant as if his pants were on fire.

And maybe they were. Because this little interview had clearly struck a nerve. The man was guilty all right. Of providing drugs to Jimmy, and maybe of something more.

CHAPTER TEN

Trent knew it was wrong, but he couldn't help feeling a surge of satisfaction that he'd rattled Brett. He stood and reached for Serena's hand. "Let's go before we end up paying for his snails."

"No kidding," she agreed, wrinkling her nose. "Disgusting."

He couldn't help but chuckle as he led the way through the restaurant, avoiding the startled glance from their server. He figured the staff here knew Brett Caine well enough to charge him for the escargot.

When they were outside, he continued to hold her hand as they walked at a leisurely pace back to where they'd parked the car. "That was interesting," Serena said thoughtfully. "And not what I expected."

"Yeah, but we didn't learn anything new about Jimmy's murder."

"Brett reacted pretty strongly to learning Jimmy's death could be deemed a homicide." She glanced up at him. "He sure acted guilty."

"He's guilty of helping Jimmy get drugs," he agreed.

"Why didn't you ever turn him in to the police?" She looked exasperated. "He should be held accountable for his crimes."

Her question stung, and it took a moment for him to respond. "You have to understand that going to the police is not a part of my DNA. Thirteen years ago, when we escaped the Preacher, we did everything possible to avoid the cops. I never reported any of the crimes I witnessed while living on the streets." He hesitated, then added, "I was stealing at the time too. "

"I understand, Trent. Especially when you and the others were underage." Her tone held compassion. "But after you became an adult, and began playing music, surely you understood the cops weren't your enemy."

"But they were." His frustration mounted. "Do you honestly think that if a drug raid took place in the hotel that I wouldn't go down with the rest of them?"

She stopped and waited for him to face him. "I get that, but later, after you left that life, you could have reported Brett Caine. I'm sure he's providing illegal drugs to other band members he's managing. Including Jed and Dave and whoever else is part of Bootleggers."

"Probably." Trent ignored the twinge of guilt. "If Brett doesn't get them drugs, they'll find some other way to get them."

"Sounds like an excuse you've told yourself to feel better about ignoring the problem." She tugged her hand from his, and he struggled with a keen sense of loss. "Whatever, that's not really the issue. Brett was there that night. Can you remember when he left the party?"

Trent suppressed a sigh. "I already told you that most of that night is a blur."

"I need you to think back anyway," she insisted. "Focus on Brett."

He crossed his arms over his chest. "Is this your way of pushing me into doing the hypnosis thing?"

"No, although I'd still like you to try it." He had to admire her honesty. "I'm not pushing that, but if you take the time to really think back to that night, it's possible something new will come to you."

"Yeah, but is it smart to trust my alcohol-soaked memories?"

"Trent." She reached out to put a hand on his arm. "I'm only asking you to try. If you can't come up with anything new, that's fine. But with Heidi in the hospital and Brett's refusal to talk, we don't have many options."

He blew out a breath. "Okay, fine. I'll do my best. Let's get out of the sun."

They continued walking to the SUV. He hated disappointing her. Yet did she really think he hadn't gone back over that night? He had. Unfortunately, the clearest memory that kept popping into the forefront of his mind was the one where he saw Jimmy's open, unfocused eyes.

A shiver rippled over him despite the heat. Jimmy's lifeless face was the one image he wished he could forget. But knew he wouldn't.

Just like he wouldn't forget the night they'd escaped from the Preacher's burning cabin.

Or the devastated expression on Cooper's face when he told him he was leaving Gatlinburg to play with Jimmy's band.

Maybe he was destined to remember every mistake he'd ever made with stark clarity. The Preacher could have been right about God punishing them for their sins.

"Trent? This is our SUV." Serena was looking at him oddly as he'd continued walking past their vehicle.

"Oh yeah." He turned and retraced his steps.

Soon they were back on the highway. "We should get something to eat," Serena said. "Then head back to the hotel where you guys were staying that night."

The familiar sense of dread washed over him. "Why? Three months have passed. You're not going to find anything significant now."

"You never know." She didn't meet his gaze. "There's a place nearby where the food isn't terrible and the prices are decent."

He didn't eat out much these days, so he decided to take her word for it. "Sounds good. Do you live around here?"

"Me? No, I live in a studio apartment off Whitsett Road." She grinned. "To be honest, it's very similar to your place, only much cleaner."

He smiled in spite of himself. "Sounds like your PI work pays about as well as my gigs."

"Probably less," she admitted. "Even in lousy buildings like the ones we live in, rent is astronomical."

"True." He'd been surprised at the high cost of living in Nashville as compared to Gatlinburg. He stared out the window as Serena pulled in and parked at the country kitchen. He really needed to reach out to Cooper. Once the danger was over, he'd call his foster brother back, see if they couldn't make some time to get together.

These past few months he'd felt like he was drifting by, going from one gig to another. Granted, he'd created a couple of new songs, but deep down, it hadn't been enough.

Being with Serena pretty much nonstop over these past few days made him realize how much he'd missed human interaction.

Shining a bright light on how lonely his life had become.

Gatlinburg was only four hours away. If he could get his truck window repaired, he should be able to get down there to see Cooper over a couple of days when he didn't have anywhere to perform.

But not until he could be sure he wouldn't drag his foster brother into danger.

The restaurant was busy, but they managed to get one of the last booths. After they ordered, Serena sat forward. "We'll head to the hotel after lunch. Being in the same room could bring back some of your repressed memories."

Yeah, that's exactly what he was afraid of. He didn't say anything, though. He sipped his water. Returning to the hotel and the scene of the crime had to be better than being hypnotized.

Their meals arrived, and this time, he was prepared for the way Serena reached for his hand in order to pray.

"Dear Lord, we ask you to keep us safe and to continue to guide us on Your chosen path. Amen."

"Amen," he responded without thinking, then he flushed. What was he doing? God surely knew he was a hypocrite.

"Thank you, Trent." Serena squeezed his hand, then sat back. "God will guide us through this, you'll see."

He avoided answering by digging into his food. To be honest, he was glad they hadn't been forced to eat with Brett. No doubt sharing a meal with the guy would have brought on a bad case of heartburn.

"When we're finished at the hotel, I'll call to check on Heidi." Serena spoke between bites of her salad.

"And if she refuses to talk to us?" Trent asked.

She frowned. "I hope she will. Otherwise we'll have to talk to Jed and Dave again."

He didn't like that idea. "Brett would have warned them by now," he said slowly. "I'm sure they're not going to tell you anything new."

"I know, but I'm running out of ideas," Serena admitted.

"What about reaching out to Anna Weiss?"

She looked surprised by his suggestion. "You think she knows something?"

"She was friendly enough with Heidi to have a picture of the two of them together on social media." He honestly didn't think Anna had anything to do with Jimmy's death, but it couldn't hurt to ask her about Heidi. "It's possible she was the one with Heidi last night."

"Leaving her friend passed out cold without a second thought," Serena said with a scowl. "Yeah, I see your point. Anna will be next on our list."

He wanted to suggest they call Anna before heading over to the hotel but held his tongue. Going along with Serena's plan was the least he could do.

After finishing their lunch, Serena drove them straight to the Grand Ole Opry hotel. The place was a huge tourist attraction, so he doubted they'd have rooms available, even to look at.

"Do you remember what room you were in that night?"

"It was a suite." He rattled off the room number, then held the door open and followed her inside.

Serena waited in line to talk to the next available desk clerk. He hung back a bit as she requested to see the same suite they'd used that infamous night. "I'm here representing Jimmy Woodrow's father, and his son lost a ring that night. I just want to look for it."

"We clean our rooms very thoroughly," the clerk said with a frown. "I can assure you no ring was found."

"I'm sure you do, but you see, Jimmy's dad is insisting I look." Serena spread her hands helplessly. "If you wouldn't mind, I'm sure it wouldn't take much time."

"The room may already have a guest."

"Yes, but it's Sunday." Serena smiled. "I'm sure there's a good chance that whoever might have been staying in there has already checked out."

The clerk looked annoyed but turned toward the computer and tapped on a few keys. "You're right, the occupants of the room have checked out. But the room hasn't been cleaned yet by our housekeeping staff."

"That's perfect," Serena exclaimed with satisfaction. "Now we can search the room without causing you or the housekeepers any inconvenience."

Trent could tell the clerk wanted to refuse, but he caved in. "Fine. I'll program this key for you. But I'm going to disable the card after fifteen minutes."

"That's fine. Thank you so much." Serena took the card and turned away, leaving Trent little choice but to follow her.

The interior of the hotel was all too familiar. He gestured toward the elevator that would take them to the expensive suite located near the top floor. "This way."

They rode the elevator in silence. He braced himself when she used the key card to open the door to the suite.

Seeing the place again hit with the impact of a sucker punch straight to his gut. He stood frozen in the entryway for a long minute before forcing himself to walk inside.

The place wasn't very messy, certainly not the way they'd left it that night. Hit by a strong sense of déjà vu, he entered the main living area of the suite. The party had spilled into the bedrooms, which was why he'd ended up crashed on the sofa. At least, from what he could remember.

Trent slowed to a stop near the glass top coffee table. In that moment he remembered the blood staining the blue and white carpet. Of course, there wasn't any blood on the floor now.

"Here." The word sounded hoarse to his own ears. "This is where Jimmy was."

"Where was his head?" Serena asked softly.

"This end." He gestured to the appropriate spot, not far from the pointed edge of the coffee table. "His feet were that way."

"Okay, that helps me visualize things." Serena lightly touched his arm. "Where were you?"

"There." He pointed to the sofa that was nearby. "My head was pointing toward that bedroom, so I didn't notice Jimmy's face until I stood and practically stepped on him." Barely missing those wide, empty, blank eyes that stared up at the ceiling.

"Okay, you're doing fine." Her fingers tightened on his arm, but he couldn't bring himself to look at her. His mind was on that horrible night when he'd found Jimmy dead.

He turned and forced himself to walk over to the balcony. He stared through the windows without seeing the city of Nashville stretched out before him. He was remembering when Jimmy was embracing the two women laughing at something they'd said.

Was one of those women Anna? He tried to remember, but the women's faces were a blur. One had been blonde, the other a brunette. Heidi was a brunette, and Anna was blonde.

Had both women been there that night? He hadn't remembered seeing Heidi and hadn't paid attention to the women hanging on Jimmy. Seeing Jimmy with women was nothing new. In fact, he'd remember more clearly if Jimmy hadn't been with anyone.

"What is it?" Serena asked softly.

"Jimmy was with two women that night, a blonde and a brunette, but I can't remember their faces." He finally turned to look at her. "Could have been Heidi and Anna, but I can't say that with any certainty."

"What about earlier, when they weren't standing here by the window." Her voice remained calm and soothing, but his gut felt like it was tied up in dozens of knots. "Did you notice them come in?"

"No." Although he found himself glancing at the door. A flash of Heidi laughing hit hard. "Yes, Heidi was there."

"You're doing great." Serena's tone was encouraging.

Suddenly, he felt as if he were back in that party atmosphere, booze bottles everywhere, drinks overflowing. The two women and Jimmy going into the bathroom, together. He blinked, tried to push the memories away.

Sweat popped out on his forehead. Suddenly he was running, through the suite and out the door. He jabbed his finger on the elevator button and fell inside when the doors opened. Without waiting for Serena to join him, he hit the lobby button, then collapsed in the corner, staring at the panel as the elevator slowly traveled downward.

It wasn't until he was all the way outside that he could take a deep breath. He found a place to sit and held his head in his hands in an attempt to stop them from shaking. He swallowed hard, trying not to throw up the lunch he'd just eaten.

If being hypnotized was anything like what he'd just been through, there was no way on earth he was signing up for that.

Not now. Not ever.

SERENA GAPED in shock for a moment at Trent's unexpected reaction, then quickly followed him out of the suite. But she didn't make it to the elevator in time. As the doors closed, she caught a glimpse of Trent looking pale and shaken as he slumped in the far corner of the car.

Not good. He looked as if he'd seen a ghost. Jimmy's ghost. The memories of reliving that night had been more than he'd been able to handle, and she felt terrible for bringing him.

She waited for what seemed like forever until she was able to take another elevator to the lobby. Sweeping her gaze over the area, she couldn't see Trent anywhere. Had he left the hotel completely? It wouldn't necessarily surprise her, but she wanted, needed to find him.

She owed him an apology.

Outside, she desperately looked around, stopping abruptly when she saw him sitting on a bench near the sidewalk. "Trent? Are you okay?"

At the sound of her voice, he glanced up, a hard glint in his eye. "Let's get out of here."

"Of course." She felt terrible for causing him so much distress. "I'm sorry. I didn't realize—"

"Whatever." A muscle in the corner of his jaw flexed. "I just want to get away from here. If you're not willing to leave, I'll grab a rideshare."

"We'll go. Just give me a sec to get the car." She crossed over and handed her ticket to the parking attendant. Within a few minutes, the kid returned with her SUV.

Trent slid into the passenger seat, staring through his

window as she left the hotel. She felt terrible for how things had gone, but at the same time, she wanted to ask if he remembered something.

The first time she'd asked about Heidi being there that night, he'd claimed she hadn't. But now he remembered a blonde and a brunette. He'd admitted that Heidi was there, and she felt certain the other woman may have been Anna Weiss.

"Trent," she began.

"Don't. Not now." His tone was harsh, and she recoiled as if she'd been slapped. "I can't do this for you, Serena. I just can't."

"All right, I understand." She risked a glance at him. "Again, please accept my apology. I didn't expect . . ." She couldn't finish.

He didn't respond, and she tried to focus on finding a place to stay. Not in the downtown area, but something on the outskirts of town.

This clearly wasn't the time to ask him to try talking to Jed and Dave. She took several furtive glances at him as she navigated the traffic that would likely grow much worse once the football game was over.

It appeared as if Trent was hanging on by a thread and that it wouldn't take much effort at all for him to snap.

She glanced over her shoulder to check her blind spot before changing lanes. Her gaze landed on a large black Jeep. The windows were tinted, so she couldn't see how many people were inside, but the Jeep followed her into the left lane.

A warning tingle danced down her spine. Was the Jeep following them? Or was she letting Trent's reaction to the suite where Jimmy had died make her paranoid?

Without using her blinker, she quickly moved back into

the right lane and from there cut off another car in order to get off the interstate. A quick glance in the rearview mirror showed the black Jeep hadn't been able to follow.

Or hadn't been following them at all in the first place.

"What was that about?" Trent asked.

"Probably nothing. I saw a black Jeep with tinted windows and worried we were being followed." She took several side streets while continuing in the same eastbound direction, looking for another place to get back on the highway. "We need to find a place to stay for tonight. Any ideas?"

He shrugged and looked away. "Anywhere is fine."

She fought a wave of helplessness. The space between them felt as wide and vast as the ocean. Trent was acting much like the way he had when they first met, as if he was a complete stranger and preferred to keep it that way.

As if they hadn't embraced, hugged, and kissed.

Or prayed together over a meal.

The loss of any hint of friendship was crippling. She opened her mouth to apologize, then held back. She'd already apologized twice. Nothing she could say would make up for what Trent had experienced.

What she'd so callously put him through.

The freeway on-ramp was up ahead. She headed back onto the interstate. It was tempting to drive all the way out of Nashville and even out of the state of Tennessee.

But running away wouldn't solve Jimmy's murder.

Frankly, at the rate they were going, she wondered if Jimmy's untimely death was one mystery that would never be resolved.

"What do you think? Is that the black Jeep you mentioned before?"

Trent's question had her checking the rearview mirror.

She sucked in a quick breath. "Yes, I think so. Although I suppose there could be more than one black Jeep with tinted windows in Nashville."

"It's hanging a few cars back, although I'm not sure how they ended up behind us, considering we left the freeway for a bit before coming back on. They should have been up ahead." He didn't turn in his seat but kept his eyes locked on his passenger side window. "You need to lose him."

"I tried that once," she felt compelled to point out. "What I really don't understand is how the black Jeep found us in the first place. I didn't notice anyone following us earlier, and trust me, I checked."

"Brett could have sent them, or maybe someone was watching the hotel." Trent finally looked at her. "I have a bad feeling about this."

"We're going to lose them." She injected as much confidence as she could muster into her tone. "But this time, I'm going to try something different."

"Like what?"

"Get off the interstate but this time get right back on heading in the opposite direction." She considered which exit to take. "How well do you know this area?"

"Not very," he admitted. He surprised her by reaching over to take her hand, giving it a gentle squeeze. "I trust your gut, Serena. Do what you think is best."

His words almost made her cry. But this wasn't the time to succumb to emotion. She needed to stay focused. The black Jeep continued to keep pace, and she knew without a doubt the driver was tailing them.

The traffic around them grew more congested, likely from the football game. She couldn't tell if that was a help or a hindrance. She managed to move over to the right lane, watching with a sick sense of dread as the Jeep mimicked her movements.

The exit she wanted to take was still a mile away. A mile that seemed like far longer as even more cars crowded onto the interstate.

At this rate, she'd never be able to ditch the stupid Jeep. Although she figured the driver of the Jeep was in the exact same predicament.

The car in front of her abruptly slammed on his brakes.

"Look out," Trent shouted.

She hit the brake in time to avoid rear-ending the guy in front of her. Thankfully, the driver behind her was paying attention as well and managed to avoid hitting her. But the black Jeep with the tinted windows was forced to go around the vehicle behind her to drive in the emergency lane.

As quickly as it had stopped, the traffic now began to move. The car in front of her eased forward, but before she could do the same, the Jeep cut her off, moving directly in front of her.

"What in the world is he doing?" She stared in horror as the rear window of the black Jeep lowered and the barrel of a gun poked through.

"Get down," Trent roared.

She ducked as low as she dared, cranking the wheel to the right to drive over and onto the emergency lane the same way the Jeep had done earlier. She'd hoped to avoid the gunfire but didn't. The gunshot was incredibly loud, and the bullet pierced the upper left-hand corner of the windshield. By the grace of God, the entire windshield didn't shatter, but the rear window did as the bullet struck all the way through the SUV.

"Watch out," Trent said as she nearly hit the concrete wall.

She managed to wrestle the SUV to a stop. Then, without taking a breath, she cranked the gear shift down into reverse and hit the gas. The SUV rolled backward on the emergency lane, a move that caused several drivers to honk their horns in protest. She ignored them, desperate to put as much distance as possible between them and the rifle in the back of the Jeep.

Trent looked surprised, but there wasn't time to argue as the sound of gunfire echoed again. This time, the entire windshield shattered beneath the force of the bullet.

Serena continued heading in reverse, hoping and praying God would keep them safe.

CHAPTER ELEVEN

Trent hated feeling helpless and unable to help with getting them away from the gunman. Not that Serena wasn't doing a great job on her own, backing up along the emergency lane was risky, but it seemed to be working.

When she reached the exit, she faced forward and cranked the wheel in an effort to get them off the interstate. Several drivers honked again, especially those trying to get off on the exit ramp too, but Serena ignored them. By some sort of miracle, they made it onto a side street. Serena pulled over and turned to face him.

"We'll get pulled over if we continue driving this busted-up SUV." Her expression was grim. "The only option for us is to grab a rideshare."

"Okay. Did you get a good look at the shooter? Or get a plate number?" He reached into the back for his guitar. It was covered in shards of glass, but he didn't pay much attention. They needed to be safe, which meant putting as much distance as possible between them and the black Jeep.

"No, did you?" She pushed out of the car, then sort of

slumped against it. "I have to admit I was focused solely on the gun."

He looped the guitar over his body, grabbed their bags, then went over to place his arm around her waist. "That was some amazing NASCAR driving skills back there." He'd tried to lighten his tone, but emotion was clogging his throat. He added, "You saved our lives."

Serena leaned against him for a moment, then straightened. "I did what I had to do, but know this, God was watching over us, Trent."

He couldn't argue. When the muzzle of that gun was pointed directly at them, he'd felt certain they were dead. Fear had overwhelmed him. Would he go to hell, the way the Preacher had told them? And what about all the things he'd left undone? He'd found himself silently begging for a second chance to make amends.

Especially with Cooper.

With his hands full, he couldn't reach his phone, but Serena had hers and was already pulling up the location of the closest rideshare.

"What about your SUV?" he asked, glancing back the windowless vehicle. "Are you really going to leave it here?"

"Yeah. It'll get towed." She grimaced. "But I can't worry about that right now. We need to find a place to hunker down and stay out of sight. Then I can make some phone calls."

He wanted to ask who she planned to contact, but a white Chevy Blazer was heading toward them. The driver pulled over and rolled down the passenger window. "Serena?" he asked. "You waiting for a ride?"

"Yes, thanks."

Trent let her go long enough to store their bags and his guitar in the back before joining her inside the vehicle. She reached out and grasped his hand as if needing the physical contact after their close call.

He needed it too.

Serena gave him the address of a cheap motel as their destination. The driver didn't chitchat as he navigated the post–Tennessee Titan game traffic to get them to the other side of town.

There was no sign of the black Jeep, and he figured that the driver had tried to get off the interstate as well, considering people in the cars around them must have witnessed the shooting. He tried to think back if he saw a license plate, but he couldn't remember noticing.

Had anyone taken down the plate number? He sincerely hoped so.

But that wasn't enough. These attacks had to be stopped. And soon.

"Trent?" Serena tightened her fingers around his. "Are you okay?"

He wasn't, and neither was she. But they were safe.

For now.

"I'll call Detective Grayson when we're at the hotel," she said in a low voice. "Let him know about the gunfire and the SUV. Coakley never bothered to follow up with us, but I should call him too."

He nodded and offered a lopsided smile. "Okay."

They reached the motel a few minutes later. They once again managed to get connecting rooms, maybe because it was a Sunday night. Trent set his guitar and duffel in his room, then carried Serena's things through the connecting doorway. She was already on the phone.

"This is Serena Jerash, please call me back as soon as possible. The windows of my SUV have been shot out by gunfire, and I left it on the side of Rover Road."

She set the phone down and ran her hand through her hair. Tiny glass pieces fell to the floor. "We should clean up."

"Yeah." He closed the gap between them and pulled her into his arms. "First, I need a hug."

Serena wrapped her arms around his waist. "Me too," she murmured, burying her face against his chest.

They clung to each other for several long minutes. He honestly didn't want to let her go. How had she become so important in such a short amount of time?

Her phone rang, and he reluctantly released her. She swiped at her face, then answered the phone. "Detective Grayson? Thanks for returning my call."

"Speaker," he whispered. "I want to hear this."

"I'm placing you on speaker because Trent is with me." She set the phone on the table and sat down. "I need you to get my SUV and search it for evidence. One bullet went all the way through, shattering the back window, but the other one may still be inside."

"Hold on, why don't you start at the beginning?" Grayson asked.

Serena succinctly repeated the sequence of events. "I didn't get a look at the Jeep's license plate because the cars were too close together. But there had to be several witnesses, the freeway was jam-packed."

"We received several calls about gunfire erupting on the interstate," Grayson confirmed. "But I'm not aware of any license plate numbers being reported."

"Great," Trent muttered. He raised his voice. "We believe the Jeep had been following us for a while. Serena tried to lose it once, but it showed back up again." He hesitated, then added, "It's possible they followed us from the Grand Ole Opry hotel."

There was a long silence as Grayson digested that information. "You're saying this is related to Woodrow's death?"

"Yes." Serena's voice was clipped, and Trent could see the flash of anger in her desert brown eyes. "Didn't you reach out to Detective Coakley as I requested?"

"I haven't heard back," Grayson said hastily. "I'll try him again."

Serena scowled and shook her head in disgust. "That would be helpful, considering we were nearly killed today."

"Give me the plate number for your vehicle." Grayson sounded all business now. Trent hoped that meant the guy was actually going to do some real investigating. It was a shame Serena hadn't been able to get into the police academy, she was far better at unraveling mysteries than the cops assigned to the case.

Serena provided the information, then added, "I'll give Detective Coakley a call, let him know he'll be hearing from you." She disconnected before Grayson could say anything more.

"Good one," he said with a tired grin.

"Idiot," she said, scrolling through her contact list. She called Coakley but was forced to leave a message with him too.

Apparently, the police didn't hold PIs in high regard. He found himself wondering if her dad had told the cops to keep her in the dark.

Wouldn't the guy want to know his daughter was in danger? Trent sure would. If he had a daughter.

A rush of shame washed over him. He didn't have any children, at least not to his knowledge, but he had six foster siblings. Brothers and sisters he hadn't even tried to find. Not that he knew their last names or had contact information for them.

Only for Cooper.

He pulled out his phone, then hesitated. He and Serena had just been shot at, twice. The last thing he wanted to do was put Cooper in danger.

But calling his brother shouldn't put in him danger. Turning away from Serena, he crossed the threshold to his room and made the call. He sincerely doubted Cooper would answer, especially after he'd blown his earlier calls off.

But he was surprised to hear his brother's voice in his ear. "Trent? Is that really you?"

"Yeah, it's me." He cleared his throat. "I'm sorry I didn't call you back sooner. I wouldn't blame you if you hung up on me right now."

"Nah, it's okay."

He sensed Cooper was downplaying the hurt he must have felt. "I know I've been a selfish jerk, Coop. But—I'd like to see you. Not right now, I'm in a bit of a mess at the moment, but hopefully soon."

"What kind of a mess?" Cooper latched onto the danger. "Something happen with the band?"

He choked on a laugh. "Yeah, something like that. It's a long story, but Jimmy Woodrow is dead. I'm on my own now and doing okay." He didn't want Coop to worry about him. "Tell me about you? I think you said something about needing a ride."

"I was in trouble, but I'm fine now. I'm, uh, married to a woman named Mia. Oh, and I've met up with Hailey and her fiancé, Rock."

Stunned at this news, he sank onto the edge of the bed. "Hailey? What about the others?"

"Hailey, Darby, and Sawyer are all doing well. We've been worried about you, Trent."

"I've been such an idiot," he admitted. "I can't believe you met up with our foster siblings."

"We don't know where Jayme and Caitlyn are yet," Cooper said. "But Sawyer has been searching for them in his spare time. He's a cop in Chattanooga."

"Ha, that's not a surprise," he said with a wry chuckle. "Sawyer liked being in charge."

"True. But listen, I'm here if you need help." Cooper's tone turned serious. "I know what it's like to be up to my neck in danger."

His words only made Trent feel worse. He should have called Cooper back. No excuse. "I appreciate that, but I'm good. We're hoping to wrap things up soon."

"We?" Cooper asked.

He flushed and was glad Serena wasn't there listening. "A woman named Serena. It's a long story, I won't bore you with the details now, but I wanted—needed to call you. To apologize, and to ask for a second chance."

"Hey, I'm thankful you called, Trent. And you don't have to apologize. We're brothers. Maybe not by blood, but we've been through many ups and down. I've learned a lot about forgiveness, and about God. You'll always be welcome in my life, no matter what."

"Thanks, Coop. I'll talk to you later."

"Bye, bro."

Trent stared at his phone, feeling as if a weight had been lifted off his chest. Just hearing his brother's voice had centered him. Made him realize what was important in life.

Cooper had learned about God? And forgiveness? Through Mia? Probably. Much the way he'd been fortunate to have Serena rushing to his rescue.

Not just protecting him physically, which irked him as

he wanted to be the one to protect her, but rescuing him emotionally.

Destroying his preconceived notions about God and showing him there may be a different way to live.

To actually live, not to simply survive.

If he were honest, he'd admit that was all he was doing the past few months since Jimmy's death. Sure, he'd quit drinking and stayed sober. Performing his music and even creating two new songs.

But his only thought was to make it through one day, and the next. Losing himself in his music was a way to avoid interacting with others.

Until Serena had come into his life.

He slowly stood and moved back to the open doorway between their connecting rooms. Serena had given him the privacy he'd needed to call Cooper. But instead of cleaning up, she was working on her computer. She glanced up, and he saw compassion in her light brown eyes. "Are you okay?"

"Yeah. Better than I have a right to be." He wanted nothing more than to haul her into his arms and kiss her, but he managed to hold himself in check. "Thanks to you, Serena."

She blushed and tucked her blonde hair behind her ear. "It was a team effort, Trent."

"From where I'm standing, it looks like you're doing all the work." He took a deep breath, then said, "If you think being hypnotized will help, I'll do it."

Her jaw dropped. "You will?"

"Yes." He told himself that while he might prefer a dozen root canals, this hypnosis thing was the least he could do. "I have no idea how to set it up, though."

Serena jumped up and ran over to embrace him. He

cradled her close, thinking about how right she felt in his arms.

And how much he'd miss her when she was gone.

SERENA COULDN'T BELIEVE Trent had offered to be hypnotized. She kissed his cheek, then pulled back to look into his green eyes. "Are you absolutely sure about this?"

He grimaced. "It's time I do something to help uncover the truth."

"But—" She stopped, unsure how to put her thoughts into words. The way he'd reacted reliving those memories at the hotel had made her feel guilty. Now he suddenly wanted to undergo hypnosis? It was difficult to wrap her mind around the abrupt change. "Are you doing this just because of the gunfire?"

He arched a brow. "Don't you think that's a good enough reason? You were almost killed, Serena. Because of me. Because someone thinks I know who killed Jimmy." He blew out a frustrated breath. "But I don't. At least, not consciously. If there's a way to unlock the memories I've buried deep in my mind, then we need to do whatever is necessary to uncover them. And soon, before the idiot who shot at us strikes again."

Logically, she agreed with him. The sooner they knew exactly what Trent had witnessed, the better. Yet she found herself reluctant to put him through the agony he'd experienced earlier that day. It seemed as if he'd been suffering some sort of post-traumatic stress syndrome, the way he'd bolted out of there—pale, sweating, and shaking.

There was a chance Trent wouldn't remember much

about behind hypnotized. Which was the whole point. But she'd know.

"Serena? You know it's the next step to solving this thing," Trent said.

"Okay, I'll look into it." She forced a smile. "May take time to arrange anyway. In the meantime, we'll hopefully hear back from Grayson or Coakley."

Trent nodded and released her. "Although if they don't call, we'll keep bothering them until they do."

She smiled. "Yep."

"I'm going to take a quick shower." Trent retreated back into his room. It struck her that he seemed lighter, happier since he'd made that phone call.

The one she'd taken great pains not to listen to.

It made her glad he'd found something positive despite the danger that dogged them. Serena quickly pulled up a search engine on her computer screen. She'd heard about using hypnosis to bring out repressed memories in college and again at the police academy. Only certain psychologists were experts and trained to do this sort of thing, and she wasn't sure how quickly any of them would be able to see Trent.

Was it crazy for her to hope they were booked solid for the next month? Yes, yes it was.

Serena made a few phone calls, leaving yet more messages. When another piece of glass fell from her hair, she decided taking a shower couldn't wait any longer.

Maybe the hot water would help wash away those terrifying moments when she thought Trent had been hit with a bullet.

The shower felt wonderful, especially against her sore muscles. Aches she hadn't noticed until now. Upon examining her face in the mirror, she was shocked that her skin wasn't marred by dozens of cuts. Her hands sported a few minor wounds, but nothing serious.

Considering her previous car crash, the one in which her mother had died, she understood she and Trent were blessed to be relatively unharmed.

Her phone rang, so she hurried to dress and went out to grab it. "Hello?"

"Ms. Jerash? This is Detective Coakley." She wasn't sure if it was her imagination or if he really sounded annoyed.

"Thanks for calling. There have been several attempts to kill Trent Atkins, and I believe it's because the same person who killed Jimmy thinks Trent can identify him."

"Yeah, I heard all about your theory from Detective Grayson." Again, she had the sense he was irritated.

"Things are heating up." She nodded at Trent who'd come in to join her. She quickly switched the phone to speaker mode. "You need to work with Grayson to find the shooter. Then we'll know the truth about what happened to Jimmy."

There was a long pause. "Ms. Jerash, I can understand your frustration, but we're not sitting around twiddling our thumbs. I asked you before, and I'm going to ask you again, to please leave the investigating to us."

She bit her lip to prevent herself from snapping back at him. If she hadn't tracked down Trent and noticed the guy watching him, Trent would already be dead and the police would be no closer to solving either crime.

"With all due respect, Detective, my questioning the band members and finding Trent Atkins has brought the killer out into the open. The least you could do is to take these attempts against him seriously."

"We are." Now his curt tone was obvious. "But we don't need an amateur like you getting in our way."

Amateur? She bristled at his derogatory tone. Trent put a warning hand on her shoulder, and his warmth helped keep her calm. "Really? Then why haven't you reached out to interview Trent? Yeah, don't bother coming up with some sort of excuse. Sounds to me as if you're letting Captain Jerash influence your decisions. Not smart since I'm the one who is going to solve this thing. Thanks anyway, Detective." She stabbed the end call button with more emphasis than it needed. "Jerk."

"Hey, it's okay." Trent gently squeezed her shoulder. "I'm sure they are taking these incidents seriously. But, of course, they don't want to upset their boss either."

"I'm sure my dad made the necessary calls to put them all on alert."

His brow puckered in a frown. "You really think he'd work against you on this?"

"He already has." And Coakley's attitude proved it. She ran her fingers through her damp hair. "I shouldn't have lost my temper. No way is he going to give us any insight into what evidence he may have uncovered."

"You're pretty when you're angry," Trent said with a grin. "I liked how you stood up for yourself, Serena. Besides, do you really think the cops would give a private investigator evidence related to an active case?" He shook his head. "Not likely."

"Probably not." Still, her little temper tantrum hadn't helped. And who did she think she was, telling Coakley she was going to solve the case? She knew from her pastor, who loved quoting from the Proverbs, that *pride goes before destruction, a haughty spirit before a fall.*

"Hey, we're going to be okay." Trent smiled encouragingly. "You're the one who convinced me that God was watching over us."

"He is." She couldn't help returning his smile. "I have to say, you seem much better since your phone call. Not that I listened to your private conversation," she hastily added. "I'm just happy for you."

"Thanks. It was a good conversation." His smile faded. "Unlike the one we just had with Detective Coakley."

"No kidding." She sighed. "Honestly, I'm not sure what our next step should be. We don't have a way to track down the black Jeep. And while I made some calls, I doubt we'll hear back from the psychologists who do hypnosis until business hours tomorrow."

"We need a vehicle," she said more to herself than to Trent. She reached for her phone. "Guess it's time to make another call."

"To your dad?" Trent's voice rose in surprise.

"No." As if her father would even take her call right now. "To Allan, Jimmy's father. He'll need to approve the expense of a rental car."

"Hold on." Trent lifted a hand. "Why does he have to approve it? Why don't we just find a rental agency ourselves?"

"We could, but the daily expense allowance . . ." Suddenly she shook her head. "You know what? It doesn't matter. You're right. I'll pay for the rental car myself. Maybe my insurance company will cover the expense."

"I have money too," Trent said with a frown. "This isn't all on you, Serena. In fact, you're only in danger because you've been with me."

"Hey, I'm glad to have been with you through this."

"I'll give you cash for the rental," he repeated stubbornly. "Let's go."

"Thanks." She relented because, really, she understood where he was coming from. His truck had been damaged too, but he was likely feeling guilty over the total wreckage that was her SUV. Not that any of this was his fault.

It was hers for poking at the hornet's nest.

They walked out of the motel room, into the humid night. Dark clouds were rolling in, bringing the threat of rain. Nashville wasn't close to the Smoky Mountains; although they could be seen in the distance, their weather was impacted by them.

She hoped her car had been towed or the interior would be completely waterlogged in a matter of minutes.

They were picked up by another rideshare, and she gave directions to the closest rental agency. She and Trent barely made it into the building before the sky opened and rain fell in sheets.

"It's not going to be much fun driving in this mess," she muttered as Trent pressed cash into her hand.

"I'd offer to get the car, but I don't have a credit card." He grimaced.

"Hey, no worries." She felt bad for complaining. "I've got this."

They went to the counter. The helpful clerk provided them the forms to fill out. Thankfully, adding Trent as a driver didn't cost anything more, so they both handed their driver's licenses to the clerk to make copies.

Ten minutes later, they were running through the rain to their burgundy Honda Accord. Trent had taken the keys but opened her door for her, before running around to the driver's side.

"Back to the motel?" she asked when they were back on the road.

"I think we should swing by to make sure your SUV

was towed away." Trent glanced at her. "I'm concerned that the Jeep could have doubled back at some point to look for it."

"I guess we should check it out. If it's not towed, I can call someone to take care of it." She scowled. "I'm not going to be happy to find out the police blew off the opportunity to get any potential evidence."

"Understandable." Trent peered through the relenting rain, driving with extreme caution.

She was impressed he was able to find the spot where they'd abandoned the SUV. It was still there, and she ground her teeth together to keep from screaming in frustration.

"Idiots," Trent said. He drove past the SUV without stopping.

She reached for her phone, but he put a hand on her arm. "Hold off a minute. Is that a black Jeep parked over there?"

Her pulse spiked, and she tried to see through the downpour. There was a dark boxy vehicle parked there, but was it a black Jeep? The same black Jeep that had followed them? It was impossible to say for sure.

"Go around the block." She told herself that the people in the Jeep would have no way of knowing they had a burgundy rental car.

Still, she couldn't relax until the black Jeep was well out of sight.

"Okay, now pull over."

Trent did but looked confused. "Why?"

"Because we need to go back and sneak up on foot and get the license plate number for that Jeep." She stared at him through the darkness. "If it's the same one that someone used to shoot at us, then we need to find out who it's registered to."

He shut down the car. "It seems unlikely they'd be sitting there, waiting for us to return. What if the police showed up?"

"The cops wouldn't tow the car themselves, and once a tow truck arrived, they'd be gone." She couldn't help feeling a surge of anticipation.

This could be the lead they needed to blow the case wide open.

CHAPTER TWELVE

Trent stared at Serena through the darkness. "Okay, but I'm the one going to check it out. Not you."

She opened her mouth to protest, but he held up a hand. "Serena, I lived on the streets for years. I know how to get around without being noticed. Besides, it's still raining, and better for me to get drenched than you."

"I know how to skulk around," she protested.

"Skulk?" Despite the seriousness of the situation, he couldn't help but grin. "That's a good one. I know you're more than capable, but I need to be the one to do this." His smile faded. "Please."

She held his gaze for a long moment, then reluctantly nodded. "Okay. But if you're not back in ten minutes, I'm coming after you."

"Give me fifteen minutes and text me before you rush to the rescue. These things take time."

"Patience, right. I got it." She pulled out her phone. "Be safe, Trent. I don't want anything bad to happen to you."

Better him than her, but he wisely kept that thought to himself. "I know."

He wished he had a baseball cap to help keep the rain out of his eyes. His cowboy hat was long gone, but it would have been too big and too noticeable. He slid from the vehicle, shutting the door as quietly as possible.

The rain pelted down on him with less force than what they'd experienced at the rental agency. He ignored the discomfort, remembering those days he, Sawyer, and Cooper had lived in the woods as they'd slowly made their way through the Smoky Mountains.

This was nothing compared to sleeping outside in the rain, with branches interwoven above them in an effort to divert the rain and the occasional snowfall.

He shook off the thoughts; this wasn't the time to go traipsing down memory lane. He wasn't that scared thirteen-year-old kid anymore, and this was nothing more than an information-gathering mission.

Moving silently, he made his way through the neighborhood toward Rover Road, estimating where the Jeep was sitting. He thought it odd that the shooter had come back to sit on the SUV. Were they hoping he and Serena would show up?

They had, so their instincts were on target.

He knelt beneath a large oak tree, swiping the water from his eyes. He could see the Jeep about thirty yards from where he was hiding.

Not a lot of cover, he silently acknowledged. Thankfully, the rain would help.

He darted toward the corner of a house. The windows were dark as if no one was home, so he paused there, then found his next location. He moved to another tree that was located directly behind the parked Jeep.

From there, Trent could tell the windows were fogged

up. He frowned. If the driver and shooter were inside watching for them, they wouldn't be able to see much.

Unless the pair weren't in the Jeep at all.

A chill snaked down his spine, and he quickly pulled out his phone, shielding the screen so the light wouldn't betray him. He sent Serena a quick text. *Jeep may be empty, stay alert in case they're on the move.*

He didn't realize he was holding his breath until his chest tightened painfully. A moment later, she returned his message. *Will do. All quiet so far.*

Good.

He tucked the phone back into his pocket. The Jeep was only about ten yards ahead of him. He could see the license plate but not the actual information. The rain clouded his vision, and he thought there was something covering the plate as well. Determined to get what they needed, he stayed low and rushed forward until he was right behind the Jeep.

Up close he could see the license plate more clearly. He was memorizing the numbers and letters when a portion of the number 8 caught his eye. Lifting his hand, he peeled away black electrical tape that had changed the number 3 to an 8.

He checked the rest of the plate, finding more black tape as the number 1 was changed to the letter L. No question in his mind, this was the same Jeep the shooter had used. No law-abiding citizen would change the actual license plate number with black tape.

After entering the real plate information in his phone, he debated heading back to Serena or checking the interior of the Jeep. In the end, worry for Serena won out, and he retraced his steps to get back to her.

Once he could no longer see the Jeep, he broke into a run. When he flung open the driver's side door, a wave of relief hit hard when he found her unharmed.

"Did you get it?" she asked, raking her gaze over him. "We should have thought to grab a towel, you're soaked to the skin."

"I'll be fine, and yes, I got it." He recited the information, then added, "They used black electrical tape to alter the plate. I don't think it would be obvious from a distance, but up close it was easy to spot. The rain may have helped loosen the adhesive too."

Serena nodded slowly. "We need to call this into Grayson. He's been more approachable than Coakley."

She was right, although he didn't appreciate the way the police had treated her, as if being a PI made her a pain rather than an asset they should be working with. "The windows are all fogged up. Why would someone sit inside to watch for us if they can't see out the windows?"

"Yeah, I have to admit that bothers me too." She frowned. "Did you try to get a look inside? Maybe around the edges of the window where it might be less foggy?"

"No, but now that I know you're safe, I'll head back out." Again, she tried to argue, but he shook his head. "I'm already soaked, no reason for both of us to be that way."

"Let's drive closer then," she said stubbornly. "It's likely they're not inside anyway. Or that they'll notice us if they are."

He hesitated, then nodded. "Fine." He turned the car on but kept the headlights off. He slowly drove two blocks down before taking a right and another right so that he would come up behind the Jeep while staying far enough back so as to avoid attracting attention.

"Be careful," Serena said.

"Always." Once again, he slid out of the driver's seat, leaving a pool of water behind. He grimaced and hoped the interior would dry enough so that they wouldn't have to pay the rental company for damaging the vehicle.

The Jeep hadn't moved, and the windows were still fogged up to the point he couldn't imagine anyone was sitting inside. Still, he decided to stay low as he headed over, just in case this was nothing more than an elaborate trap.

He crouched behind the rear of the car, taking a moment to feel the side where the tailpipe was located. That the car was cool to the touch made him think it may have been sitting there for a while.

An hour? He glanced around at the houses nearby. Doubtful that the occupants lived nearby. More likely the vehicle had been abandoned there the same way Serena had abandoned the damaged SUV.

Curious location, though, to ditch the Jeep near Serena's SUV. A message? He couldn't figure out what was going on in the shooter's mind.

Swallowing hard, he eased up along the passenger side of the car. Lifting his head, he tried to see through the foggy window, staring through the edge where the fog wasn't as heavy.

Nothing.

He edged forward a few more inches, then tried again. It was no use. The windows were pretty much impossible to see through. And the way no one flung open the door to confront him convinced him the Jeep was empty.

Reaching up, he tested the door handle. It wasn't locked, so he carefully opened the door, half expecting to see the barrel of a gun pointing out at him.

Instead, he saw the pale white skin of a hand draped over the edge of the seat. Another warning tingle raised the hairs on the back of his neck. No way did he believe the passenger had simply fallen asleep.

He opened the door wider and rose up to get a better look. When he saw the blood staining the woman's chest, he recoiled, stumbling backward with such haste he plowed into the car door.

There was no doubt in his mind she was dead. But he forced himself to inch forward to check for a pulse.

Nothing. Her skin was so cold, he knew she must have been dead for a while now. He looked but didn't find a gun.

It wasn't difficult to recognize her as the woman who'd been dancing with the man at Whistlers the night he'd nearly been shot.

But where was that same guy now? And why had he shot his dance partner in cold blood? Leaving her there for them to find?

He fought the urge to be sick, then realized he didn't want his fingerprints anywhere on this crime scene. Using his wet shirt, he wiped off the edge of the door, the handle, then used his clothing-covered hand to slam the door shut.

Then Trent turned and ran like the devil himself was on his tail until he was back in the burgundy sedan. Without saying a word to Serena, he turned on the car, put it in gear, and drove away, gripping the steering wheel with shaky hands.

There was no doubt in his mind the dead woman was a message of some sort.

One that made him seriously consider leaving Nashville and the entire state of Tennessee for good.

SERENA PUT a hand on Trent's arm. He looked awful, and she had no idea why he was driving away from the Jeep with such haste. "What happened? You look like you've seen a ghost."

"I saw something far worse." The words were barely a whisper.

Her stomach churned. "What do you mean? The Jeep wasn't empty?"

"No." He didn't so much as glance at her. "The woman that guy had been dancing with at Whistlers was sitting in the passenger seat with a hole in her chest."

"Wait, what?" Serena heard her voice rising in panic and tried to wrestle it back under control. "Dead? You're saying that woman was murdered?"

"Oh yeah. I don't think she shot herself in the chest, do you? I didn't see a gun anywhere nearby." There was a hard edge to his tone.

She could barely grasp the implication of what they'd found. And now she really needed to call Detective Grayson. "I don't understand. Why would that guy kill her and leave her in the Jeep parked so close to the damaged SUV?"

Trent dragged in a deep breath and finally looked over at her. "When you run the plate number, I'm sure we're going to find that the Jeep is registered in her name. I also believe she was probably the driver, while the guy who shot at me at Whistlers was the shooter that blew out the windows of your SUV in an attempt to kill us both. Attempts that failed."

His theory made sense. She reached for her phone. "I need to call Grayson. Not only has there been another murder, but there's a good chance the shooter left his prints somewhere inside that Jeep."

"Hold on a minute." Trent reached out to put a hand over her phone. "I don't know that we want to be the ones to alert Grayson to this most recent crime. Maybe the reason the shooter left the woman there was to throw suspicion on us." He paused, then added, "On me."

On Trent? Realization dawned, and she realized he could be right. "But you don't have a motive to kill her."

"We've already figured out this is all connected to Jimmy's death, which means I'm neck deep in motive." He let out a harsh laugh. "Someone could be trying to make it look as if I'm the one who killed Jimmy. And that I'm setting someone else up to take the fall."

She gaped at him, then realized he was feeling a bit paranoid. "No way, Trent. I'm sorry, but that doesn't make any sense. I've been with you since that first night when the guy tried to stab you with a knife, and then again when you narrowly escaped gunfire, not just once but several times. Only a complete idiot would believe you set this all up to divert suspicion off you as a suspect in Jimmy's murder."

"Keep in mind, you're the only one who has been with me for most of these attempts." Trent continued driving toward their motel. She couldn't seem to make herself pick up the phone to call Grayson about the dead woman. "Other than the gunshot inside Whistlers, witnesses are few and far between."

"Someone saw something on the freeway earlier today," she protested. Although he was right that she was the only one who had seen the knife guy and the gunshot that took out his driver's side window. "There has to be something more going on."

"Yeah, well, I think it's time for me to get out of town for a while." Trent's face looked as if it were carved out of stone.

Panic gripped her around the throat. "You can't leave, Trent. What if the killer follows you?"

"He won't. I'll make sure of it." Trent glanced at her. "You have to leave this alone, Serena. Tell Jimmy's dad to turn the investigation over to the police. Now that there's been another murder, I'm sure they'll take Jimmy's death more seriously."

The police probably would be all over the potential connection between this recent murder and Jimmy's death, but she wasn't giving up. Not now. But the thought of Trent leaving filled her with a sense of dread. "Please don't leave yet," she begged.

There was a long silence before he responded. "Serena, it's safer for you if I leave the city. I can't bear the thought of something happening to you."

"I feel the same way about you, and if you're gone, I'll never know if you simply found a way to disappear or if Jimmy's killer found and silenced you too." She clutched his arm as if holding on to him would prevent him from leaving. "Please, Trent, just give me a little time. I feel like we're getting close to the truth."

"Funny, I feel like we're farther from the truth than ever before," he said grimly.

Maybe it was just her innate stubbornness, but she refused to accept defeat. "I know the Jeep is probably a dead end, but we should be able to learn the identity of the female victim." If she had to call in every favor she had to get the woman's ID from the locals, she would.

Even if that meant calling her father.

"Hang in there with me for just a little while longer," she urged when he didn't respond.

Trent pulled up in front of the motel and shut down the

engine. For a long moment no one spoke. The rain continued to fall but with less intensity. It didn't take long for the windows to fog up, much like the Jeep's had done.

"Please, Trent." She wasn't above begging. "Don't leave me yet."

He drew in a choppy breath and slowly nodded. "Okay. I'll wait. But not for much longer."

At this point, she'd take what she could get. They climbed out of the car and headed inside their connecting rooms. She expected Trent to close his side, but he didn't. Instead, he muttered something about changing into dry clothes before disappearing into the bathroom.

She took out her phone and considered how she might be able to let Detective Grayson know about the dead woman in the Jeep.

Or could she simply call and ask where her SUV was towed? Without giving a hint to the fact that she knew it hadn't been taken anywhere yet? She didn't like being dishonest, but she wasn't about to do something that would send Trent running out of state either.

She set the phone aside and dropped her chin to her chest. Closing her eyes, she prayed for God to guide her through this dilemma. To show her the way to save Trent without forcing him to give up the life he'd made for himself here in Nashville.

His music.

Deep down, she felt certain that Trent's talent would be used for something good. Maybe even Christian music, although he hadn't seemed interested in that possibility. Yet the two songs he'd composed offered a thread of hope to the listener, filling her with joy in a way that convinced her God had plans for Trent.

Trent just needed to open himself up to receiving those plans. And they didn't include running away.

As far as Jimmy's case, they were clearly onto something. So much had happened in the past forty-eight hours that she felt certain things would come to a head soon. She thought about the dead woman in the car. About how Anna and Heidi had been on a social media post together, and about the two wine glasses in Heidi's house.

She picked up her phone and called Grayson. It was late, so she doubted she'd reach him, but to her surprise, he answered. "Detective, this is Serena Jerash. I'm sorry to bother you, but can you tell me where my SUV has been taken? I need to make arrangements with my insurance company to get it repaired."

"Uh, I'm not sure." She could hear papers rustling on his desk. "Actually, I don't think it's been picked up yet. The storm caused a multi-vehicle accident on the interstate, so routine tows were put on hold."

"I see." She sighed loudly. "Okay, can you call me when you do know where it's been taken?"

"Sure. I'll send the tow truck there now."

"Okay, but don't forget to look for the bullet." It occurred to her that her SUV could be towed away without anyone bothering to notice the Jeep parked nearby that just happened to have a dead body inside.

"Right, right. I'll send an officer too."

"And there haven't been any other reports about the Jeep that opened fire on us?" she pressed.

"I'm not sure, there's a stack of messages here that I haven't gotten to. But don't worry, we'll track it down."

She didn't share his confidence. Even with the Jeep in question being near her SUV, she doubted they'd realize it was one and the same. Still, she forced a smile. "Thanks."

When that call was finished, she scrolled through her phone to find the hospital closest to where Heidi Lawrence lived. Unfortunately, when she called the operator and asked to speak with Lynn, aka Heidi, she was informed the woman wasn't a patient.

She slowly lowered the phone. Wasn't a patient because she was discharged home? Or because she'd died?

No, Heidi hadn't been that bad. They'd gotten to her in time. Then it occurred to her that someone as wealthy as Heidi might request not to be listed as a patient in the directory. Especially considering she'd come in as an overdose.

When she'd been in the hospital after the car crash that had taken her mother's life, Serena had learned about the federal privacy laws governing hospitals. Each person had a choice whether or not to be listed on the main directory as a patient. *Something I should have thought of earlier*, she thought with a sigh.

Although being shot at had a way of clouding your judgment.

She set her phone aside, deciding that her brain was too fried to keep working. Sundays were supposed to be a day of rest.

Today had been anything but.

"Are you hungry?" Trent asked from the connecting doorway.

She wasn't really, but if she didn't eat now, she'd probably be famished later. "I could eat. What did you have in mind?"

He lifted a brochure. "How about a pizza? They deliver."

"Perfect." She realized she was still sitting in her damp clothes. "I'll eat anything but anchovies. Order what you'd like. I still need to shower and change."

"Will do."

As she washed up and changed, her thoughts returned to the dead woman in the Jeep. She could easily picture her dancing with the guy at Whistlers moments before he pulled the gun from beneath his shirt and fired.

A co-conspirator who was now dead. Because she'd failed in her mission? And maybe as a way to frame Trent, making it look as if he'd done the deed?

Or because the killer was simply cutting off all loose ends?

The latter seemed the most likely, yet that wasn't at all reassuring. Because even if she didn't believe Trent was being set up as having killed the woman and Jimmy, he was right about one thing.

He was a loose end. And so was she.

She left the bathroom, surprised to note the enticing scent of tomato sauce, pepperoni, and garlic bread. On cue, her stomach began to growl, making her smile wryly. Guess she was hungry after all. She went over to peer through the connecting door. "Something smells amazing."

"It just arrived. Sit down," Trent gestured to the chair he'd pulled from her room. She squeezed through the small space and sat down, her knees bumping into his.

"Sorry." For no reason whatsoever, she was suddenly self-conscious. After all they'd been through, sharing a pizza in a motel room shouldn't bring on a case of the nerves.

Yet somehow she was seeing Trent as a man, a partner. Not just a singer with amazing talent.

But someone she wanted to be with. More than anyone else.

Yeah, she really needed to get over this weirdness. Maybe her brain was rattled more than she'd realized.

"Uh, I'd like to pray. If, er, that's okay with you." Trent's tone was hesitant as if he regretted saying the words as they left his mouth.

A warmth washed over her. "I'd love that." She reached over and gripped his hand. "And if you get stuck, I'll help."

"Good to know." He cleared his throat. "God, we thank You for continuing to keep us safe, especially as we seem to be facing danger at every turn. You, uh, we need Your guidance to find those responsible for this. Please help us do that. Thank You."

"Amen," she said, thinking she'd never heard a more beautiful and heartfelt prayer in her life.

"Right. Amen." He flushed and shrugged as he released her hand to reach for a slice of pizza. "Hey, I can only get better, right?"

"Trent, there's no reason to be embarrassed. God sees what's in your heart. And what's there is beautiful, sweet, and kind. That's what's important."

"You're giving me far more credit than I deserve." A tiny frown puckered his brow. "I'm not even sure God is listening to me."

"He is." She spoke with absolute certainty. As she reached for a slice of pizza, she asked, "Do you mind if I ask what made you change your mind? About praying?"

After a moment, he admitted, "I spoke to Cooper."

Her eyes widened. "Your foster brother?"

"Yeah. He's doing well and is married to a woman named Mia. He mentioned God had taught him about forgiveness." He smiled wryly. "To hear Cooper even mention religion and that he believed in God was a shock. And made me realize that I might be wrong to turn my back on religion. That maybe God is real. Maybe He is watching over us."

Yes! Her heart swelled with hope as she beamed at him.

"Oh, Trent, I'm thrilled to hear you say that. Think back to everything you've endured. Your life before the Preacher, during those terrible years, and afterward. You're so much stronger now, and I know with God's help you can accomplish anything you want."

His green gaze met hers. "You're giving me way more credit than I deserve."

"No, I'm really not. You deserve that and more."

"Thanks to you, Serena." He flushed and looked away, then took another bite of his pizza. "If I'm going to stick around for at least another day or two, what's our next move?"

"We need to rest and recharge." She was troubled by the way he'd indicated he might still leave. She was about to explain how she'd called Grayson to ask about her SUV when her phone rang.

She stood and eased between the chair and the bed to get back to her room. When she saw Grayson's number on the screen, she thought of the dead woman in the Jeep and answered warily. "Hello?"

"Ms. Jerash? This is Detective Grayson. We found a bullet in your SUV."

She wasn't expecting that. Through the connecting doorway, Trent motioned her over. She quickly put the call on speaker. "I'm glad you found a bullet in the SUV, at least now you know we were telling you the truth about the Jeep."

"Oh yeah, the Jeep." There was a pause before he asked, "Do you know Gabrielle Mason?"

Her gaze locked with Trent's. In that moment, she knew the dead woman Trent had found was Gabrielle Mason. Unfortunately, the name meant nothing to her. She lifted a brow, but Trent shook his head to indicate the name wasn't familiar to him either.

They finally had a name to match with the woman who'd danced with the shooter. Too bad the name was nothing more than another dead end.

CHAPTER THIRTEEN

Gabrielle Mason.

Trent rolled the name around in his mind but couldn't come up with any idea of who she might be. To be honest, he hadn't paid that much attention to the woman while she'd been dancing at Whistlers. Seeing her now, though, didn't bring any sort of recognition either.

"Thanks, Detective. Let me know if you need anything."

Trent realized he'd missed the bulk of their conversation. When she lowered the phone, he said, "Did he have any ideas about what happened?"

"None that he'd share with me." Serena sighed and rubbed her temple. "I'm surprised he shared the victim's name with us. Usually, they hold off until next of kin has been notified. Prevents anyone from leaking information to the press."

"I can understand that." He glanced at her, thinking she sounded just like a cop. That she should be a cop. From the very beginning, her instincts had been right on target when it came to solving Jimmy's murder.

And now there'd been another murder. Thinking it through, he felt certain Heidi's overdose may not have been an accident either.

"Time to learn more about Gabrielle." Serena turned and went back into her room. He followed, knowing she was going to be searching social media sites again.

He didn't quite understand the allure of putting your picture out on a website for people to look at and comment on. Then again, he'd spent the bulk of his life trying to avoid being seen. Until he'd joined Jimmy's band. Then his picture had been splattered all over the internet. Mostly along with the other members of the band.

Serena nimbly typed in Gabrielle's name and began to search. It wasn't difficult to find her, and looking at her smiling face made him feel bad to know that she was now dead.

Murdered, just like Jimmy. To protect the shooter? It was the only explanation he could come up with.

"She's definitely the one dancing with the shooter at Whistlers," Trent said somberly. The carefree smile made him feel slightly sick to his stomach. Seeing her dead body would stay with him for a long time. "I wonder if she was innocent in all this."

Serena glanced up at him over her shoulder. "If she was driving the Jeep while her boyfriend shot at us, she was an accessory to attempted murder, which is hardly innocent."

He nodded. Serena was right. Still, he couldn't help but think Gabrielle had been sucked into this mess by some guy, only to get in way over her head.

In a sense, wasn't that what had happened to him? He'd gotten sucked into Jimmy Woodrow's band, seeking fame and fortune, only to lose himself along the journey. The money had been nice, more than he'd seen in his entire lifetime, but along with the steady stream of cash had been the alcohol, drugs, and women.

Looking back, he could honestly say the money hadn't been worth it.

Or maybe the real problem was that he personally couldn't handle it. No one had forced him to drink. To party until all hours. No, that had been his decision.

And a lousy one at that.

Would he have found the strength to walk away if Jimmy hadn't been murdered? He was afraid the answer was a resounding *no*.

"What do you think? Does this guy look anything like the shooter?"

Serena's question broke into his thoughts. He looked at the face on the screen and shook his head. "No, this guy looks younger. Judging from the cheekbones, I'd say he's Gabrielle's brother."

"Good eye," she said in admiration. "She hadn't tagged him in this post, so I have no clue what his name is." She continued delving deeper into the social media site, finding a list of friends. Did the police delve into suspects' social media sites? Probably, which was another reason he'd always avoided that kind of stuff.

He remembered hearing from Brett that they'd taken down the Jimmy Woodrow Band's website a few weeks after he'd died. Brett had let them know the website had gotten more hits after Jimmy's death than they'd ever gotten before. Typical, he supposed that someone would become more famous after they died.

It made him wonder who would take down these photos for Gabrielle now that she was gone.

"Weird, I can't find this guy listed as one of her friends." Serena scowled as she sat back in the chair.

"Apparently, he's not on social media." Trent didn't see that as weird.

"I know you're not on any of these platforms," she said with a wry smile. "But trust me when I tell you that zillions of people are. Far more are on social media sites than not."

"I guess." For a moment, he wondered if any of his foster siblings were on these types of sites. Somehow, he didn't think so. Cooper hadn't been, he knew that much. Like Trent, Coop hadn't owned a computer.

The urge to return to Gatlinburg was strong. He wanted to see Cooper again. Along with Sawyer, Hailey, and Darby. They needed to find Jayme and Caitlyn too.

"It doesn't look like we're going to find the shooter on her social media sites," Serena said with a grimace. "I guess he's too smart for that."

"Maybe he's disappeared completely. Decided killing us wasn't worth getting caught."

"I highly doubt a man who's capable of shooting his accomplice is going to back off his mission to kill you." Her gaze bored into his. "Just the opposite. By killing Gabrielle, this guy has gone all in. He's more dangerous now than ever. Because we won't know what he's driving or where we'll stumble across him."

She was right. He knew it, even if he didn't want to accept it. "All the more reason I should leave town."

"You promised you'd stay," she reminded him.

"For a couple of days, but not necessarily forever." His mind was a jumble of thoughts, and he suddenly felt exhausted. "I won't leave without telling you, okay?"

Serena nodded, but her gaze was full of concern. "I'm worried that even if you leave, this guy will track you down. He hasn't hesitated to kill and seems to have unlimited resources."

"Unlimited resources remind me of Heidi Lawrence," he said. "Yet it makes no sense that she'd hire someone to kill me."

"Don't forget Brett Caine," she said. "I'm wondering if he isn't the one behind all this."

"No way does he have as much money as Heidi," he protested.

"You don't know that," Serena countered. She sat up and turned back to the computer. "In fact, maybe there's more to Jimmy's murder than we realize. Maybe Brett was skimming money from your band."

He stared at her in shock. "I—hadn't thought of that."

"From the way he acted at lunch, Brett enjoys the finer things in life." She typed *Brett Caine manager* into the computer's search engine and hit enter. "And he'd gotten very upset to hear the meeting wasn't about his representing you as a musician but a request for information related to Jimmy's death."

"But the end result of killing Jimmy is that a big source of revenue had been shut down, forever."

"Is it really, though? Doesn't royalty money keep coming in over time?"

"I haven't seen any royalty money coming in."

"That's exactly my point. Maybe Brett is keeping the royalties rather than sharing them with the rest of you. Who else had access to the band's finances?"

He shook his head. "I have no clue."

"Brett Caine probably controlled everything." She frowned at the screen. "I'm not finding much about him. You'd think he'd want to advertise his band manager services."

"I get the sense a lot of that happens through word of mouth." He couldn't help replaying that brief encounter at

Hathaways. It was possible that Brett's wanting to be his manager again was a ploy to prevent Trent from signing up with another manager. Maybe one who would question where the previous royalties were.

He'd been a complete fool to let Jimmy and Brett handle the financial side of things. Especially once he'd realized Jimmy was doing more and more drugs. Brett could have easily taken money without Jimmy realizing it.

And if Jimmy had confronted him, it was also possible that Brett had gotten enraged, similar to how he'd acted at Hathaways. Brett could have hit Jimmy harder than he'd intended and, once he realized Jimmy was dead, left the suite before Trent had come to.

He tried to push through the fog surrounding his memories of that night. He vaguely remembered an argument. But he had never considered the argument to be about money. He'd figured the women had gotten upset and argued about Jimmy's lack of fidelity.

Serena stood and yawned. "I'm having trouble keeping my eyes open. Let's get some sleep. We can keep searching for information on Brett tomorrow."

"Sure." He hated to broach the subject, but he forced himself to ask, "Do you think we should call those psychologists back about getting hypnotized?"

Serena smiled and put a hand on his arm. "Yes, if no one responds to my messages, I'll make more calls. It means a lot to me that you're willing to do this."

"The sooner we find the person responsible, the sooner we can go back to our lives, right?" His attempt to sound casual failed. "Okay, to be honest, if I'm going to do this, I'd rather get it over with."

"I'll do my best to make that happen." Serena surprised him by going up on her tiptoes to kiss his cheek. "You're an amazing man, Trent Atkins. And I'm blessed to have been able to get to know you."

It was all he could do to stop himself from pulling her into his arms and kissing her the way he so desperately wanted. But he wasn't that guy any longer. He couldn't allow himself to start something with Serena that he wouldn't be able to finish.

She deserved better than a recovering alcoholic average musician.

"Are you okay?" She was gazing up at him with wide clear eyes. Was it his imagination or was she thinking of kissing him again?

Wishful thinking on his part. He cleared his throat and forced a smile. "I'm good. And you're right, it's been a long day. We need to sleep."

She nodded but didn't move. It took him a minute to realize he was in her room. Feeling like an idiot, he turned and headed through the connecting door.

"Trent?"

He glanced back at her. "Yeah?"

"I have faith that God will lead us to the person responsible for this."

"I know you do." He turned and closed the door partway to give Serena privacy.

He washed up and stretched out on the bed. During those moments when the guy in the back of the Jeep had shot at them, he'd prayed that God would protect them. Easy to do when you were staring down the barrel of a gun.

But now? He stared up at the dingy ceiling. He tried to pray for God to guide them to finding Jimmy's killer, but he felt like a fraud.

Was there really a God? One who wouldn't care about all the terrible things he'd done?

He closed his eyes and batted back a surge of panic. Even if God existed, why on earth would He answer his prayers? Maybe he hadn't killed anyone, but he certainly had broken several laws.

And been a terrible drunk.

Then he thought of Cooper, and the tension eased from his body. Cooper hadn't become an alcoholic the way he had, but Coop had been with him as they'd lived on the streets. Pretending they were like Robin Hood, stealing from the rich to give to the poor.

Only the poor was the two of them. Not all the poor people they'd encountered.

At some point, he fell asleep because he abruptly awoke and sat straight up in bed, his heart pounding in his chest from a really strange dream. He'd been sitting on the mountainside with Cooper, and slips of paper were falling from the air like giant snowflakes. He'd reached out to grasp one. And another. And another.

The message on each slip of paper was the same. In block letters, every single note read:

God is real. God is real. God is real!

AFTER A RESTFUL SLUMBER, Serena emerged from the bathroom and followed the enticing aroma of coffee. She was normally up before eight o'clock in the morning, but the past few days had been long on action and short on sleep.

She knocked on the connecting door. "Are you decent?"

"Yep. Want coffee?"

"Yep." She smiled as she entered his room. He handed her a steaming cup of coffee, then poured another for himself. She eyed him curiously; he seemed different today. Of course, maybe it was just the ability to get a decent night of rest.

"I was thinking I should call Jed and Dave to set up a meeting." He glanced at her. "They should know there's a possibility Brett can't be trusted."

"Makes sense. Although we don't have proof."

"I know. But at the very least they should be paying close attention to the money they're earning." Trent grimaced. "Not ignoring it like when we were with Jimmy."

"You're right, they need to do that much." She sipped her coffee. "I checked my phone, no responses yet to the hypnosis request. But it's probably too early. I don't think it will help to make follow-up calls until later this afternoon."

"Understood." He didn't seem nearly as concerned about the thought of undergoing hypnosis. "Unfortunately, Jed and Dave won't be up early either. But I'm thinking we can find where the Bootleggers last played and see if we can track them down that way."

Thirty minutes later, they had their destination. The Bootleggers had played at a nightclub near the Stardust hotel. "I'm sure that's where they stayed," Trent said. "No way would they have driven very far after a performance."

"It's strange that they'd be playing on a Sunday night," she mused.

"Not necessarily." Trent shrugged. "It's not unheard of to have nightclubs have bands playing on Sunday nights, especially in Nashville. They have a lot of live music playing downtown. What is interesting to me is that they weren't offered a Friday or Saturday night spot. The night-club is very popular, and that they were playing on Sunday makes me think the band isn't doing as well as they'd claimed. Certainly not at the level of Jimmy's band."

Since her experience with the music business was limited, she couldn't argue. "Well, all the more reason to warn them about Brett Caine."

"Yeah." Trent narrowed his gaze. "I plan to recommend they find a different manager."

Serena nodded, although she wasn't convinced the guys would take Trent's word for it. "Let's grab something to eat before heading over to the Stardust. Maybe we'll miss the worst of the downtown traffic."

They packed their things in the rental car and hit the road. She found it amazing that Trent's guitar hadn't suffered any damage from the gunfire they'd experienced. Her phone rang, an unknown number flashing on the screen. One of the psychologists maybe? "Hello?"

"Ms. Jerash? This is Detective Coakley."

"Yes, Detective. What can I do for you?"

"Are you still with Trent Atkins?"

Warning bells jangled in the back of her mind. "Why are you asking?"

"Answer the question, is he still with you?"

She didn't have a good feeling about this. "I know how to get in touch with him if need be. Why?"

There was a long silence. "I need him to come in for questioning."

She could feel Trent's questioning gaze. "Didn't you already question Trent about Jimmy's murder?"

"I need to talk to him again." From the tone of his voice, she knew Coakley was losing his patience.

"Does that mean new evidence has come to light?" She tried to smile reassuringly at Trent, but his expression remained somber.

"Can you please ask Atkins to call me?" Coakley asked.

"I need to understand if Trent is a suspect. Because if

that's the case, he has a right to have a lawyer present when he talks to you."

She could practically hear Coakley's teeth gnashing together. "Are you pretending to be a lawyer now rather than a cop?"

His sarcasm stung, but she did her best to ignore it. "I'm not his lawyer, but you can rest assured I'll make sure he finds one." She disconnected from the call and let out a sigh. "This isn't good, Trent."

"Yeah, I kinda gathered that."

"Listen, let's head to the Stardust hotel now. You're not going to be able to avoid going in to talk to Coakley for long. Maybe Jed or Dave can shed some light on what's happening."

"Not likely," he muttered. "Why do I have the feeling I'm being set up?"

"I share that feeling." She thought back to everything that had transpired since Friday night. Then it occurred to her. "Heidi Lawrence."

"What about her?"

"Maybe she decided to turn against you." Serena's mind raced. "Heidi could have gone to the police with some story that implicates you in Jimmy's death."

"Why would she do that? Unless she's somehow involved." Trent grimaced. "I guess I answered my own question."

"Either that or she's protecting someone. If Heidi is the one who went to the police. Or it could have been Brett too."

"Wouldn't Brett be opening himself up to further scrutiny by doing that?" Trent asked. "I mean, if he did steal money from Jimmy and the band, he wouldn't want that information to come out."

"True, but criminals often think they're smarter than the police." There were too many possibilities, and none of them good. "I don't like this, Trent."

"Hey, if they really are going to arrest me, that's my problem, not yours." His smile didn't reach his eyes. "And maybe I'll be safer in jail."

"Don't count on it." She took a deep breath in an attempt to calm her racing heart. She stared down at her phone, then dialed her father's work number.

"Serena? What's going on? Are you consorting with a criminal?"

His response wasn't unexpected. "Dad, I know you don't believe in me and my ability to investigate this case. But I'm telling you, Trent and I have been under attack since Friday night. The man who shot at us from the back of a black Jeep almost killed us."

"That's exactly why you need to bring him in!" Her father thundered loud enough to make her wince. "Why would you risk your life for some low-life musician?"

On one level, she was surprised her father cared if she risked her life. "You're a good cop, Dad. Think this through. Someone is trying to kill Trent, very likely the same person who killed Jimmy."

"It's a police matter," he said curtly.

"I'm aware of that. But answer this, Dad. If Trent is guilty of killing Jimmy, why is someone so determined to silence him? And me?"

He was silent for a long moment.

"I'll tell you why," she continued. "Because we're close to uncovering the truth. And that has made the real killer extremely nervous."

More silence. She looked at the screen, wondering if he'd hung up on her. It wouldn't be the first time.

"You may be right. I . . . don't want to lose you." Her dad's voice was so soft she wasn't sure if she'd heard him correctly.

"I love you, too, Dad. But I need you to trust me on this."

"Aiding and abetting a known felon is against the law." He wasn't telling her anything she didn't already know. But the fact that he calmly stated the words rather than shouted at her spoke volumes.

"I know. And we'll be in to see Detective Coakley soon. Take care, Dad." She pressed the end button and slumped back against the seat. "Wow. That was surreal."

"I heard part of it." Trent reached over to take her hand. "I'm glad you and your dad have found some common ground."

"Not sure I'd go that far, but that conversation was definitely a breakthrough." She couldn't believe her dad had actually mentioned not wanting to lose her. After three years of nothing but disappointment, she wanted to rush to the police station where he worked to give him a big hug.

Since that was the same precinct Detective Coakley worked in, that wasn't an option. Not yet.

But hopefully soon.

"I should have trusted in God's plan," she said wryly.

"I have to admit, I'm putting my faith in God's plan too," Trent admitted.

She glanced at him in surprise. "I'm glad to hear it."

"Thanks to you." He smiled and squeezed her hand before releasing it. "The hotel is just a few miles from here."

"Do you think the clerk will tell us what room they're in?"

"We can only try. If nothing else, we can hang around

and wait for them to check out." Trent sighed. "That could take a while, though."

"Time isn't our friend." She hoped Detective Coakley wouldn't send out a BOLO, a notice for all cops to be on the lookout for Trent. Or for her.

The idea of having the entire Nashville PD looking for them was not reassuring.

She sent up a silent prayer as Trent navigated the streets toward the Stardust hotel. It wasn't anything super fancy, but it was far better than the places she and Trent had stayed in.

He found a place to park, then surprised her by pulling his guitar out from the back seat and looping it around his body. "What are you doing?"

"I figure the clerk is more likely to let another musician into the room." Trent sent her a sidelong glance. "I can pretend to have lost my key."

She couldn't help but admire his plan. "Okay, let's do this."

He paused. "Maybe you should wait here."

"Oh no. You're not going in without me." She linked her arm with his. "We'll pretend to be a couple. Nothing suspicious about that."

He grinned. "You're catching on."

They walked inside the lobby. Serena made sure to lean against Trent, gazing up at him as if she were besotted. Never in her life had she been a groupie, but her feelings for Trent were complicated enough that it wasn't difficult to pretend.

"Hey, I'm with Jed Matson and Dave Jacoby. Forgot my key." Trent offered a sly smile and kissed Serena's temple. "Got distracted, if you know what I mean."

"Oh, sure." The young woman looked flustered and

tapped the keyboard. Seconds later, she nodded. "Yes, suite 2 1 1 1. I'll get a new key for you."

Serena could hardly believe it was that easy. Because it shouldn't have been. The clerk should have asked for Trent's name and noticed he wasn't listed as an occupant for the room.

Then again, for all she knew, Jed and Dave had others staying up there with them. Maybe there was a note in the computer to allow other guests to go up.

Or maybe the young woman was an idiot.

"Thanks, darlin'," Trent drawled, shooting her a wink. Serena had to swallow a snort when the clerk practically melted into a pile of goo at Trent's feet.

Was this how he'd gotten women when he'd been a part of Jimmy Woodrow's band? If so, she was shocked that he'd walked away from it all.

She continued snuggling up to him until they were safely in the elevator. "That woman should be fired."

"Hey, we got the key, what more could you ask for?" Trent asked with a knowing grin.

They got off the elevator and headed down the hall. She and Trent paused outside the door to room 2 1 1 1 and listened.

Nothing.

Trent knocked at the door, but there was no response. He knocked again and finally used the key to access the door. The scent of alcohol and weed was so overpowering she purposefully left the door ajar. Serena wrinkled her nose and followed Trent inside. The place was a mess, but no one was sleeping on the sofa or on the floor, which she figured was a good sign.

Trent went to the first bedroom and cracked the door

just enough to peer inside. Then he closed the door and did the same thing with the second bedroom.

"They're still sleeping," he said in a low voice. "Or more likely passed out."

"Alone?"

"Surprisingly, yes." Trent glanced around. "I guess we can wait."

"I thought I'd find you here," a male voice said from the doorway. Serena whirled around in time to see Brett Caine standing there, holding a gun pointed directly at them.

CHAPTER FOURTEEN

Trent stared grimly at his former band manager. At some level, he wasn't surprised to see him with a gun, yet it wasn't smart of Brett to threaten them in a hotel full of people. "Put the gun down, Brett."

"No, see, I'm calling the shots here." Brett glared at him with such malevolence that Trent almost took a step backward. "You both need to come with me. Right now."

Trent didn't move, and neither did Serena. He knew she was armed, but she couldn't grab her gun without drawing Brett's attention. And a move like that would likely make the manager start shooting. "Or what? You'll start shooting in the middle of a busy hotel? I don't think so."

"You think I can't set this up to look like you pulled the trigger on Serena, then turned the gun on yourself?" Brett slowly and deliberately moved the muzzle of the gun so that it was centered on Serena's chest instead of his. A bead of sweat rolled down the back of Trent's spine as he tried to come up with a way out of this. "Oh, I think I can."

"The gunfire will wake Jed and Dave," Trent said calmly.

"Not fast enough to save either of you." Brett's scowl deepened. "Now you're both going to come with me. Understand?"

"This is all about the money you siphoned from the band, isn't it?" It had been a shot in the dark, but the flicker of surprise that crossed Brett's eyes confirmed he'd nailed it. "Is that why you killed Jimmy? Jimmy found out about the money you stole and confronted you. An argument broke out, and you shoved him too hard."

"We argued, but I didn't kill him. Enough talking, we're walking out of here." Brett's tone was clipped, and the way he jacked the hammer of the gun back caused another bead of sweat to roll down his spine. "Now."

Trent forced himself to take a few steps closer, willing Serena to hang back, out of the way. When she kept pace with him, he shot her an annoyed look. "Let's talk this through, Brett. If you didn't kill Jimmy, then there's no reason to hold us at gunpoint."

"I'm not going to let you hang me out to dry," Brett said between clenched teeth.

"You know Serena's dad is a police captain with the Nashville PD, right?"

Another flicker of surprise darkened Brett's eyes as his gaze bounced between the two of them. "You're lying."

"I'm not." Trent was doing everything possible to distract Brett long enough to make a grab for the gun. He didn't want Serena caught in the crossfire and found himself praying for God's strength as he anticipated his next move.

One thing for certain, he couldn't allow Serena to be hurt.

"Trent is correct, my father is Captain Jerash, and he works out of this district." Serena lifted a brow. "You can call to verify, but understand my dad knows all about my investigation into Jimmy's death. No way is he going to believe Trent shot me and then himself. Not when he knows we've been in danger over the past few days."

"He'll track you down, Brett," Trent pointed out as he took another step closer. "Jerash dotes on his daughter. Trust me on this, the captain will not rest until her killer is brought to justice."

"I'm not worried as it's going to look as if you killed her." Brett didn't appear the least bit fazed by his comments.

"I'm telling you, my father isn't stupid." Serena's voice sharpened, and Trent could tell she was trying to get loud enough to draw attention either from someone in the hall or from the two band members. "You're going down, Brett. Unless you decide to be smart about this. If you just lower your gun, we'll come up with a plan to help you."

Brett didn't say anything, but Trent could see his finger tightening on the trigger. One small movement and he'd be dead. No one could survive a gunshot wound in the chest at this close range.

"Hey, what's going on?" a sleepy voice asked.

The moment Brett's gaze darted over toward Jed, Trent rushed forward, jamming his arm up beneath Brett's wrist in an effort to knock the weapon loose. Or at least cause the muzzle to point at the ceiling rather than at him and Serena.

Crack!

Trent ignored the extremely loud gunshot deafening his ear as he slammed into Brett. The manager stumbled backward beneath the force of his weight. When he brought his knee sharply up into his groin, Brett grunted with pain. Trent managed to grab Brett's gun hand by the wrist, pinning it up and over his head against the wall. Serena came up beside him and added her strength to hold Brett in place.

"What's going on?" Jed asked again, all hint of sleep evaporating from his voice. "Trent? What's the deal with Brett? Is that a gun?"

With Serena's help holding Caine, he wrenched the gun from the man's hand and tossed it into the far corner of the room. "Good ole Brett embezzled money from our band. I believe that when Jimmy confronted him about it, Brett killed him."

"Embezzled money?" It figured Jed would focus on that part of the story rather than on Jimmy's death. "From us?"

Trent suppressed a sigh. "Yeah, from us. Get over here and help me get him secured in a chair." He could hear pounding footsteps out in the hallway. "Sounds like the cops will be here any second."

"Cops?" Jed glanced warily around the room, no doubt looking for evidence of drug use.

"I've got him," Serena said. She was stronger than she looked, and between the two of them, they were able to drag Brett over to a chair.

Moments later, the door burst open. A security guard held what was likely a master key card while the two Nashville police officers approached with their weapons drawn. "What's going on?"

"We've unarmed him," Serena said.

"Yes, his gun is over there in the corner," Trent added.

"Officers, these people attacked me. When I fought back, the gun went off. It's not my gun but theirs," Brett said, his gaze earnest. "I'm the victim here."

Trent hated to admit his prints would be on the gun. "That's not true, officers. Brett Caine has been embezzling money from the bands he's managing. When we found out, he threatened to kill us." He glanced at Jed. "And we have a witness that will corroborate our story, right, Jed?"

"Right." Jed scowled at Brett. "How long have you been stealing from us, old man? Since the beginning? Or did that only start once we hit it big?"

"I want to see some IDs," the officer said curtly. "Now!"

"Not until you secure Brett Caine," Trent said, hoping his fake ID wouldn't raise suspicions. It had gotten him this far, but he'd managed to keep his interactions with the police to a minimum. "He's the one who fired the shot when I tried to take the gun away."

"No, you're the one who tried to shoot me," Brett shot back. There was a wild look in the band manager's eye as he began to realize the police weren't buying his version of the event. "I want these two arrested. I fully intend to press charges against them."

Serena pulled her ID out and handed it to the cop who hadn't said much. "I'm a private investigator and have a gun in my shoulder holster." Moving very carefully, she pulled the gun out and handed it over to the cop. "My father is Captain Denis Jerash."

"You're the captain's daughter?" The cops exchanged a glance, clearly recognizing the name. It was the first time Trent had ever been relieved to know someone within the police department. The cop handed Serena's gun back. "Okay, we'll take this man into custody, then get your side of the story."

"You may want to talk to Detective Coakley and Detective Grayson too. There have been a series of attacks against us, all likely related to this guy here." He jerked his thumb toward Brett. "Including several attempts to shoot us."

"Trent is right, we've reported the incidents to the

police," Serena said firmly. "You can check with either detective. And with my father."

"We will," the cop assured her. He went over to place Brett Caine in handcuffs. Trent relaxed once he knew the manager wasn't getting away with his ridiculous story.

"Thank you," Trent said, meaning it.

"In the meantime," the cop went on, "we need all of you to come down to the police station to be formally interviewed."

The small bit of relief faded. Trent told himself there was nothing to be afraid of. He hadn't done anything wrong, at least not recently. And he wasn't the target of this investigation. Once they dug into Brett's finances, he was sure the police would find all the motive they needed to arrest him for Jimmy's murder.

Yet old habits were tough to break.

"Of course, we'll come down to the station," Serena said calmly as if sensing he wasn't thrilled with the idea. "We're happy to help."

"Yeah," he added in a lackluster tone.

Dave staggered from his room, his eyes deeply bloodshot as he glanced around in surprise at the amount of people in the suite. His gaze eventually landed on Jed. "Dude, what's going on?"

Trent could tell both men were suffering bad hangovers, and he felt extremely relieved that he'd quit drinking. He didn't miss feeling lousy all the time.

Never again, he silently vowed.

"Brett was stealing from us, man," Jed said. "Even back when we were with Jimmy."

"Whaaaat?" Dave drew the word out in surprise as he scratched his chest. "No way."

After yelling about how he was going to have his lawyer

sue them all, including the entire Nashville Police Department, Brett had finally clammed up. The two officers rolled their eyes as if that empty threat was something they heard several times a day.

Trent drew Serena aside. "Are you sure you're okay?" He hadn't had time to verify that she hadn't been injured.

"I'm fine. More worried about facing my dad than anything else."

He frowned. "I'll stick with you. You don't have to face him alone."

"Thanks." She smiled. "I'm not worried he'll physically hurt me, but he's not going to be happy about what went down here."

"Not our fault that Brent threatened us at gunpoint." Then he winced. "Well, sort of, since we were investigating Jimmy's death."

"After being told not to," Serena agreed. "But it will be all right. The good news is that we're safe now. No more attacks against us."

"Yeah." It made sense that Brett must have hired the gunman and the woman to come after them. What didn't seem right was Brett showing up at the hotel with a gun. How had he known they were coming? Or had he just stumbled across them and always carried a weapon?

Too many questions that were still unanswered. Hopefully, the cops would straighten everything out.

While he was relieved to know the danger was over, and that Serena had solved the mystery around Jimmy's death, his gut tightened over the idea of never seeing her again. Yet he knew this was it. Their time together was over.

He loved music, but even the thought of returning to his regularly scheduled performances didn't make him feel better.

Instead, he felt as if he was losing the only life jacket keeping him afloat in a stormy sea.

———————

WHEN SERENA and Trent arrived at the police station, they were instantly separated and taken into different rooms. Serena was relieved that she didn't have to face off with her father right from the start.

She recited her side of the story as succinctly as possible. Of course, the cop made her go through it twice, then informed her a detective would be coming in.

Coakley didn't look at all happy to see her. "I told you to leave the investigating to us!"

Whatever. She sighed. "Brett Caine never denied embezzling the money from the bands he's managing, although I think it's pretty clear he did. He assumed we were onto him, which was why he threatened to kill us."

"In the middle of a hotel." The droll statement wasn't a question.

"I know, stupid, right? But hey, if the crooks weren't stupid, we'd never catch them, would we?"

"We?" Coakley scowled. "You're not a cop, remember?"

She didn't respond. If he was looking for an argument, she wasn't about to play along.

"Okay, start at the beginning." Coakley picked up a pencil and waited.

She swallowed a groan. "Which beginning? From the moment I began investigating Jimmy's murder? Or just what happened today?"

He heaved a sigh. "Today."

That was easy as it wasn't a long story. When she

explained how Trent rushed Brett to disarm him, the detective's eyebrow rose.

"He's lucky he didn't get killed," Coakley muttered.

Serena knew God has been watching over them, but she decided the detective wouldn't be interested in hearing that. She'd gone a little crazy herself when Trent had rushed Brett. When the gunfire rang out, she'd feared the worst, that Trent had been shot. But he wasn't.

"Ms. Jerash?"

Right. The story. "We pinned him against the wall, and Trent took the gun and tossed it in the corner. Then we hauled him over to the chair. We'd just gotten him seated when the officers arrived."

"I heard you were armed," Coakley said.

"Yes." She'd had to lock up her weapon before coming inside. "But I couldn't draw my weapon without causing him to shoot."

Coakley made a couple of notes on his yellow pad. "What else did Caine say?"

She thought back to the sequence of events. Easy to understand why witnesses didn't always include all pertinent details the first time around. It wasn't easy to think clearly when facing the wrong end of a gun. And things had happened so fast. "He just kept saying he would make our deaths look like a murder-suicide." Then she remembered something else. "I was surprised when he admitted to arguing with Jimmy but denied killing him."

"Criminals lie," Coakley pointed out.

"I know. But if he thought we were going to die, why bother to lie? He didn't deny embezzling the money."

Coakley nodded and made another note on the yellow pad. "What about the two band members? What's their role in this?"

"I don't believe they're involved," Serena said honestly. "They both sounded stunned to hear about the allegation of Brett embezzling their money. In fact, I'm sure that's how Brett found us there. He must have known we'd warn Jed and Dave about his embezzling."

It occurred to Serena that stealing from music stars who drank too much and took drugs was fairly easy. It seemed as if these guys didn't bother to pay attention to all the financial details.

A shame, really, because people like Brett Caine didn't hesitate to use that to their own favor. Much like some of the sports agents did when it came to handling big contracts.

Thinking back, though, she wondered again about why Brett had denied killing Jimmy. She wanted to find Trent, see if he remembered anything more about that fateful night. It was possible that hearing about Brett's argument with Jimmy had caused him to remember something important.

She crossed her arms over her chest. "How much longer are you going to keep us here? I'm sure once you get the ballistics from the gun, you'll find a match to the bullet found in my SUV."

Coakley stared at her for a long moment. "Why did you drop out of the police academy?"

"What?" His question threw her for a loop. "How did you know I went to the academy?"

"Everyone knows you dropped out. You're the captain's daughter."

She winced, thinking about how proud her father would have been. Before everything had gone sideways.

Before the accident that had killed her mother. And cost her the opportunity to follow in her father's footsteps.

"Why do you care?" She wasn't being snarky, she was honestly curious about why Coakley had broached the subject.

He shrugged. "You think like a cop. Act like a cop. Seems to me you're wasting your talent working as a private investigator."

It was a backhanded compliment, but she couldn't deny it made her feel good. Her gaze instinctively fell to her injured ankle. "Physical limitations after the car crash."

He nodded slowly. "I'm sorry, I should have known it was something like that. Although you could always try again."

Try again? Trent had suggested that too, but she was afraid to go down that road. To get her hopes up, only to have them pummeled into dust once again.

A knock at the door prevented her from responding. Coakley rose to open it.

Her father. She tried not to let her dismay show on her features.

"Captain," Coakley said with a nod.

"I'd like a word with the witness," her father said with barely a glance in her direction.

The witness, not his daughter.

"Of course." Coakley glanced back at her and offered what she interpreted as an encouraging smile.

When the door closed, her father finally met her gaze. "Are you okay?"

His question surprised her. "Yes, I wasn't hurt."

For a moment, she saw a flash of relief darken his eyes. She mentally braced herself for another tirade, but he surprised her once again. "I was shocked to hear you were involved in another shooting incident."

She winced. "I'm sorry, I didn't intend to worry you."

Her dad dropped into the chair across from her, his expression haggard. "It's one thing to go into danger when you're armed, wearing body armor and a shield, with other cops there to back you up. But this?"

"It wasn't as bad as it sounds. I was armed, but my weapon was in my holster. Caine held his gun at us, so I couldn't get to it. Trent is the one who risked his life to disarm Caine."

"I heard. Strange for a musician to do something like that." His derogatory tone compared Trent to a zookeeper, but she didn't take offense. She understood that her father preferred what he deemed to be real jobs rather than contributing to the arts.

The fact that her father had come here out of concern rather than to yell at her was amazing. Even though he was wrong, in that the arts were important, she wasn't about to throw his effort back in his face.

"A very good musician," she agreed. "But he's also a great guy. He saved us today. I ended up backing him up rather than the other way around."

Her dad nodded slowly. Serena pushed to her feet, came around the table, and bent over to wrap her arms around his broad shoulders. He reached up to cover her small hands with his larger ones.

"I love you, Dad," she whispered in his ear. "I'm sorry if you were worried."

"I don't want to lose you too." His voice was low and gruff.

She kissed his cheek. "I feel the same way about you, Dad."

He turned in his seat to gather her into his arms. It was their first hug since her mother died. Tears rolled down her cheeks. She'd missed spending time with her father and hoped this meant they could move on from her mother's death.

"I'm so sorry about Mom," she whispered.

"It's not your fault, Serena. I was wrong to blame you." After all this time, his admission filled her with relief.

Another knock at the door interrupted the moment. She released her father and swiped at her face.

"I'm buying you body armor for your birthday," her dad said gruffly.

She laughed. "Works for me. I love you, Dad." She opened the door, expecting to find Trent, but it was Detective Coakley.

"Sorry to interrupt." The detective addressed her father. "The chief is looking for you, sir."

Her dad stood and moved away. Then he turned back to face her. "Call me later, we'll schedule some time to have dinner together."

"I will." She shifted her gaze to Coakley. "Am I free to go?"

"Yes. Do you need a ride?" Coakley asked.

"I have a car, but where's Trent? We rode together."

The detective frowned. "I think he left."

What? "No, he couldn't have. He doesn't have the car keys." She patted her pockets, belatedly remembering that he did in fact have the car keys. Pushing past Coakley, she quickly went outside to find the burgundy rental.

It was still parked in the same spot. She crossed over, opened the door, and looked around. When she flipped down the visor, the keys fell into her hand.

He'd left her the car. Interesting. She raked her fingers through her hair, trying not to scream in frustration. Why would Trent leave her like this? He'd just saved her life. It didn't make sense that he'd take off, leaving her stranded.

Swallowing her anger, she marched back inside to retrieve her gun and holster. Then she went back to the rental, wondering where Trent had gone.

Back to the hotel to talk to Jed and Dave? Or to his apartment? She pulled out her phone and called him but got his voicemail. Her gut told her he must have gotten a ride home.

"Idiot," she muttered as she navigated through the Nashville traffic. "Probably blames himself in some way for what happened."

It took longer than she liked to reach his apartment. She pulled up and parked next to his rusty truck that still had the driver's side window blown out from the gunshot that seemed like eons ago, rather than a couple of days.

She sat for a moment, trying to understand what had gone through Trent's mind. Did he know she'd reunited with her dad? If so, it didn't explain why he'd leave so abruptly.

Without even bothering to say goodbye.

She slid out from behind the wheel and slammed the door shut with more force than was necessary.

Trent Atkins had a lot of explaining to do.

She went inside and made her way to the second floor. As she approached Trent's apartment, she listened intently. Was she wrong about his coming here? Maybe he'd gone to the hotel to talk through the missing money Brett had embezzled.

Then she heard muted voices from the apartment. The speaking was quiet enough that she couldn't understand what was being said. She honestly couldn't even be sure that they were two real people talking or just the TV.

Wait a minute. She froze. Trent didn't have a television.

At the time, she'd thought it strange because she didn't know anyone who didn't own a television.

A warning tingle rippled along the back of her neck. She eased her weapon from the shoulder holster and slid forward, reaching for the door handle.

It wasn't locked.

Putting her ear to the door, she could hear the voices a little better. Enough to identify one of them as female.

Was she wrong about what was going on here? Women flocked to musicians. Should she leave? Maybe this was his way of telling her he wasn't interested in continuing their friendship.

"You're wrong." Trent's sharp tone came through as clearly as if he'd been standing there. That's when she realized things in the room might not be the way they seem.

She slowly turned the handle and silently pushed the door open. Instantly, she saw Trent's gaze flicker as he noticed her over the woman's shoulder.

Not Heidi, as she'd assumed, but a different woman. It took a minute for her to recognize her as the woman in the photograph on Heidi's social media page.

Anna Weiss, the daughter of Wayne Weiss, the owner of the Country Blues record label.

"Get back," Trent shouted.

Serena didn't move. As Anna turned toward her, she belatedly saw the gun.

CHAPTER FIFTEEN

Trent was mighty tired of people pointing guns at him. The moment Anna turned toward Serena, he leaped forward and shoved the woman off balance, praying the gun wouldn't go off and hit Serena.

Two gunshots reverberated through his apartment. He'd landed on top of Anna's small frame. His heart pounding, he glanced frantically toward Serena. He was shocked to see her leaning on the doorway, almost as if her legs wouldn't hold her upright. He didn't see any blood, which was reassuring. "Are you okay? Were you hit?"

"Fine," she managed. "But I think Anna's hit."

He glanced down, noticing a small pool of blood forming on the floor beneath Anna. There was also a bleeding wound on her back.

The pain in his side didn't register until he'd realized the bullet had gone through Anna and hit him. He ignored the pain as he scrambled off the woman.

While he rolled Anna over onto her back, he heard Serena calling 911 requesting an ambulance and officers to respond to the shooting. She also reassured the operator that the shooter was down.

Anna's gun was nearby, but her eyes were dazed as if she was in shock. He could see the wound on her lower abdomen and knew he should do something to help her. He felt a bit like he was moving in slow motion, his head slightly fuzzy.

"I'll get a towel." Serena moved through the apartment to grab a kitchen towel off the counter. She returned to kneel on Anna's other side and pressed the towel against the bleeding wound.

"Y-you shot me . . ." Anna said weakly, her eyes wide with surprise.

"You shot me first." Serena's tone held no sympathy. "Thankfully, you missed."

Trent realized his knocking Anna off her feet had disrupted her aim. He closed his eyes, silently thanking God for keeping Serena safe. Another wave of dizziness hit hard, and he put his hand on the floor to keep himself from toppling over.

"Why did you kill Jimmy?" Serena asked as she held pressure against Anna's wound.

"I told Heidi it was an accident . . ." Anna's voice trailed off, her eyes drifting closed. Trent could tell the pain was getting to her, and he could pretty much relate.

His side ached like crazy, and he hadn't experienced the full impact of Serena's bullet. Although, now that he thought about it, where was the bullet? He surreptitiously felt along his back, but there was no exit wound.

Which meant the bullet was still inside him. Fun times. Yet it could have been so much worse. He owed Serena his life. He looked over at her. "How did you know to come here?"

"Why did you leave without me?"

The wail of police sirens grew louder. In another few minutes there wouldn't be time to talk. He knew he owed her an apology. "As I was leaving, I saw your father going inside to talk to you. I could tell he was upset and worried about your welfare, so I felt it was better to give you the chance to smooth things over with him."

"That's a big fat load of baloney sausage," Serena snapped back. His jaw dropped in surprise; it was the first time she'd been really angry with him. Frustrated, yeah, but never angry. "Why don't you just admit you didn't want anything more to do with me? And were too chicken to tell me to my face?"

"That's not true . . ." He was interrupted by the pounding of footsteps coming down the hallway toward them. Seconds later, cops swarmed the small apartment.

It was going to be a repeat of what had just gone down in the hotel suite, only this time with Serena being the center of the investigation. He moved aside as two paramedics brought over their supplies to begin providing care to Anna.

He staggered to his feet, wincing at the pain in his side. He put his hand there with a grimace. There was more blood than he'd realized, considering the bullet was still lodged somewhere inside him. He didn't mention the injury as Anna's wound was more serious.

He understood the shooting was her own fault, but that didn't mean she shouldn't get care.

A cop had taken Serena off to the side. When his knees threatened to buckle, he sank to down onto the sofa and watched as she handed over her weapon, then turned and pointed at the bullet hole in the doorframe. The cop placed her gun in a plastic bag, then retrieved Anna's weapon, placing that one in another bag.

Seeing the bullet hole so close to where Serena had been standing caused a wave of nausea to wash over him. Trent leaned forward, pressing his hand against the entry wound in his side, trying not to throw up. If Anna's aim had been just a little better, Serena would be dead.

Dead.

He swallowed hard. In that moment he knew she was right. He hadn't left her behind at the police station for noble reasons. Sure, he'd hoped she'd reunite with her father, but as she'd pointed out, that was a handy excuse.

The truth slapped him in the face. He'd been a coward and had assumed she'd go back to being a private investigator, moving on with her life. While he went back to his music career, such as it was. He'd left because he hadn't wanted to hear her tell him things between them were over. That their kisses had taken place in the heat of the moment while being on the run for their lives.

That they didn't mean anything more than two people seeking comfort in the midst of danger.

Only now he understood just how much he loved her. A variety of emotions cascaded over him. He'd never felt like this about any woman.

He couldn't lie about his past. He and Cooper had enjoyed more than their fair share of women. Joining the Jimmy Woodrow Band certainly hadn't hurt. They'd come to him.

Yet he'd never given one his heart.

And he'd never prayed with one either.

"Trent? Are you bleeding?" Serena's voice interrupted his thoughts. He wondered if his love for her was reflected on his face.

"Yeah. I think the bullet that went through Anna is lodged inside me."

"What?" Serena paled and rushed over to lift the hem of his T-shirt. He longed to pull her into his arms, but she seemed intent on probing the site of his injury. "Why didn't you say something?"

"Because I'm fine." He glanced at Anna Weiss. "Better than her."

"This man needs medical attention," Serena said loudly. "He's been shot too. The bullet is still inside him."

He was ridiculously pleased with her concern. "Serena, I'll be okay."

The EMTs lifted Anna onto a gurney. One fiddled with her IV while the other one came over to check him out. "Wow, you need to get to the hospital too. I'll ask the cops to call for another rig, we can't take two patients at a time."

Trent was beginning to feel light-headed. Maybe all the talking about his injury was making him feel worse than the injury itself.

One of the cops called for another ambulance while the other approached to sit beside him. "The rig will be here soon. Is this your place?"

Trent tried not to groan at the lengthy interview that he'd have to go through all over again. "Yeah. My name is Trent Atkins." The EMTs bundled Anna on the gurney and wheeled her out of the apartment. He couldn't deny being glad to see the last of her.

"What happened?" the officer asked.

"He's been shot," Serena said, sounding like a broken record. "This interview can wait until he's received medical care."

"It's okay, I can answer," Trent assured her. He turned toward the cop. "I walked in to find Anna Weiss waiting for me. I knew Anna from when I was with the Jimmy Woodrow Band. She's the daughter of Wayne Weiss, the owner and producer of Country Blues Records."

The cop's brow lifted in surprise. "I've heard of Country Blues. Go on," he encouraged.

"She and Jimmy had a fight over his unwillingness to be faithful." When Anna had started talking, fragments of his memories of that night fell into place. "She wanted Jimmy to be with her exclusively, Jimmy told her to get a life. Then she threatened to tell her father, who would refuse to sign our recording deal, if he didn't go along with what she wanted. Jimmy got mad, but he was also drunk and high, so he wasn't exactly a physical threat. She pushed him, and he fell against the glass table. She rolled him over, and when she realized he'd died, she took off." He swallowed hard as another wave of nausea hit.

This getting shot deal wasn't much fun.

It hurt way more than he could have imagined.

"Do you remember any of that argument?" Serena asked.

"Yeah, some of it. But I was pretty drunk that night too." It pained him to admit his failures for these guys to hear. If he hadn't been drunk that night, he might have been able to intervene in the argument between Anna and Jimmy. "But I can testify as to what she told me as she threatened to kill me. And she'd mentioned telling Heidi Lawrence that she'd killed Jimmy too. I think she must have given Heidi drugs and left her to die. Only we found Heidi in time and managed to call an ambulance."

"Did Anna Weiss admit to hiring the guy in the Jeep?" Serena pressed. The cop glanced at her in surprise but didn't interrupt, apparently realizing there was far more to the story than what had just transpired here.

"Yes. She was really mad that he'd failed her," Trent admitted. "And she wanted to know how much you knew, Serena. I think when she finished with me, she planned to come after you."

The cop looked between him and Serena. "I'll need both of you to talk with the detective assigned to this case. This is above my pay grade."

"I know," Trent and Serena said at the exact same time.

Trent let out a chuckle. "It won't be our first time," he added.

"He's right. We've already spoken to Detective Coakley barely thirty minutes ago," Serena said with a sigh. "But Trent isn't going anywhere except to the hospital. Even if I have to drive him there myself."

Trent tried to smile, she was cute when she was upset, but his strength was fading rapidly. Is this what shock felt like? Maybe.

He didn't like it.

The officers moved off to the side. One used his radio to notify Detective Coakley about the shooting involving Serena and Trent. It was easy to hear Coakley's incredulous tone as he stated he'd be there ASAP.

"Tell him Trent's on his way to the hospital," Serena called out to the officer. "The ambulance is here."

Trent blinked, wondering where the EMTs had come from. He swayed again, and this time, Serena forced him to stretch out on the sofa.

As she moved away to make room for the emergency personnel, he reached out to grasp her arm. "I'm sorry."

"For leaving me at the police station?" Serena asked.

Clearly she wasn't going to give him any leeway here. "Yes, for being a coward. I figured you weren't interested in pursuing anything more between us, and I didn't want to hear you say it."

"Idiot," she muttered. "I wasn't going to tell you any such thing."

He eyed her warily. "You weren't?"

"Trent . . ." She sighed and rubbed her temple. "We'll talk about this later."

The EMTs began to work on him, listening to his heart and lungs, putting patches on his chest, and then starting an IV.

But all he could think about was that Serena wasn't going to leave him.

Whatever medication they gave him made his eyelids droop. He tried to focus on Serena's face but couldn't see her clearly.

He wanted to tell her how much he loved her, but blackness pulled him under before he could say the words out loud.

They only echoed in his head.

I love you.

SERENA COVERED her mouth with her hand as Trent was lifted off the sofa and onto the gurney.

She'd shot him.

Oh, not on purpose, but there was no denying the bullet she'd fired at Anna had gone through the woman and into Trent. Was still lodged in Trent's abdomen, causing who knew how much damage.

Dear Lord, what had she done?

Serena bowed her head in prayer, begging God to watch over Trent. She wanted nothing more than to follow him to the hospital, but when she'd tried to leave, the officers insisted she stay there until Coakley arrived.

Her new best friend.

Not.

Serena forced herself to leave Trent's well-being in God's hands. She found Trent's phone and noticed the dead battery. She slipped it into her pocket, then turned to the doorway when she heard someone enter. It hadn't taken Coakley long to get there.

"You shot a suspect?" The first words out of his mouth were not reassuring.

"She shot at me first." Serena took a deep breath and tried to calm her racing nerves. She'd never shot anyone before, and this incident had been far worse as she'd nearly killed the man she loved.

The realization gave her a surprising surge of strength. She loved Trent, and she wasn't going to give up on him. On them.

He'd just have to find a way to deal with it.

Serena lifted her chin and faced Coakley. She calmly went through the events as they'd unfolded, including showing him the bullet hole in the doorframe just two inches above where she'd been standing. Then she informed him of what Trent had mentioned about the conversation between him and Anna before she'd arrived. And finally, she included what Anna's last words had been.

I told Heidi Jimmy's death had been an accident.

"Unbelievable," Coakley muttered.

"Tell me about it," Serena agreed. "I still think she's guilty of reckless homicide in relation to Jimmy's death, but it's more the things she did to cover up that so-called accident that will sink her boat. She's the one who hired that guy to come after us. She's responsible for all the acts of violence against us even if she hadn't done them herself. When I came into the apartment, I wasn't expecting her to have a gun."

"You should have called for backup," Coakley snapped.

"Backup? I'm not a cop, remember?"

"You should have called it in rather than confronting her by yourself," he continued as if she hadn't spoken. "You're lucky no one died here today."

"I know." Her voice trembled, and she held herself together with an effort. "Do you think I'm happy to have wounded Trent? Anna deserved what she got for trying to kill me, but Trent put his life on the line to save me. And I nearly killed him instead."

"I'm sorry, I know shooting a person is never easy." Coakley actually patted her on the shoulder like some sort of awkward big brother. "Don't worry, I'm sure both of them will survive. We have good trauma docs here."

She forced a nod. "I know. Look, can we do the rest of this later? I've given my statement and handed over my weapon. I'd like to get to the hospital to see Trent. He doesn't have any family in the area."

Coakley swept his gaze over the area. "Yeah, okay. I know where to find you."

"Thanks." She hurried out of the apartment and back to her rental car. After sliding behind the wheel, she took a moment to steady herself. Trent didn't have family in Nashville, but he had foster siblings.

One that he'd mentioned in particular. Cooper.

She glanced at the phone she'd taken from his apartment. Thankfully, her power cord would fit to charge it back up. Maybe she could figure out how to call this Cooper to let him know about Trent's injury.

After all, what kind of private investigator would she be if she couldn't track him down?

When she reached the hospital, she learned Trent was in surgery. She prayed God would provide the surgeon the skills needed to successfully remove the bullet. Using her power cord, she charged Trent's phone and scrolled through the numbers.

Most of the calls were local, but when she stumbled across a number outside the area, she used her phone to look up the location. Gatlinburg. Did Cooper live in Gatlinburg? It appeared there were two missed calls, then Trent had returned one call, all to the same number.

There was only one way to find out.

To her surprise, the phone was answered almost immediately. "Trent? Is that you?"

"This is Trent's phone, but I'm Serena Jerash. Is this Cooper?"

"Yes, but what's wrong? Why do you have Trent's phone?" There was no mistaking the panic in Cooper's tone.

"Trent is in surgery to remove a bullet from his abdomen. I, uh, well, it's a long story. I mainly wanted to let you know in case . . ."

"Which hospital?" Cooper demanded. "We can be there in four hours."

"Oh, do you have your foster siblings with you?"

"I'll reach out to Hailey and Darby, but the others don't live as close. My wife and I will come right away, just tell me where you are."

Serena gave him the information. "Call me when you get here."

"I will. And Serena? Thanks for calling." Cooper disconnected before she could respond.

A solid ninety minutes went by before Serena learned Trent was out of surgery. And another hour before he was brought to his room. The surgeon had informed her the procedure went well overall. A small portion of his small intestine was removed, but the large bowel hadn't been hit. All in all, she was assured Trent would recover without a problem.

Serena sat at his bedside, holding his hand. She thanked God for watching over him. When Trent stirred, she rose to her feet. "Hey, how are you feeling?"

"I've been worse." He gazed up at her. "I'm surprised to see you."

"I'm not going anywhere." She hesitated, then added, "Don't be mad, but I called Cooper. He's on his way here."

"What? Really?" Thankfully, Trent didn't look upset. "He's coming?"

"Yeah, he and his wife. Sounds like he was ready to drop everything to get here."

Trent looked stunned. "Wow. I can't believe I'm going to see him after all this time."

"You might want to get some rest so you don't fall asleep in the middle of their visit." She leaned over to kiss Trent's cheek. "Try not to worry, the doc says you're going to be fine. No major damage."

"Yeah, she told me that too." Trent tightened his grip on her hand. "There's something I need to tell you."

His voice grew faint, as if he was losing his strength. "Don't worry, Trent. I'm not going anywhere. I'll be here when you wake up."

The corner of his mouth kicked up in a smile. "Thanks for that. But that's not it. I wanted you to know how much I love you."

She blinked. Had she really heard him correctly? "I, uh,

think you need to get some rest. We'll have time to talk later."

"I love you," he repeated, his voice stronger now. "I want you to know I've never said those three words to another woman. Not once. I made a lot of mistakes, Serena, too many to count. But that's in the past. I know God brought us together for a reason. And I don't want to lose you."

"Oh, Trent." She couldn't be absolutely sure it wasn't the pain meds talking, but his words still touched her heart. "You won't lose me. I love you too. But there's no rush, we have all the time in the world."

"But if we don't, if God has other plans for us, I want you to know how much I love you. More than anything." His eyelids began to droop. "I want us to be together . . ."

In a heartbeat, he fell back to sleep. She stared down at him, telling herself not to put much credence into his ramblings. Trent had seemed to know what he was saying, but being wounded, then undergoing surgery probably made him keenly aware of his mortality. It certainly had done that to her. When he was fully recovered and out of the hospital, he may look at things differently.

Still, she held his declaration of love close to her heart as she sank back into her chair, keeping his hand cradled in hers.

Detective Coakley stopped by. She left Trent sleeping to talk to him.

"I spoke to Heidi Lawrence, she confirmed Anna admitted to killing Jimmy by accident. Heidi said she'd gotten really upset since she felt certain Jimmy's band was going places, which is why she'd arranged for Jimmy's band to open for Luke Bryan."

"I thought as much," Serena admitted. "So that must be when Anna slipped drugs into her wine."

"Exactly," Coakley admitted. "Heidi and Rob both wanted me to thank you and Trent for saving her life."

"Rob was with her?" Serena was a little surprised when Coakley nodded. "Wow. Sounds like the near-death experience made her realize what was important."

"That was my impression too. They seemed willing to try again," Coakley agreed. He glanced at his watch. "I have to go, I'll come back later to get Trent's statement."

"Okay, thanks for coming and filling me in on the details."

"You're welcome," Coakley said gruffly.

Serena went back into Trent's room, thankful to know the case of Jimmy's death had been solved once and for all.

Trent woke again two hours later. He smiled when he saw her. "I still love you."

She had to laugh since he was clearly reading her mind. "I love you too."

There was a knock at the door, and when it opened, a handsome guy with longish blond hair and arresting blue eyes stood there, a pretty dark-haired woman at his side. As they entered the room, Trent's eyes widened in shock.

"Cooper?"

"Yeah, it's me." Cooper gave Serena a quick nod, then took his foster brother's hand. "And this is my wife, Mia. I'm so glad Serena called to let us know you were hurt, but what on earth happened?"

Trent grimaced. "It's a long story."

"Yeah, that's what Serena said." Cooper gazed down at Trent. "I'm glad you're doing okay. The last time we talked, you said something about being in a mess. To be honest, I'd prepared myself for the worst."

"Yeah, sorry about that," Trent agreed. He winced as he shifted in the bed. "Serena can fill you in on the details. I can't believe you're here. That after all this time you came rushing to see me."

"Anytime, brother." Cooper smiled. "I want you to know that Hailey, Sawyer, and Darby are all anxious to see you too. I convinced them we'll get together in the near future, so don't make a liar out of me."

"I won't. Still no word about Jayme and Caitlyn?" Trent asked.

"Haven't found them yet. But Sawyer is working on that. In fact, Sawyer called me earlier this morning to let me know he found your address here in Nashville." Cooper shook his head. "If Serena hadn't called, I would have shown up on your doorstep in the next day or so. Mia and I live in Knoxville now so she can attend nursing school."

"I'm glad you didn't just show up at my apartment, or you'd have been in danger too," Trent said with a frown.

Cooper glanced at Serena. "Maybe it's time to tell us that long story."

"Later," Trent said. He reached out to take Serena's hand. "All you need to know right now is that I love Serena."

She smiled. "And I love Trent."

"Glad to hear it." Cooper grinned, then turned somber. "Sorry to hear about Jimmy. What have you been doing now? Did you find another band?"

"That's part of the long story," Serena admitted. "And you should probably know that I'm the one who shot Trent. Not on purpose, I was aiming at a woman who shot at me. She missed, I didn't. The bullet went through her and into Trent."

Cooper and Mia glanced at each other in surprise. "Now that is a story," Cooper drawled.

"Oh, there's more." Trent held Cooper's gaze. "The most important part is that I've been sober for three months, so there's no need for you to worry about me."

"I wasn't," Cooper said a little too quickly.

"Yeah, right." Trent shifted again. "Serena opened my heart and my mind to God."

"That's great, brother. Really great." A broad smile bloomed on Cooper's features. "Mia and I have been attending church too. Oh, and you need to heal up fast, Hailey and Rock are getting married mid-October. They'll want you to be there."

"Married." Trent smiled. "I'm happy for her. Serena and I will make it, no matter what."

Cooper winked at Serena, then took a step back. "Listen, we'll leave you alone to get some rest, but don't worry, we're sticking around Nashville for a while. Figured we'd do some sightseeing while we're here."

"Okay." Trent looked as if the conversation had worn him out. "Thanks for coming."

"Of course." Cooper gave them a nod, then ushered Mia from the room.

"I'd better go with them," Serena said. "I'm sure they're anxious to hear the entire story. Although I have information from Coakley to share with you too."

"I can't wait to hear it, but I should have asked if you were interested in coming to Hailey's wedding." Trent's green eyes sought hers. "I shouldn't have assumed you would."

"Of course, I'll go with you." She leaned over to kiss him again. "I love you, Trent. We'll figure everything out once you're feeling better."

"I know we will." His eyelids slid closed, but he opened them quickly. "Serena? Would you find some Christian music for me to listen to?"

"I'd be happy to." She plugged in his phone and scrolled through to find the music app. Then she selected the Christian music station she normally used and put it on speaker. Music filled the room, bringing joy and light.

And peace.

"Thanks." Trent smiled, nodded, and closed his eyes.

Her heart swelled with faith, hope, and most of all, love.

EPILOGUE

Three weeks later . . .

Trent watched as Serena ran two miles in seventeen minutes. More than good enough to pass the police academy training requirements. There were other requirements too, but this and the agility run were the two that had given her the most trouble.

And she'd nailed it.

"Congrats, babe!" He pulled her into his arms for a long kiss. "I knew you could do it."

"I'm all hot and sweaty," she protested, but her eyes gleamed with excitement. "My ankle is holding up far better than I could have hoped."

"God is giving you the strength and endurance you need." He kissed her again. "I'm so happy for you."

"Are you sure you don't mind dating a cop?" Her tone was teasing, but her gaze was serious. "I know you haven't always held the police in high regard."

She knew everything about how he and Cooper had lived on the streets, the multitude of laws they'd broken.

"I've learned the police are there when we need them the most. And I want you to be happy."

"I'm very happy, Trent. Especially with you."

They'd learned Anna Weiss had been charged with manslaughter for Jimmy's death and with murder for hire in the attempts against him and Serena, and for the attempted murder of Serena. She'd be in jail for a long time, which was what she deserved. If she'd have just come clean early on . . . but she hadn't. The police picked up Kurt James, Anna's hired gun, and charged him for the murder of Gabrielle and attempted murder of him and Serena. Anna claimed Kurt had killed Gabrielle on his own without her knowledge, but that was a matter for the lawyers to sort out.

Thankfully, Serena's shooting of Anna Weiss had been deemed to be done in self-defense, which was all Trent cared about.

Brett Caine had been charged with multiple counts of embezzlement and was facing prison time. Jed and Dave had asked Trent to join Bootleggers, but he'd declined. He'd discovered that playing Christian music filled the emptiness in his soul, and he had no intention of ever going back. He was working on creating more music, which was his true love.

He and Serena had gone to Gatlinburg to see Cooper, Hailey, Sawyer, and Darby. Their reunion was amazing, although they still needed to track down Jayme and Caitlyn. Hailey had asked him to perform at her wedding, and he'd readily agreed.

He'd found peace and happiness with Serena, but there was more that he wanted. Much more. He wanted it all.

Grasping Serena's hand, he led her over to a maple tree with leaves that were just beginning to change color. He'd had the ring for a week now and couldn't wait a moment longer.

Still holding on to her hand, he dropped to one knee and reached into his pocket for the ring. "Serena, will you please marry me?"

Her jaw dropped, and he was secretly pleased that he'd been able to surprise her. She was always so in tune to his feelings, her cop instincts such that he'd figured she'd guess his intentions long before he had the chance to act on them.

"Oh, Trent. Yes, yes! I'd be honored to become your wife." She laughed, then added, "I can't believe you're proposing marriage while I'm hot and sweaty!"

"I love you, no matter what." He stood and pulled her into his arms. He kissed her to prove it. "By the way, I talked to your dad last week. He gave me permission to propose."

"You asked my dad to marry me?" A smile bloomed on her face. "That's the sweetest thing anyone has done."

"I won't even tell you how nervous, hot, and sweaty I was during that conversation," Trent said dryly. "Talk about pressure."

She laughed again, then drew his head down to hers for a long, deep kiss. "I love you, Trent Atkins."

"And I love you too." He tucked her close and glanced up through the green and yellow leaves to the blue sky beyond.

He thought about his dream where he was sitting beside Cooper with little pieces of paper raining down from above containing the words *God is real*. Trent nodded, knowing that God was smiling down at them, pleased with how they'd followed their hearts and His plan.

. . .

I HOPE you've enjoyed Trent and Serena's story! I'm having fun reuniting the fosters, but they won't all be together until the next book, *Jayme's Journey*. Are you ready to read Jayme's story? Click here!

DEAR READER

I hope you've enjoyed *Trent's Trust* and all the other books in my Smoky Mountain Secrets series. I've wanted to show how amazing God's love can be, and these books are a testament to His love. Jayme's story will be out next month, and I can't wait to have the big reunion. You won't want to miss it!

Reviews are critical to authors, so if you enjoyed this book, please consider taking a moment to write a brief review. I would very much appreciate your time. Thank you very much.

I also adore hearing from my readers! I can be found on Facebook at https://www.facebook.com/LauraScottBooks, Twitter at https://twitter.com/laurascottbooks, Instagram at https://www.instagram.com/laurascottbooks/, and through my website https://www.laurascottbooks.com. If you enjoy my books, you'll want to sign up for my monthly newsletter as I offer a free novella to all subscribers. This novella is not available for sale on any platform, it's exclusive to those of you who join my list.

Thanks again for your support! I'm blessed to have wonderful readers like you!

Until next time,

Laura Scott

If you're curious about *Jayme's Journey*, I've included the first chapter here.

JAYME'S JOURNEY

The pungent scent of smoke pulled Jayme Weston from sleep.

Fire!

She sat upright in bed, her heart pounding, fear clawing up her back. She swept her gaze frantically over the room, searching for the yellow and orange flames. It took a moment for her to register that the fire was from her dreams.

Her nightmares.

Swallowing hard, she pressed a hand to her chest and willed her pulse to slow down. She instinctively massaged her scarred hand, bending her fingers back and forth. But then she wrinkled her nose again.

The smoke scent lingered. Maybe even getting stronger.

It wasn't her imagination!

Jayme scrambled out of bed, jammed her feet into running shoes, and pulled a sweatshirt on over her sleep shirt and shorts. She grabbed her phone, grateful Caitlyn had moved out with her college friend at the start of the semester. Yet being alone in the small house only emphasized her vulnerability.

Never again, she thought grimly as she tiptoed down the short hallway to the living space. She wasn't a victim, she was a strong and capable woman. The smoke scent was stronger now, a haze hanging in the room. But she still couldn't see any sign of an actual fire. And the smoke wasn't enough to trigger the alarm.

Yet she wasn't going to take any chances either. She swept her thumb across the phone screen and quickly dialed 911. When the operator answered, Jayme did her best to remain calm.

"My name is Jayme Weston. I live on Oakdale Road in Sevierville and smell smoke inside my house. I don't see a fire, but I would like you to send the fire department out to investigate."

"What's the house number?"

Jayme relayed the information, still searching for the source of the smoke. Was she making a big deal out of nothing? Maybe the fire was somewhere nearby and not actually in her home? They hadn't had a lot of rain recently, so it could be that a portion of the woods was burning. And it would explain why her smoke detectors weren't going off.

"Ma'am, are you able to get out of the house?" the dispatcher asked.

On cue, the smoke detector in her living room began to blare loudly. She winced and shouted into the phone. "Yes!" She instinctively grabbed her purse off the counter on her way to the front door. Outside, it was easier to hear the dispatcher. "I didn't see any flames."

"The fire could be in the attic or basement. Please stay outside, far enough back to remain safe. I've sent the fire department to your location."

The fire might be in the attic or basement? The basement was empty except for the washer and dryer. Jayme glanced up at the roof of her house. There was no indication the fire was in the attic, yet she wasn't an expert on house fires.

Although she had started one. A long, long time ago.

Taking a deep breath of fresh air, she shoved the old memories away. She stumbled across the lawn, glancing back over her shoulder at the house.

She hadn't turned on any lights, so it was completely dark, with no sign of anything amiss.

But the smoke had to have come from somewhere. She was tempted to run around to the backyard to see if she could figure out where the smoke was coming from, but the wail of sirens convinced her help was on the way.

The early October air was relatively cool, especially at night. Maybe she should have changed into jeans because her legs were chilled. She wrapped her arms around herself, trying to stop from shaking. A reaction to the smoke and her dream of the fire rather than to the cool temperatures. The scent of smoke clung to her clothing, reassuring her that it was real. Not some figment of her overactive imagination. And the smoke detectors were still screeching.

The sirens grew louder, overwhelming the smoke detector. Soon she could see the swirling red lights cutting through the darkness. The fire department had made good time. Granted, Sevierville wasn't that large, and it wasn't that late, just past midnight.

She felt silly standing out on the sidewalk. But the team of firefighters pretty much ignored her as the fire engine pulled up in front of her house. They jumped down and spread out around her property. They were all dressed from head to toe in heavy coats, hats, and carrying a lot of gear. One of them crossed directly to her. "Are you Jayme

Weston, the homeowner? You called about smelling smoke?"

"Yes, the smoke woke me from a sound sleep, and you can hear the detector going off. I looked around and could see a haze in the house, but no source of the fire." She rubbed her hands over her arms. "Is there a forest fire nearby that may have caused this? It doesn't look to me like my house is on fire."

"No other fires have been reported nearby. Please stay back, we'll take a look." The firefighter lifted a hand and gestured toward the door. Two firefighters went inside while he and another firefighter walked around the outside of her property.

A few of her neighbors' lights flipped on, no doubt woken by the sound of the fire truck. She glanced around, noticing faces pressed against the windows. Her cheeks flushed, and she ran her fingers through her red hair. This was going to be mighty embarrassing if it turned out to be a false alarm.

Her closest neighbor, Mrs. Katz, hurried outside. "Jayme dear, are you okay?"

"I'm fine." Mrs. Katz had a kind heart and certainly meant well, but she was also extremely nosy. Jayme forced a smile. "No need to be concerned. I'm sure it's nothing."

"Well, the fire department must be here for *something*," the woman insisted. "I'm glad you're okay, though." Despite her nosiness, Jayme did her best to stay on good terms with the woman. Mrs. Katz had often treated Caitlyn like a granddaughter.

Her experience of living with family was limited to the foster homes she'd been in. The last one in particular she'd suffered physical and emotional abuse. And more. There was no point in dredging up the past now, but she edged closer to Mrs. Katz, once again grateful not to be alone. "Did you happen to smell smoke?"

"No, dear. Is that what this is about?" Mrs. Katz's eyes widened with interest as she scanned the area. "I don't see any source of the fire."

"I didn't either." She lifted her arm to Mrs. Katz's face. "But you can smell the smoke clinging to my clothes, right?"

Mrs. Katz sniffed. "Yes. That's so strange. Maybe a part of the woods is on fire?"

"But we'd see the flames, wouldn't we? And the firefighters would have known about that."

"Over here," a voice shouted.

Her heart leapt into her throat, and she found herself gripping Mrs. Katz's arm. Had they found something?

Jayme watched as a fireman pulled the long hose toward the right side of her house. It didn't take long for the crew to douse whatever they'd found, and within minutes, the crew had brought the hose back and returned to the fire truck.

Maybe she'd woken up just in time. Calling for the firefighters who'd found the source before it had time to spin out of control. Thank goodness for smoke detectors.

The same firefighter who'd spoken to her on arrival came over to join her. For once, she didn't mind Mrs. Katz hanging around. "Ms. Weston? We found the source of the fire."

"Where? Is my house damaged?"

"Not from what we can tell. The fire was found outside the east part of your home near the heating vent. That's how the smoke was sucked into your house."

Jayme frowned. "But I don't understand. What was burning? Did my furnace malfunction?"

"No." The firefighter took her arm and drew her away from Mrs. Katz. He lowered his voice and said, "Ms.

Weston, you need to know I've called in the arson investigator. The fire was small, but it was also deliberately set."

She blinked, wondering if she'd misheard him. "Deliberately set? Are you sure?"

"Positive." There was no room for debate in his tone.

"But—who would do such a thing? Kids?"

The firefighter shrugged, eyeing her steadily. "I don't think it was kids. The fire was set in a way that it wouldn't spread but would cause enough smoke to be sucked into your home to be noticeable."

A shiver snaked down her spine. That certainly didn't sound like something kids would do. She cleared her throat, striving to remain calm. "I'm glad it wasn't more serious, but please tell me, have you seen this happen anywhere else?"

"No. And I haven't heard about it either. That's the reason I called the arson investigator. Lincoln Quade covers the entire city and would know if this particular type of signature had been used anywhere else recently."

Signature? It sounded like something out of a movie. She nodded dumbly, grappling with what he was telling her. The fire had been set on purpose, but only enough to cause smoke to fill her home, to set off the smoke detectors, but not enough to engulf the house in a huge blaze.

It didn't make any sense. The firefighter must be wrong, this particular incident had to be something a bored teenager had come up with.

"Oh, there Linc is now," the firefighter said.

Jayme saw the twin headlights grow bright as a large SUV pulled over to park near the large fire truck. When the firefighter she'd been talking with crossed the yard to meet up with the driver, she followed more slowly, in no hurry to join them. She veered back toward the sidewalk where Mrs. Katz was standing.

Watching the two men speak in low tones was easier than trying to understand what had happened here. They walked over to the side of the house where her air-conditioning unit was located.

"Is everything all right, dear?" Mrs. Katz asked.

"Yes, everything is fine." She forced a smile. "Apparently, it was a small fire set by kids. It made a lot of smoke but didn't cause any real damage." She patted the woman on the shoulder. "Nothing for you to worry about, Mrs. Katz."

"Kids?" Mrs. Katz tsk-tsked. "I just don't understand this new generation."

Jayme smiled. "Me either." She was twenty-nine years old but felt decades older. Living in the woods, then on the streets while caring for Caitlyn had forced her to grow up real fast.

Too fast.

But Mrs. Katz didn't need to know that. "Get some sleep, Mrs. Katz. The fire is out, and we're all safe. That's what matters."

"Of course, dear." The woman's curious gaze darted back to where the men were still talking. "Jayme, if you need a place to stay, you're welcome at my house."

"Thank you, that's very sweet." Jayme was truly touched by her hospitality. She knew from personal experience that not everyone would have made the offer. "But since the fire was outside and didn't cause any damage, I'll be fine."

"If you're sure." Mrs. Katz gazed around with frank curiosity, clearly not satisfied there'd been enough drama.

"I'm sure. Get some rest." Jayme moved away, walking over to where the arson investigator and the firefighter were talking. The two men had large flashlights they used to illuminate the area. Even as she approached, she could see the black soot, which had been caused by the fire, staining the white siding of her house.

Thankfully, it wasn't anything worse than a black sooty stain. Nothing like the cabin she and the other foster kids had watched go up in flames thirteen years ago.

"Clever setup," a deep male voice said. "Thanks for calling me in."

"Figured you'd want to know." The firefighter caught sight of her. "Linc, this is Ms. Jayme Weston, she's the homeowner."

"Linc Quade, arson investigator." The tall man shifted his flashlight and offered his hand. She forced herself to take it, ignoring the way his fingers wrapped around her scarred hand. She didn't doubt he could feel the raised burn scars. "Ms. Weston, can we go inside to talk?"

"I, uh, sure." She hadn't expected that. "I assume the house is safe for me to go inside?"

"Yes, it's safe. The remaining smoke should dissipate soon. There wasn't enough to cause any real damage."

She let out a tiny breath. "Good to know."

"Shall we?" Linc Quade seemed anxious to get her away from the scene of the fire. Maybe he was worried she'd mess up any remaining evidence.

She walked across her dew-damp lawn and led the way inside, flipping on the lights that were bright enough to hurt her eyes. The smoke detectors were still blaring, but the fire investigator quickly reset them. She crossed over to the small kitchen table. Up close, she could see Linc Quade's handsome features more clearly. His blond hair was cut military short, a shadow of scruff covered his cheeks as if he hadn't shaved in a day or so, and his piercing dark eyes were intense enough to knock her off-kilter. She turned away and tried to focus. "Ah, do you want some coffee?"

"No thanks." He was polite as he gestured for her to sit before dropping into the chair across from her. For a long moment, he simply looked at her. "As you've already been told, we know the fire was set on purpose."

"So I hear. Kids, right?"

"Not likely." Linc Quade stared at her for another long moment, then his gaze dropped to her scarred hand and wrist. "Looks like this isn't your first close encounter with a fire."

She instinctively covered the scars with her uninjured hand as if that alone would make them disappear. "That was from an accident thirteen years ago."

"What happened?"

Jayme shifted in her seat, unsure why he was asking about the past. "Does it matter? Thirteen years is a long time, and that event doesn't have anything to do with today."

He leaned forward, propping his elbows on the table. "Ms. Weston, I've been investigating fires for over three years now. I'm the best judge of what matters and what doesn't."

She wanted to snap but managed to control her redheaded temper. Since he didn't seem willing to let it go, she decided to give him the bare minimum information. Even telling him that much wouldn't be easy. Caitlyn was the only person who knew the varnished truth about what happened that night in the Preacher's cabin, and as far as she was concerned, that was one person too many. No one else needed to hear the gory details. She held Linc's dark brown gaze. "I accidentally broke an oil lantern, and some of the hot oil spilled on my hand and wrist."

He surprised her by reaching across the table to lightly grasp her injured hand. He examined it closely. Why on earth she noticed the gentle strength in his fingers was beyond her. "Thirteen years ago? These scars are pretty bad. Why didn't you get appropriate care?"

Linc Quade knew far too much about fires and burns for her peace of mind. "I was too far away from civilization when this happened. By the time I was able to get anywhere close to a place offering medical care, it was too late." She tugged her hand from his, gripping them tightly in her lap. "Why don't you explain to me why my injury from thirteen years ago matters?"

His dark gaze bored into hers. "Sometimes victims of fire become obsessed with the dancing dragon. It wouldn't be the first time that a fire victim became an arsonist."

Never in her life had she heard of fire being called the dancing dragon. Then the rest of his words registered, and her jaw dropped in shock. "Me? You think I started the fire outside my own house? That's ridiculous. Why would I do that, then call you? Especially when I'm terrified of fire."

He shrugged. "Why are you terrified of fire? I thought the burn on your hand was from hot oil?"

She felt like he'd punched her in the gut. He was smart, she'd give him that.

Or maybe she was an idiot to think she could fool him. The spilled oil had in fact started a fire. That night thirteen years ago was seared painfully into her mind. The Preacher, as he called himself, had ranted and raved at the foster kids in his care, screaming about how they were all going to hell for being terrible sinners. He'd hit them with switches to hammer the point home.

If that wasn't bad enough, he'd set his sights on her. The evil leer in his gaze when he looked at her chest, her thighs made her want to throw up. She had no idea what to do, how to keep him from acting on his sick attraction, but escape was impossible.

When he made his move, she'd been grossly unprepared. He grabbed her, dragged her down, and began unfastening his pants. Horrified by what he was trying to do, she tried to call out to wake Ruth, but the woman was sleeping as if she'd been drugged.

And maybe she had been.

Panicked, she'd grabbed the oil lantern and swung it at the Preacher in an effort to get away. The oil had burned her hand, but she hadn't noticed because the Preacher screamed in agony as the hot oil burned the side of his face and his chest. Seconds later, the sofa erupted into flames as the Preacher stumbled toward the bedroom in an effort to save himself.

That moment she knew she needed to get away, no matter what. Ignoring her burns, she'd rushed over to yank up the cellar door, which was where they were forced to sleep. She'd been surprised to see Sawyer and Hailey already at the top of the stairs. Jayme had helped them up and out of the cellar. By the time they'd stumbled outside, the cabin was engulfed in thick smoke and flames. Coughing, nearly gagging, they'd managed to survive the fire by running and hiding in the woods.

The Preacher and Ruth, however, hadn't made it out of the fire.

"Ms. Weston?" His deep voice drew her from her troubled thoughts. "Are you okay? You look upset."

Upset was putting it mildly. Jayme squared her shoulders and met his gaze head-on. "I'm not upset," she lied. "And yes, if you must know, the hot oil did cause a small fire. Thankfully, I managed to escape without a problem.

Only my right hand and wrist were burned." She tried to smile, but it felt like her face was frozen. "Please be assured that I am not obsessed with fire. And I did not set the fire outside my own house. I would never do something like that." She rose to her feet. "If that's all, I think it's best if you leave."

Linc slid his business card across the table and rose, forcing her to tip her head back to look up at him. The man was tall, well over six feet, and came across as rather intimidating. Still, she hadn't survived in the wilderness without being strong, so she simply tilted her chin and stayed right where she was. His dark eyes seemed to look right through her to the hidden secrets she had buried deep within.

"Ms. Weston, my only goal is to uncover the truth about what happened here."

"I'm happy to hear that because it's a goal we share. I sincerely hope you can find out who did this awful thing." She kept her voice steady and calm, despite the emotions churning in her gut. "Now, if you don't mind, I have to work in the morning. Good night."

Linc stared at her for another long moment before turning toward the door. He got halfway when he abruptly stopped and glanced back over his shoulder. "If you didn't set the fire, you need to take some time to think about who did. Who could possibly be holding a grudge against you to do something as serious as this? While the fire turned out to be relatively harmless, the next time you may not be so fortunate. Another attempt could be far more deadly. You really need to consider who might be targeting you for some reason. Maybe someone you angered in the past?"

Bands of fear tightened around her chest making it difficult to breathe. Another attempt? She couldn't bear to think about it. "I'll try, but I'm not involved in a relationship and haven't been for eighteen months. I work as a physical therapy tech at the clinic in town. I highly doubt one of my patients hates me enough to do something like this." Although there were the occasional circumstances where patients had lashed out at her. Being in pain wasn't easy, as she knew all too well. She flexed her scarred fingers. Yet to go as far as to set a fire? No, she couldn't see it.

"Think harder," he said ominously before leaving through the front door.

Jayme drew in a deep, jagged breath as she went over to close and lock the door behind him. Then she slumped against the wood, sliding down until she was sitting with her back against the wall, her knees cradled up to her chest. She lowered her forehead to her knees and tried to quell the rising panic.

What was going on here? This whole thing didn't make any sense. A small fire set on purpose to send smoke into her house, but not enough to burn the place down? Who on earth would do something like that? And why?

As much as she desperately wanted to cling to her theory of neighborhood kids pulling some sort of prank, she couldn't deny there was a sinister tone to the vandalism. Granted, the fire had been contained, but what if it hadn't been? She had to think there was always the possibility it could have spiraled out of control.

Which left her with no choice but to accept Linc Quade's preposterous idea.

To think about who from her past was carrying a grudge against her. Honestly, her first instinct would be to name the Preacher. Except he and his wife were dead. She and the other foster kids—Sawyer, Hailey, Darby, Cooper, Trent, and Caitlyn—had all hidden in the woods, watching and waiting for the adults to emerge from the fiery cabin.

They hadn't. And the way the cabin had burned so fast and so quickly, she felt certain there wouldn't have been time for the adults to get out. Especially since the Preacher had already been badly burned.

None of them had gone in to help rescue the Preacher or his wife either. A better person would have felt guilty about that, but she hadn't experienced an ounce of remorse. Not after the way he'd groped her, pinned her down with the intent to rape her. No, she hadn't gone in to rescue him.

By tacit agreement, she and the other foster kids had simply watched and waited.

When they heard the fire engines rushing toward the cabin, they finally began to move away, hiding deeper in the woods. They'd stayed together only briefly, long enough to agree that none of them were ever going back into the foster system.

To avoid being found, they'd split up and scattered. Sawyer, Cooper, and Trent had gone south. Hailey and Darby had gone due west, and she'd kept Caitlyn with her heading in a northwest direction.

From that point on, she'd never seen her foster siblings again. Well, other than Caitlyn, whom she'd kept with her over the years, telling everyone the girl seven years her junior was her younger sister. To be honest, Jayme knew she'd mainly survived for Caitlyn's sake.

Sure, she could think about who might be carrying a grudge against her, maybe someone from the early days when she'd been forced to lie, cheat, and steal to stay alive. But that didn't seem at all likely.

And she highly doubted her old boyfriend Eli cared about what she was doing now. They'd parted amicably enough.

No, the simple answer was that this was some sort of

mistake, that someone had chosen her house instead of the one they'd really wanted.

But as she turned off the lights and tried to go back to sleep, she tossed and turned, her mind whirling.

She'd survived by trusting her instincts. And they were screaming at her now. Jayme knew deep in her bones the fire had been set on purpose to frighten her. And worse? Whoever had done it had succeeded.

She was scared to death and had no idea what to do about it.

CPSIA information can be obtained
at www.ICGtesting.com
Printed in the USA
LVHW080222040723
751510LV00013B/106

9 781949 144574